THE FIGHT OF THE ASURAS

WHEN THE GUARDIANS ARISE

ARPITA CHAKRABORTY

LAUNCHPAD
An imprint of
Srishti Publishers & Distributors

Srishti Publishers & Distributors
A unit of AJR Publishing LLP
212A, Peacock Lane
Shahpur Jat, New Delhi – 110 049

editorial@srishtipublishers.com

First Published by Launchpad,
an imprint of Srishti Publishers & Distributors in 2025

10 9 8 7 6 5 4 3 2 1

This is a work of fiction. The characters, places, organizations and events described in this book are either a work of the author's imagination or have been used fictitiously. Any resemblance to people, living, or dead, places, events, communities, or organizations is purely coincidental.

Superheroes aren't fictional – this was a truth I knew from the very beginning. God has been kind, for I have been blessed with real-life superheroes all around me.

Prologue

Welcome, seekers of truth, to the realm of Eldoria, where the veils of mysticism are lifted, and the echoes of the ancient power resonate through the ethereal currents. I'm the Spirit of Eldoria, an entity that transcends time and space, and I shall guide you through the enigmatic tale that unfolds within this hallowed domain.

Eldoria, a realm born from the dreams of gods and forged in the crucible of celestial energy, is a testament to the interplay between mortal existence and the supernatural.

Within the ethereal realm of Eldoria, a tale of ancient power and fateful encounters unfolds. The air seems to crackle with ancient magic, welcoming those visiting Eldoria into a realm where secrets are whispered, and destinies are forged. In the sprawling city of Eldoria, nestled amidst towering mountains, and enchanted forests, lies Eldoria Academy, a school unlike any other.

Eldoria Academy, a haven of revellation, became a stage where light and shadow danced, where the very fabric of existence was tested, and where heroes were chosen to bridge the divide between the mortal and celestial realms, fight Kalyuga (Armageddon), and restore the balance of the realms.

Within this extraordinary school's hallowed walls, the battle between light, and darkness unfolds. Destinies are shaped, allies, and adversaries emerge, and their true intentions are veiled beneath layers of deception. It is a land where trust is elusive and motivations are masked by an intricate web of secrecy. Within its enchanted halls, alliances were formed, and shattered, as truths, and half-truths wove a convoluted tapestry of deception.

Legend has it that Eldoria Academy was established by the enigmatic figure Kalki, who serves as the school's guardian and guiding light.

Born with extraordinary abilities, gifts that set him apart, yet cursed with a weight of darkness in his soul. He walks a precarious path, torn between his duty as the school's guardian and the dark impulses that surge within him. He must maintain a delicate balance, for the consequences of his true nature being exposed could be catastrophic to both the school and the realm.

As the Spirit of Eldoria, I watched Kalki guide his students through the corridors of knowledge. He encountered challenges that tested his resolve and forced him to confront the literal and figurative demons that not only haunted him but threatened to engulf Eldoria. Within the halls of the school, allies, and adversaries emerge, their motivations often veiled by deception.

In this pivotal moment, he must draw insight from his ancestors, the Rakshasas, who were once revered as 'Suras' or deities. He must tap into the wisdom of his forbearers, channelling their legacy to guide his actions, for it is in their stories that the answers lie.

As the encroaching darkness casts its shadow upon the realm, they embark on a journey guided by signs and synchronicities that will test their courage and resolve.

Let's unravel the secrets within the ancient chambers and hidden realms. Let us witness the convergence of mortal champions and celestial beings, for it is in this convergence that the fate of Eldoria hangs in the balance.

Gather close, for I shall unveil the mysteries and mythical tales of Eldoria, woven through the ages, and etched upon the tapestry of time.

It is the story of Eldoria, a tale of cosmic forces, extraordinary destinies, and the eternal battle between light and darkness. Welcome to a world where mortal and celestial realms converge and where the realms and their beings shall play their part in shaping Eldoria's destiny. Together, we shall witness an epic battle, where the clash between light and darkness will shake the foundations of Eldoria. Emotions will run high, as Kalki must confront the present and the past, where a grave secret lies.

Welcome to Eldoria Academy, where the battle between light and darkness, good and evil, and right, and wrong takes root within the heart of its realm.

The Gathering Shadows

The heavy wooden door creaked open. Kalki did not look up immediately.

"You're late, Rudrama," he murmured, his voice weighted with unspoken concern.

A woman stepped inside, the flickering lanterns casting long shadows across her regal form. Her silver-streaked hair fell in waves. She carried a satchel, its worn leather marked with ancient symbols.

"You've been troubled," she noted finally. "More than usual."

"This is sooner than I expected." His voice was measured.

"It was never a matter of 'if', only 'when'," she said. "And now, it seems that 'when' is upon us."

A long silence stretched between them. Outside, the night pressed against the windows, casting elongated shadows across the chamber walls. The flickering light of enchanted lanterns illuminated the ancient maps and relics surrounding them.

Kalki exhaled. "There's a disturbance in the eastern provinces," he said, his voice laced with restraint. "Something unnatural."

Rudrama's expression darkened. "Then the rumours were true."

Kalki finally met her gaze, his own unreadable. "Tell me everything you know."

Rudrama reached into the satchel and withdrew a bundle of scrolls. "There have been sightings of creatures – things that should not exist in our world. Shadows moving without bodies, whispering in tongues lost to time. The air itself feels… wrong. And then, there's this." She unfurled a weathered parchment, revealing an intricate sigil drawn in dark ink. "It was found at the site of a vanished village. No bodies. No signs of struggle. Just this, burned into the ground."

Sweat prickled at Kalki's brow. The darkness had not gone – it had only bided its time. Now, its claws scraped at the edges of their world once more.

Kalki's jaw tightened as he studied the symbol. It was familiar in a way that sent a slow, crawling dread down his spine.

"You recognize it." Rudrama's words were not a question.

Kalki didn't respond immediately. "It is older than the Rakshasas," he murmured. "Older than even when the Rakshasas were considered the Suras."

Rudrama inhaled sharply. "Then it is as I feared."

The silence between them deepened, stretching like an unspoken omen.

"We cannot act recklessly. If this is what I suspect… we may be dealing with something far beyond our reach. Maybe it is the knock of the abyss…"

Rudrama frowned. "You have never feared the unknown before."

"It's not the unknown that I fear, Rudrama," he said, his gaze distant. "It is the known. The things that existed long before this time, long before the fall of the Rakshasas. It is the part of our history that we tried to erase, the legacy we chose to forget, because it was no less than an Armageddon. A 'Kalyuga' in itself. And I have a sombre feeling about this. This symbol, these omens… it all feels too familiar."

For the first time, a flicker of hesitation crossed Rudrama's features. She did not confirm his words, but did not deny them either. Instead, she set her hands on the desk, steadying herself.

"If that's true," she said at last, "then we are standing on the edge of something far worse than we imagined."

Kalki nodded. "Then, Eldoria must prepare for war. Summon our best, summon the 'Yodhas'," he said. "This war begins now."

Rudrama nodded, her fingers tightening around the hilt of her sword. She stepped forward, placing a stack of reports onto the table.

"Then you already know what's in these."

"I don't need to read them to know the truth." He turned away from the darkened sky, his jaw tightening. "The veil is thinning, Rudrama. I can feel it. In the same way, our ancestors must have felt it before the last war. Before the world shredded itself apart."

She said nothing. She felt it too.

For centuries, the Rakshasas had been reduced to whispers, myths twisted beyond recognition. Few knew the truth—that they had once been gods, before power, and greed had dragged them into darkness, before they had become something the world feared.

But history had a cruel way of repeating itself.

A knock at the door shattered the heavy silence.

"Enter," Kalki commanded.

The door creaked open, and Maya stepped in. The young warrior's face was tight with barely concealed urgency.

"There's been an incident," she said. "At the southern gates."

Kalki's gaze sharpened. "What kind of incident?"

"No signs of forced entry. No struggle. But the sentries are gone." Maya hesitated. "Vanished."

The last time soldiers had disappeared without a trace, the world had bled for it.

Kalki strode to the balcony again, eyes scanning the darkness beyond Eldoria's walls. Fear thrives in whispers. And whispers often hold a sliver of truth.

"Things aren't right, and my gut is having a grave feeling about this," he murmured. "And I can sense that you know exactly what I'm feeling, Rudrama."

She nodded, her fingers tightening around the edge of her cloak.

Kalki turned back to Maya. "Maya, prepare the Yodhas now, and go for a quick scout, but discreetly. No alarms. No panic. We don't know what we're dealing with yet."

Maya gave a sharp nod. "Consider it done, Acharya. My team of Yodhas and I'll scout the places where these reports originated."

Without another word, she turned on her heel and strode toward the door.

Rudrama turned to Kalki, "Are you sure this is wise? What if they don't return?"

"Then we'll have our answer," Kalki declared. "Make sure that the Yodhas are fully prepared for this mission. I need you to keep a vigilant eye on their well-being. Please keep me updated. Their safety is paramount."

Rudrama had seen the darkness before—felt its hunger creeping through the cracks of the realm. It had left scars on her soul, whispering its venom even now. But she would not falter.

"Consider it done, Kalki." Her voice held steady. "I will assemble the team at once. We'll move carefully, unseen. Eldoria's fate depends on it."

Kalki's gaze bore into her, sharp as a blade. "There's something else. Keep a watchful eye on the twins – Maya and Ayyappan. You know what I mean, Rudrama… I only trust you with the truth."

Rudrama's brow furrowed. They knew Maya and Ayyappan were… different and mysterious—more than mere warriors. There was a force within them, raw, and unpredictable. A force that neither of them could yet define.

"I understand." Rudrama's voice softened. "They walk a path unlike any other. Their gifts make them invaluable, but also vulnerable. I will do my best to protect them."

"They are powerful – more than they know. But power without control can be treacherous. I have pushed and trained them beyond their limits, but…" He hesitated, a rare crack in his usual certainty. "With the reports we've received… I fear it may not be enough. I fear that the guilt inside me may prove to be the reason for the extinction of our realm."

Silence thickened between them. The air itself felt charged, as if the very walls of the Academy understood the weight of his words. Rudrama placed a firm hand on his arm. "We cannot control the future, Kalki. But we can prepare them. Train them. Guide them." She met his gaze, unwavering. "I do not claim to know the future, but this – I swear upon my very soul: even if we falter, even if the heavens shatter and the realm crumbles, the twins, and Eldoria shall not stand defenceless. You and I, Kalki, have walked through the depths of darkness and felt its whispers coil around our very bones. But we've seen something greater – darkness is never absolute. Even the faintest spark can set an inferno ablaze. In the battle against the dark, when hope seems but a whisper, the cosmos itself sends that spark… that ray of light that aids our warriors of righteousness, and in that sacred moment, our chosen hero shall emerge to light our path. May I remind you, Kalki, that no one understands this truth better than you?"

A flicker of gratitude softened Kalki's face. "With you watching over them, I can fight without hesitation."

Rudrama nodded and turned, her long white Angarakha whispering against the floor as she left.

Kalki's eyes fell upon the weathered journal on his desk as the door shut behind her. His ancestors had stood against the same darkness, wrestled with the same fear. And now, it was his turn.

He opened the journal. A passage caught his eye.

A chamber. Hidden within Eldoria Academy itself. A sanctuary of lost knowledge. And within it, the key to strengthening the veil.

Kalki rose, moving through the darkened halls with silent purpose. His steps echoed against the stone, each one drawing him closer.

At the end of the passage, an ancient door loomed before him. Its surface was marked with symbols that pulsed faintly under the burning 'mashals'. A big silver lock, wrapped in sacred red cloth, sealed its entrance.

Kalki whispered the incantation. The symbols flared to life. A deep, resonant hum filled the air as the door groaned open.

Inside, the chamber shimmered with an ethereal glow. Crystals lined the walls, their light casting dancing shadows. In the centre, a stand stood – a thick, ornate container resting upon it. Within, a small flame flickered, impossibly still.

Kalki stepped forward, brushing his fingertips against the fire.

The world shifted.

Visions flooded his mind—chaos, blood, an endless night swallowing Eldoria. He saw the Academy in flames, its walls crumbling. Maya and Ayyappan stood at the heart of the storm, their eyes alight with something terrifyingly powerful.

The darkness was coming. And they were at its centre.

Kalki yanked his hand back. The chamber spun around him, the weight of the prophecy pressing against his ribs.

For a moment, fear clawed at his resolve. In that instant, his trident-shaped mark radiated a luminous glow. He cast aside the suffocating clutches of fear and uncertainty. With a determined swipe, Kalki straightened. He would not let this happen.

Kalki reached for the flame again. This time, his hand did not waver. The fire curled around his fingers, its warmth sinking into his skin, its knowledge embedding into his soul. As the ancient power awakened within him, Kalki made his vow.

The darkness would come. But so would he.

And this time, he would be ready.

Hours Earlier…

The golden light of the setting sun bathed Eldoria Academy. The air thrummed with energy – students hurrying between lessons, laughter, and conversation mingling with the wind. Some pursued the arts, others trained in combat, and a select few grappled with the untamed force of their awakening powers.

Yet amid the bustling life of the Academy, one figure moved with quiet authority.

Kalki.

To those who walked these halls, he was a mentor, a guardian, and a leader—his presence alone was enough to command respect and reverence.

They did not know the truth.

They did not know about the legacy of his clan – 'The Rakshasas', a race once revered as gods. Nor did they see the cost of that legacy – the cataclysm that had shattered their celestial status and cast them into the shadows of history.

The world remembered them as monsters.

But Kalki knew the truth.

He walked with measured steps through the Academy's open courtyard, his sharp gaze sweeping over the students, always watching, always searching. Darkness did not announce its arrival. It seeped in, slow, and unseen, like poison in a well.

Beside him, a young Yodha named Ayyappan, Maya's twin brother, struggled to match his pace.

"Acharya," Ayyappan ventured hesitantly. "There's a rumour spreading among the initiates. Some claim to have seen…" He hesitated, then lowered his voice. "A shadow moving through the eastern dormitories. A presence. They say it watches them."

Kalki did not break stride. "Quiet voices whisper secrets capable of toppling empires."

Ayyappan swallowed. "You believe something is watching?"

Kalki finally stopped, turning to face him. His eyes – dark as the depths of the cosmos – held a quiet intensity.

"I believe," he said slowly, "that maybe the storm we have been waiting for is already here."

The Yodha paled but nodded. "Should I alert the sentries?"

Kalki considered. “Not yet. Watch. Listen. Darkness reveals itself to those who do not chase it away too soon.”

Ayyappan bowed his head in understanding. “Yes, Acharya.”

As the young man hurried off, Kalki stood, gazing toward the eastern horizon. The reports from the provinces lingered in his mind. The veil is thinning. Since the dawn of time, greed, ambition, and the lure of immortality have driven men to ruin. Even the Rakshasas—his kind—had fallen to that temptation. Kingdoms had crumbled beneath it. Heroes had lost themselves to it.

But Kalki was different.

Where others had faltered, he stood firm – a warrior who carried the burden of his bloodline with pride. He had founded Eldoria Academy not just to train warriors, but to restore what had been lost. To reclaim the truth buried beneath centuries of deception.

One day, the Rakshasas’ legacy would rise again.

Not in the shadows. In the light.

The Whispering Veil

The news spread like wildfire but carried something more sinister than curiosity – an eerie unease. The grand hall of Eldoria Academy, where voices had once risen in spirited debate and scholarly discourse, was now thick with silence – an oppressive, expectant stillness. Kalki spoke.

"We are being watched."

A shudder passed through the assembly. A single torch flickered violently, its flame shrinking as if recoiling from the truth in his words. Kalki's voice was neither raised nor frantic, yet it held the weight of a thousand unsaid warnings.

"The veil that separates our world of light from what lies beyond is growing weaker. The balance that has protected us, the force that has kept the darkness at bay for centuries, is fraying." His gaze swept across the faces before him, lingering on those who looked away, unwilling to accept what their hearts already knew. "And when the veil falls, so too will the walls we have built to keep the horrors of the past from returning."

A breathless moment passed. The air seemed to tighten, as if the unseen forces at play had drawn closer, listening.

Ahilya, one of the youngest members of the Yodhas in Maya's team, was the first to break the silence.

"Then we must act." Her voice was unwavering, but the tension in her stance betrayed the storm brewing beneath. "Acharya, the Yodhas will lead the mission themselves. We will scout the realm from where these disturbances are surfacing. We will uncover the truth. We, the finest of warriors, shall march with unyielding resolve, sparing nothing in our path. This war will be fought with our souls until victory is ours."

Kalki met her gaze. His silence was not one of uncertainty, but of calculation.

"The truth is not hiding, Ahilya," he said at last. "It is waiting."

Ahilya's brow furrowed, but she did not waver. "Then we will find it before it finds us."

She turned sharply, motioning to the warriors. Their footsteps echoed as they made their way toward the armoury, each movement a silent vow to the battle ahead. But before she could disappear into the corridor, Maya stepped forward.

"And if the darkness is already among us?" she asked, her voice barely above a whisper. "What if it's already here, waiting for us to look the other way?"

A hush fell over the hall. The torches dimmed. The air shifted, as if the question had invited something unseen to lean in closer.

"Then we were never meant to stop it," he murmured. "Only to survive it."

Kalki continued, "We don't know the future. We can only imagine it. All we truly have is the choice to walk our path with intention, integrity, and towards the light.

"The future is a mystery, ever shifting, ever unknown. But the present, this moment, is ours. It is here that we can act, here that we can learn from the past – both ours and others – and here that we begin to shape what lies ahead.

"Not by certainty. But by conviction."

Maya's fingers curled into fists. "Then we have no options but to be ready," she said, her voice laced with determination. "The Yodhas will ensure that they are fully prepared, that their minds remain sharp, and that their spirits are undaunted."

Kalki nodded, but there was something else in his gaze—something he did not say aloud.

Not all would withstand what was coming.

The first battle had already begun. They did not realize it yet.

He turned back to the gathered Eldorians, his voice steady, unwavering.

"The darkness does not announce its arrival with war horns or marching armies," he said. "It seeps. It slips through the cracks of our resolve, whispering our fears in voices we cannot ignore. It does not need to conquer us. It only needs to make us doubt. It only needs to make us question our existence."

The 'Mashals' flickered again. The walls groaned, as if the very foundations of the Academy were straining against an unseen pressure.

Kalki stepped forward. His voice dropped, low, and commanding.

"You will hear it," he warned. "It will call you by name. It will take the shape of your deepest regrets, your most painful losses. It will make you believe that you are alone. It will make you believe that your near and dear ones are your foes. It will make you envious of others, and dissatisfaction may start brewing in your mind."

"We must forge a shield that thrives on love and acceptance," Kalki continued, his voice unfaltering. "See beyond the veils that grief, guilt, ambition, and greed can cast upon us. Recognize the inherent light within every being and strive to ignite it with the radiant flame of our compassion."

As Kalki continued his impassioned address, the word "guilt" momentarily pierced the air, casting a shadow of pain upon his countenance. In that fleeting moment, the images of twisted creatures danced before his mind's eye, threatening to consume him in a vortex of guilt and anguish. However, his mark, the glowing trident in his palm, jolted him back to the present, a symbol of his purpose and the strength he carried within him.

A gust of wind rushed through the hall, rattling the ancient iron sconces. Someone inhaled sharply, as if they could already hear the whispers beginning to form.

"But you are not alone." Kalki's voice rose, cutting through the invisible chill that gripped the room. "You will never be alone. And when the veil is torn and the darkness spills forth, we will stand when the time comes. We will not falter. And even if we falter, we will not break."

After Kalki's resolute declaration, a wave of unwavering determination coursed through the room, electrifying the air with undeniable energy.

As his words settled, the room erupted in a symphony of voices, a chorus of Eldorians united in perfect harmony.

"For Eldoria!" They roared, their voices intertwining like the strands of an unbreakable bond. In that moment, doubt, and fear faded into insignificance, replaced by an indomitable spirit that blazed within the hearts of the Eldorians.

A fierce rush of wind snuffed out a torch, casting a hall section into shadow. A collective breath caught in the throats of the Eldorians.

Kalki did not flinch.

Outside, the wind howled—a long, bone-deep sound, neither entirely natural, nor entirely of this world. A sound that carried a message, though none could yet understand it.

Somewhere, unseen but ever-present, something listened.

And in the silence that followed, it smiled.

The Astral Council and the Mortal Awakening

The night sky above Eldoria shimmered with an unsettling stillness, as if the heavens themselves held their breath. A realm of enchantment and ancient secrets, Eldoria had long stood as a beacon of balance between celestial forces and mortal existence. But that balance was fraying.

The Astral Council convened within their ethereal realm, where the constellations shimmered in silent harmony. These were no ordinary beings; they were the keepers of equilibrium, their luminous forms shifting between radiance and shadow, woven from the very fabric of the cosmos. They had witnessed the rise and fall of civilisations, watched as the forces of light and darkness clashed in an eternal waltz. But tonight, an unease rippled through their sacred chamber – something beyond mere fate was at play.

At the heart of the gathering stood Parvati. Her vast and iridescent silver wings glowed with an otherworldly sheen as she surveyed her fellow council members. Her presence commanded not just respect but something deeper—awe. Where others saw mere celestial duty, she felt the weight of destiny press against her like an unrelenting tide.

Parvati's voice rang out, both melodic, and resolute. "Threads unravel in ways unseen, yet undeniable. Darkness does not always arrive with fury; sometimes, it whispers, slipping through the cracks we fail to mend… And this time it seems that the Lord of the Darkness has fully prepared and is determined to engulf Eldoria."

A murmur spread across the council.

"The signs are clear," she continued, her silver eyes gleaming with a knowledge beyond time. "The wall dividing the realms is fading, unravelling the balance that upholds Eldoria. If we do not act, the consequences will ripple far beyond this realm – even the celestial order may falter."

For a brief moment, silence reigned. Then, a low hum resonated from the chamber's depths – a sound older than time. Agreement.

A celestial elder, his form flickering like a dying star, stepped forward. "Intervention is not taken lightly, Parvati. To disrupt mortal fate is to defy the natural course of existence."

Parvati's wings unfurled slightly, her presence a mixture of patience and unwavering determination. "And to remain silent is to forsake the very reason we exist. We are far more than passive onlookers; we are the steadfast protectors of what matters."

Parvati's voice echoed like thunder wrapped in silk – ancient, commanding, and undeniable.

"Darkness isn't just where light fades – it's the cruel delight taken in others' pain. It is the cold delight when others choke on despair.

"But light… light begins when you step outside yourself. When you wear another's agony as your own, and their pain no longer feeds your pride but shakes your spirit.

"To walk in the light doesn't mean you must fall for others. But those who choose to bear the weight, who bleed not for glory but for balance – they are not just in the light – they are the warriors of it… they are the 'Yodhas'.

"And let it be known – we are not meddling with fate. We aren't defying the natural course of mortal lives. We aren't simply stepping in but answering the solemn call of duty.

"What we do now is not interference – it is restoration.

"We do only what must be done… to keep the balance of the cosmos intact.

"For the world doesn't endure by those who merely witness the light, but by those rare souls who become it."

A pause. Then nods of reluctant agreement.

She had expected resistance but not surrender, which, too, was a sign. The council had always sought balance, but something about this moment felt different. Taking a slow breath, Parvati lifted her hand. A soft glow coiled at her fingertips, forming shifting threads of light – each thread a story, a fate, a possibility. They wove together in a delicate dance, until only one thread remained, gleaming brighter than the rest.

"In this critical hour," she spoke, her voice laced with an urgency she could not suppress, "we must find the one who can stand at the threshold of both worlds, the mortal who belongs to neither radiance above nor the shadows below. A soul of fire and wisdom. A heart of battle and peace."

She closed her eyes. And she saw her.

A figure bathed in flickering light stands upon the precipice of fate. A warrior whose very existence defies the natural order. The mortal is untethered to light yet unclaimed by darkness, a force of nature unto herself.

And yet, she did not know it.

Parvati exhaled, her celestial glow intensifying. She did not need to name the chosen one, for she had seen the prophecy in visions both waking and dreaming. Instead, she wove her words into an ancient verse, a celestial chant carried upon the unseen winds of fate:

"In a mortal guise, this champion stands tall,
A fusion of bravery and grace, poised for the call.
Her heart beats with compassion, her spirit alight,
A leader born, destined to ignite.
With eyes that reflect wisdom's gentle glow,
And a soul ablaze, ready to bestow.
She carries the weight of ancient lore,
Guided by the celestial forces, forevermore.

Clad in attire that mirrors celestial might,
Rust-coloured garments, radiant in light.
A sacred thread adorns her wrist,
Anklet bound with purpose, black as night's mist,
Born to great sages, the cosmos' gift,
Kashi is where this mortal exists.
Upon her forehead a divine tilak,
Of red and white sandalwood, a sacred sign.
Armed with bow and arrows, true,
She commands the elements, both old, and new.
Her presence commands attention and respect,
A beacon of hope, our trust she'll protect.
To find her, we must unite,
Peer into mortal lives, seek her celestial light.
Through signs and synchronicities, we'll be led,
To the chosen one, where destiny has tread."

As the final words of the verse resonated through the chamber, a shift occurred. The celestial realm seemed to stir, as if the very stars acknowledged the revellation.

The council members, their luminous forms flickering with the weight of realization, turned to Parvati.

"She is already walking the path," one murmured, their voice tinged with reverence.

Parvati nodded. "But she does not yet know it. And that, dear council, is where our challenge begins. Kalki stands vigilant for Eldoria, and across Eldoria, even though ancient prophecies made no mention of a chosen one, hope quietly takes root—whispering that perhaps the cosmos will rise to join their stand against the looming storm of Armageddon."

For the first time in centuries, the celestial beings felt something akin to anticipation.

The chosen one had been revealed.

But she was still just a girl.

A girl who had no idea that the fate of Eldoria – and the cosmos itself – rested in her hands.

The celestial chamber hummed with energy as the Astral Council intensified their search. Their luminous forms flickered like cosmic flames, their collective power coursing through the vast expanse of fate's intricate web. With Parvati's guidance, they peered into the unseen, tracing the invisible threads that bound the chosen one's destiny to Eldoria's survival.

"The signs are undeniable," one of the council members murmured, his voice like the distant chime of a sacred bell. "The omens align. She is the one."

Parvati's silver wings arched slightly as she nodded. "Then we must ensure she heeds the call," she said, her voice carrying a gravity that made the chamber tremble. "The road before her would not only challenge her – it would shatter her, should she face it unready. But she must rise."

The council members raised their hands in unison, their celestial energy weaving through the very fabric of existence.

Chitrangada was not foretold in their legends. Yet she will soon be walking among them—a storm wrapped in silence, a prophecy unfolding in real time.

The skies above Kashi darkened momentarily, a brief eclipse casting long shadows over the sacred city. The night air hung thick with the scent of incense and the rhythmic hum of ancient chants. The Ganges flowed like a liquid mirror, reflecting the scattered constellations above, while temple bells rang in solemn cadence.

A lone figure stood by the river's edge.

The girl from the prophecy.

Chitrangada.

She did not yet know of the celestial council's decree.

To others, the world breathed as it always had. But to Chitrangada, it spoke.

The air carried frequencies only her soul could decipher – subtle hums woven with cryptic meaning. When she paused, she could hear them whisper: "The gates are opening... Eldoria waits..."

Leaves didn't just fall; they descended in a rhythmic cadence, like dancers in a forgotten ritual. Each flutter seemed to murmur: "Kalki awaits you... The time draws near..."

The old and wise trees groaned with purpose in the wind. Their trunks pulsed with deep vibrations, telling her, "You are the keeper of balance. Walk the path. Awaken the flame..."

The river wasn't merely a flowing current; it pulsed with a resolute, almost sentient purpose. It's rushing water sang in a language older than time: "He waits at the turning of the tide... find him before the eclipse swallows the light..."

Birds cut through the sky, their wings slicing coded messages into the air. Their chirps rose and fell like mantras: "To Eldoria... to destiny... go now, chosen flame..."

Even the beasts in the underbrush paused when she passed—as if in reverence, as if they knew. Their sounds were layered echoes of warning and wonder: "The world is tilting... bring the balance back..."

Everything... everything was trying to tell her something.

The universe wasn't just guiding her – it was summoning her.

Chitrangada remained oblivious to the invisible powers stirring in the shadows, silently reshaping fate with every step she took. To her, the world was as it had always been – harsh yet beautiful, a test she had long learned to endure.

With her bow slung across her back, she gazed at her reflection in the river, the flickering torchlight dancing across her sharp, determined features. Her russet garments clung to her frame, dusted with the remnants of training, while the black anklet upon her foot shimmered ever so faintly in the moonlight. A gift, she had always thought—a trinket of little consequence.

She did not know it was a marker—a seal of fate.

A sudden gust of wind whipped through the air, carrying a whisper-not of mortal tongues, but something far older. Chitrangada felt it before she understood it. It wove silently through the reeds, coiling around her like a phantom whisper born of shadows.

Chitrangada's eyes narrowed. The sensation was foreign, yet it did not frighten her. She had long been attuned to the world in ways others were not. It was never unusual for her to feel the world shift – she had always sensed the subtle tremors in reality, the quiet rearranging of fate. But this time, it was different. In the past few days, she had been inundated with signs – flooded by a chorus of unspoken messages. Everything around her carried whispers or murmured secrets, and even silence had begun to speak.

All pointed to one undeniable truth:

A realm called Eldoria was calling her. And at the centre of that call – like a heartbeat in the distance – echoed a single name: Kalki.

It was not a request. It was destiny's demand. And something far more significant than destiny had begun to stir when the balance between the seen and unseen wavered.

And tonight, Chitrangada could feel as she spoke to herself: "Something is coming."

And she was right, as she heard a voice.

"You stand at the precipice, child."

The voice was neither near nor far, neither loud, nor soft. It did not belong to man or beast, yet it carried the weight of both.

A sudden weight pressed against Chitrangada's chest, as though unseen hands were pulling at the very essence of her being. Her hand grabbed the blade so tightly, it was as though she could feel every pulse of her heartbeat in the metal. She did not turn. Did not flinch.

"Show yourself." Her voice was firm. Unwavering.

A soft chuckle echoed through the air, laced with amusement. "Ah. You are indeed as the prophecy foretold. No hesitation. No fear."

A ripple coursed through the river as a figure materialized from the shadows of the trees. It was not a man, not entirely a spirit—something in between. His robes were woven from the night itself, and his eyes were two glowing embers, shifting between warmth, and unreadable depths.

Chitrangada did not move. But she understood. This was not a mortal being.

"Who are you?" she asked, voice steady.

The figure tilted his head slightly, as if appraising her. "A messenger," he said. "And you, Chitrangada, are no ordinary girl."

She tensed. The name he spoke – how he said it – was laced with meaning beyond mere recognition. It was a summons.

"I know who I am," she said carefully, keeping her stance firm. "A warrior. A guardian of my people."

The figure exhaled, the sound less of breath and more of shifting wind. "No. You are more. Far more."

A sharp sensation – neither pain nor pleasure – rippled through her veins, like cinder waiting to ignite. The air crackled around her, and in that fleeting moment, she knew.

She had been chosen.

The realization sent a shiver down her spine, but the world around her shifted before she could fully grasp its meaning. The rustling trees whispered louder, their voices forming half-spoken words she could almost understand. The earth beneath her seemed to thrum, as if responding to her presence.

Chitrangada felt something tighten in her chest, an instinctive resistance. She had always fought against expectations, against the fate others tried to thrust upon her. But this—this was different. It was not a mere expectation. It was true.

Still, she did not yield. "And if I refuse whatever it is you've come to demand?"

A pause. Then, a slow smile. "Then the realms will burn."

The words struck like thunder, yet the night remained eerily still. Chitrangada's heartbeat quickened – not in fear, but in recognizing something inevitable.

She had felt the growing unease, the shift in the wind, the silent cries of the planet.

Something was coming.

Something ancient.

But even as her mind screamed for logic, a deep voice resonated within her.

"The time has come."

Chitrangada's heartbeat thundered in her ears. Was she losing her mind? Or was she truly hearing something beyond this realm?

Before she could question it further, the winds rose. Leaves swirled around her like a cosmic dance, carrying the scent of sandalwood and something ancient and divine. And then – she heard a distant yet familiar voice weaving through the very air.

"Come forth, child of fire and fate. The path is set. The journey begins."

The voice was neither cruel nor kind. It was absolute.

A sudden surge of energy coursed through her, and with it came clarity. This was not madness. This was destiny.

Just then, the figure stepped forward, his voice dropping lower. "You have always felt it, haven't you? The pull. The knowledge that you are not meant for an ordinary life."

Chitrangada clenched her fists. She hated that he was right.

She had spent years pretending otherwise, clinging to the illusion of normalcy, of control. But deep down, she had always known.

The figure lifted a hand, and with it, the river stirred. The once calm waters now swirled in restless currents, images forming upon their surface. Scenes of cities engulfed in shadow. Of warriors falling before unseen enemies. Of a darkness that did not belong to the mortal realm but seeped into it like ink through parchment.

A war was brewing.

Not of kings and conquerors, but of forces far greater.

Chitrangada exhaled slowly. Then, with deliberate precision, she unstrapped the bow from her back and held it before her.

A test.

She did not know why, but instinct guided her hands. She nocked an arrow, drawing it back, feeling the weight of the moment settle upon her.

"If I am to be part of this, then let me see."

The messenger's ember eyes flickered with something faint. Approval, perhaps. And then, without another word, he raised his hand. A burst of energy surged from his palm, crackling through the air like lightning, aimed directly at her.

Chitrangada did not flinch. She released the arrow.

The impact sent a shockwave through the clearing. The ground trembled, the trees groaned, and the river recoiled from the force. For a heartbeat, silence reigned.

And then, the messenger smiled.

"You are ready."

Chitrangada lowered her bow, breathing heavily, but her gaze remained locked onto his. The weight of everything – the prophecy, the celestial decree, the war yet to come – settled upon her shoulders.

But she did not cower.

Because deep down, she had always known.

The Yodhas of Eldoria

Kalki stepped into his chamber. The grand hall had erupted with cheers at his speech – voices of unwavering faith in him, the Yodhas, and the battle against the encroaching darkness. And yet, beneath the fire of their devotion, he had sensed something else.

Fear.

It hung in their gazes, a shadow in their eyes, as their voices trembled on the edge of applause. Not just faith had drawn them to him tonight – it was desperation. The world outside was shifting, crumbling under the weight of the looming sinister. Kalki knew that his leadership alone would not be enough. He needed the Yodhas, his warriors, his guiding light in this war against the darkness.

His gaze fell upon a stack of sealed scrolls resting on his desk—the latest reports from the eastern provinces. A shiver of foreboding ran through him as he unsealed the first parchment, its weight pressing against him like a silent omen. The words etched across it were grim.

Greed festers in the hearts of rulers.

Corruption coursed through Eldoria's veins like poison, silent but relentless.

Blood staining the once-sacred lands.

A chilling increase in disappearances, kidnappings, and murders.

And in the whispers of terrified citizens, tales of shadows moving where none should exist.

Kalki exhaled sharply, setting the parchment aside as he rose. He strode towards the large open balcony of his chamber. The moon loomed heavy over Eldoria, its pale light slicing through the night, spilling silver veins across the jagged spires below. The city was beautiful, still untouched by the destruction that loomed at its borders. But for how long?

"They sense the ripples, but remain oblivious to the unstoppable tide churning in the depths below. The storm doesn't announce itself – it moves in silence until it is too late." The realization settled over him like a quiet warning. Fear had taken root in the beings of Eldoria, but fear was never the true enemy – the true nature of the living beings who are naturally pulled and easily lured towards shortcuts and darkness was. And if left unchecked, it would open the door for what lurked beyond.

His thoughts turned to the Yodhas, the warriors chosen by fate itself. They were more than just soldiers. They were symbols of resistance. Each was a force unto themselves, carrying the weight of past battles and unseen scars. Together, they were the last line of defence against the coming storm.

They had not been chosen at random. Their selection had been a whisper of destiny, an orchestration of cosmic design. It was as though the universe itself had willed them into being – each with a skill, a purpose, and a burden.

And if Eldoria had any hope of surviving the coming war, it would begin with them.

The first name that surfaced in his mind was Maya, the eldest of the Yodhas, the unsaid leader of the pack, and the silent architect of unseen battles.

The Weaver of Illusions: Maya, the Enigma

Maya – the name itself meant illusion. And like her name, her existence was a mystery wrapped in shadows.

No one could fathom the true essence of who she was beneath the mask she wore.

She moved through the world like a mirage—untouchable, unpredictable, unknowable.

Yes, she was a warrior—fierce, unyielding, forged in battle. But whispers always followed her, hushed, and trembling. Some claimed that in the silence between stars, she could hear the darkness calling—low, patient, and inevitable. Others said that she danced on the edge of both realms—light and shadow—never fully belonging to either.

There wasn't any doubt that she fought for the light. But a few said that Maya was a story half-told, a flame flickering with purity and something far more dangerous.

She was a sorceress of unparalleled talent, weaving illusions as effortlessly as a painter brushes colour onto a canvas. She walks in the space between light and shadow, unseen, and unbidden.

There was a fluidity to her magic, a dance of deception, and beauty. She did not just create illusions—she commanded them, made them breathe, made them whisper truths hidden beneath layers of deceit.

Maya's presence was both alluring and unsettling. She was as much a mystery as the magic she wielded. Some said she was born from the remnants of a celestial storm; others believed she had no origin, merely appearing one day, draped in shadows.

She moved through the world like a whisper, her dark attire merging with the night itself. The silver patterns on her six-yard dark cloth shimmered faintly, tracing symbols no one understood. She was illegible, a woman who smiled with command yet held a thousand secrets behind her piercing sapphire eyes.

Even her allies treaded cautiously around her. They respected her, even admired her, but trust? That was another matter. Maya had no known past, no history to anchor her existence. She had built herself from the ruins of something no one could name and carried that weight alone.

Everyone had a vision of her. And yet, no one truly knew Maya.

Perhaps that was her greatest weapon, or her greatest weakness...

But beneath the enigma, there was something undeniable—a

fierce loyalty and devotion to those she called her own. And above all, there was Ayyappan.

Her twin brother. The last thread binding her to anything that felt real. Where Maya walked, Ayyapan followed.

The Warrior of Discipline: Ayyappan, the Unyielding Blade

Ayyappan was a warrior of terrifying skill, a swordsman whose blade never wavered. He had trained relentlessly, each strike more precise than the last, each movement honed to perfection. While Maya wielded deception, Ayyappan was raw power, a force that could not be stopped once unleashed.

His dark eyes burned with the same fire that coursed through his veins. He carried himself with discipline, and his broad frame was a testament to years of relentless training. His blade, its grip adorned with intricate engravings, was not just a weapon – it was an extension of his soul.

Together, the siblings were a paradox. Maya thrived in the shadows, her illusions weaving trickery and deception. Ayyappan was the opposite—undaunted, unyielding, heart like a child, a warrior who met his enemies head-on.

Yet, despite their differences, they were bound by something more profound than blood.

A shared wound. A past that neither spoke of, but both felt in the hollow spaces of their souls. Maya never let Ayyappan out of sight, her protective instincts as sharp as the daggers she concealed beneath her sleeves. Ayyappan, in turn, carried a quiet devotion to her, an understanding that needed no words.

The darkness they had encountered as children left scars that had never fully healed. Perhaps they never would. Maybe that was why the shadows unsettled them in ways they couldn't explain.

But if they feared the darkness, they vowed to conquer it.

Their fight was not just for Eldoria—it was personal. It was vengeance. It was redemption.

The twins had a past, of that, there was no doubt. No one knew it. No one dared ask.

What couldn't be questioned was the bond they shared. Thick as blood. Fierce as war. Unbreakable.

They were each other's shield, sword, and sanctuary.

Not just siblings – they were all the family they had left, perhaps. All they ever needed.

And if the world came for one... it would have to go through both.

As Kalki thought of them, his chest tightened. He knew their power. He had seen them fight, watched them turn battles in their favour with nothing but instinct and skill. But he also knew that if the darkness was creeping into Eldoria, it would come for them first.

Because the strongest warriors were always the first to be tested. And the Yodhas were about to face their most significant test yet. A whisper of cool air stirred in the chamber, carrying the scent of night jasmine and something more elusive – an aura of the unknown, a presence that flickered between reality and illusion. Kalki barely had time to register the shift before the shadows at the far end of the chamber seemed to ripple.

And then, the Yodhas entered...

Maya did not arrive like the others. She appeared, emerging from the folds of darkness, her silhouette a seamless extension of the night. She circled the chamber slowly, her fingers brushing against the ancient scrolls stacked on the table, her touch as light as a whisper. "Interesting," she mused, glancing at Kalki. "These reports speak of shadows rising, but the real question is – do you truly see what lurks beneath them? Do you think that the beings of Eldoria will stand with us... and not be seduced by darkness? What's the guarantee?"

Kalki exhaled, not allowing himself to be drawn into her verbal dance. "That's why you're here."

Maya tilted her head, a smirk playing at the corner of her lips. "Indeed."

Her role among the Yodhas was not merely to fight with steel and strength but to manipulate perception itself, to deceive the deceivers, and to unravel secrets shrouded in darkness. While others fought battles with weapons, Maya fought in the realm of minds and illusions, where the enemy never realized they were losing until it was too late.

She was not just a warrior. She was the shadow that danced between realities, blurring the lines between truth and trickery.

If Maya was the whisper of the night, Ayyappan was the roar of the storm.

The chamber doors swung open with a resounding force, revealing a towering figure clad in sturdy battle-worn armour, his dark raven hair cascading in untamed locks over his shoulders. His deep brown eyes carried the wisdom of one who had seen too much yet refused to be broken by it.

He strode into the chamber, his movements powerful but controlled, like a perfectly balanced blade. Strapped to his back was his legendary sword—the embodiment of his absolute swordsmanship. The base bore intricate engravings, each a testament to the countless battles he had fought and the victories he had claimed.

Kalki met his gaze, and for a moment, neither spoke. There was no need. Their understanding went beyond words—both warriors bound by duty, the scars of their past, and the unspoken weight of what was yet to come.

Ayyappan exhaled, resting his hand around the cold handle of his sword. "Acharya! The East is worse than we feared." His voice was calm, but a restrained fury streamed beneath it.

Kalki nodded. “We expected as much.”

Ayyappan clenched the weapon, his knuckles a storm of white against the dark steel, before he released a slow breath and regained control.

Silence hung in the chamber momentarily before a soft clink of metal echoed from the doorway. The sound was deliberate—a presence making itself known not through force but through precision.

Ahilya stepped into the light.

The Mind of the Battlefield: Ahilya, the Strategist of War.

She was not the tallest or most physically imposing in the room, but her presence was undeniable. A regal elegance surrounded her, a quiet authority that commanded attention without a single word. Her piercing, storm-grey eyes held a calculating sharpness, as if she had already read the entire room before entering.

Her armour gleamed, polished yet practical, each piece designed for efficiency rather than mere display. The wreath of brahmi leaves and jasmine flowers woven into her midnight-black hair symbolized her wisdom—an intellect that had outmatched countless foes and turned battles before the first strike was even made.

She did not fight with brute force alone. She fought with her mind.

Kalki leaned back slightly. “You’ve seen something?”

Ahilya nodded, her mind already several steps ahead. “The enemy won’t stand idle while we hesitate. They’re positioning themselves, weaving chaos where order once stood. If we hesitate, we’ll be reacting rather than controlling the battlefield.”

Maya exhaled. “Then we move.”

Ayyappan smirked. “Finally, something exciting.”

Chitragupta remained silent, his gaze distant, as if already seeing the consequences of their next moves.

The Keeper of Balance: Chitragupta, the Arbiter of Fate

As the chamber settled into a charged silence, a presence unlike the others filled the space, not of brute force, or deception, but of something far more profound.

Chitragupta stood at the far end, his presence neither commanding, nor subdued—yet it held an undeniable gravity. Clad in a yellow dhoti and a blue silk kurta, his appearance was deceptively simple, but those who knew him understood that he carried the weight of justice. A single gold bracelet gleamed on his wrist, an anklet on his right leg chiming softly as he moved. But it was his eyes—deep and endless like the night sky that bore the knowledge of countless fates, an abyss where every truth and lie converged.

He advanced, his eyes scanning the scattered reports before locking with Ayyapan's gaze. "You seem to be restless," he observed, his voice even, unwavering.

Ayyapan sighed, running a hand through his hair. "Restless is an understatement. The province is suffocating beneath the weight of corruption and shadow. And we still do not know the true force behind it."

Chitragupta picked up a parchment, his fingers ghosting over the ink as if reading more than just words. "It is not just what lies in the present that we must consider, but the ripples of past actions that have led us here."

Ahilya exhaled sharply. "We don't have time for philosophy. We need a plan."

Chitragupta tilted his head slightly. "Philosophy and strategy are not so different, warrior. One seeks wisdom before action. The other acts without knowing the wisdom behind it."

Maya smirked. "He's right, you know."

Ayyappan scowled but said nothing.

Kalki tapped his fingers against the table, his mind racing. "Then tell me, Chitragupta—what do you see?"

For a moment, the seer was silent. Then, his voice dropped just above a whisper.

"I see fate twisting, the scales tipping. The balance is fragile. If we stumble, there may be no turning back."

Ahilya narrowed her eyes. "Then we don't falter."

Chitragupta nodded once, satisfied. "We move."

Ahilya leaned forward. "Do you have a lead?"

Chitragupta crossed his arms. "A pattern. The disappearances aren't random. They're following the ley lines – points of power across Eldoria."

Ahilya's brows lifted. "That means someone is tapping into the very essence of the land for power."

"Or corrupting it," Chitragupta added.

Maya's grip tensed on the bow resting across her back. "Whichever way this turns, remaining still will cost us more than we can afford."

Kalki turned to the rest of the Yodhas. "Then we act now," he declared. "No more waiting. No more reacting. We take the fight to them."

The Yodhas nodded, their resolve unshaken.

The war had already begun.

And the Yodhas were ready.

The Guided Encounter

The eastern province of Eldoria had become a battlefield of silent suffering. The darkness had slithered its way into the hearts of the people, tainting their desires, twisting their morals, and breaking the fragile fabric of trust that once bound them together.

The team of the warriors of Eldoria had come across instances of senseless executions, brazen kidnappings, and ruthless tortures. The atmosphere was thick with the foul scent of suffering and wrongs left unrighted.

The Yodhas moved cautiously, every step measured, every whisper exchanged in hushed urgency. They had trained for battles of strength and skill, but this—this was something else. This was a war that seeped into minds and twisted them from within.

Yet despite their caution, the darkness was cunning. It did not always roar; sometimes, it slithered unseen. And on this fateful evening, it found them.

A sudden chill wrapped around them, unnatural and biting. The air thickened, turning stale, as if the very essence of the land recoiled from the presence of what approached. The shadows lengthened unnaturally, creeping toward them like fingers of some unseen entity. And then, they rose.

Figures materialized from the darkness—twisted minions, their grotesque forms shifting as though the laws of the mortal realm did not bind them. Their eyes glowed with malevolence, and their bodies were a monstrous fusion of smoke and flesh. They did not attack immediately; they relished the fear in their victims' eyes.

Maya's voice cut through the tension.

Maya, raising her sword, took the charge, "Yodhas! Stand

your ground! These creatures thrive on fear. Do not give them the satisfaction."

The warriors tightened their grip on their weapons. They had faced monstrosities before, but there was something different about these entities—something ancient and insidious.

Without warning, the creatures lunged.

The battlefield erupted into chaos. Blades clashed, arrows sliced through the thick air, and spells crackled as the Yodhas fought with everything they had. Yet for every shadow they cut down, another seemed to rise in its place.

Ayyappan gritted his teeth as he parried a blow, "They're not scrambling – they're striking! This isn't a reaction… It's a perfectly laid trap. They knew. They've been watching us, studying us like predators in the dark. We didn't walk into an encounter – it's like we walked into an ambush. We're right where they wanted us."

Chitragupta spun gracefully, his dagger slicing through a shadowy form, "We can't keep this up forever. We need to regroup!"

Ahilya looked at the others with resolve, "Then we change the game."

She lifted her arms, and a radiant shield shimmered into existence before her. The minions screeched, recoiling from its radiance, but they did not disappear. They circled instead, waiting for the shield to weaken.

Then, amidst the turmoil, something shifted.

A presence entered the battlefield—one that did not belong to the darkness or the desperate warriors struggling to hold their ground. It was neither loud nor violent, yet it carried an undeniable force.

A huge one lunged toward Ayyappan, its claws gleaming in the dim light. In one fluid motion, he brought his sword up, catching the blow before it could land—"Bow down. NOW." The voice commanded.

Instinct took over. Ayyappan dropped as an arrow whizzed past his ear, striking the creature in its forehead. The beast let out a blood-curdling shriek before disintegrating into a cloud of blackish-red mist. Ayyappan turned sharply, his heart pounding.

A lone silhouette emerged and stepped forth at the edge of the battlefield.

She was unlike anyone he had ever seen. Clad in armour that bore intricate golden patterns, her stance poised, and her bow raised. The wind carried her long, dark locks behind her, and her eyes – fierce, unwavering – were locked onto the battlefield with an intensity that sent chills down his spine.

Another arrow left her bow before anyone could react, striking a minion creeping up behind Maya.

Ayyappan asked, still in shock, "Who-who are you?"

Aiming another arrow without looking at him, Chitrangada replied, "Not the time for introductions."

A minion lunged at her from the side. She didn't even turn—she shifted her bow, released another arrow, and dropped the beast mid-air. The precision, the confidence—it was like she had fought this battle a hundred times before.

The Yodhas exchanged glances. Whoever she was, she was on their side.

Ahilya grinned as she slashed a creature in half, "Now that's impressive."

Chitrangada didn't respond. She moved through the battlefield with the grace of a dancer and the precision of a warrior, every shot finding its mark. With her by their side, the battle shifted. The Yodhas fought harder, pushing back against the tide of darkness.

Minutes passed like hours until the last twisted shadows finally let out a squeal and dissolved into the night. Stillness. The Yodhas stood amidst the ruins of the battle, their breaths heavy, their bodies aching. But they had won.

Maya rushed to Ayyappan's side, her gaze shifting from her brother to the mysterious warrior who had saved him, "You saved my brother. Thank you."

Chitrangada was calm, "I did what was necessary."

Ahilya tilted her head, studying her, "Who are you?"

Chitrangada hesitated and then spoke with quiet certainty, "I am Chitrangada. And I was guided here for a purpose."

Ayyappan, still shaken yet intrigued, exchanged a glance with Maya. Maya looked sceptical but interested, "Guided by whom?"

Chitrangada's gaze wavered slightly, but there was no hesitation in her voice, "By the Astral Council."

The words sent a ripple of unease through the group. They had heard of prophecies and celestial guidance before, but the Astral Council rarely interfered so directly.

Observing her, Chitragupta asked, "And what is your purpose?"

Chitrangada's fingers brushed against the shaft of her blade, as if grounding herself, "I was led to Eldoria… to meet Kalki."

A hushed silence fell over the group. Chitragupta was wary when he spoke, "Kalki? The leader of the Yodhas?"

Chitrangada nodded, "Yes. He holds the answers I seek."

Chitragupta cleared his throat, "So… Chitrangada. You were guided here by the light?"

Chitrangada didn't turn to face him, but there was a flicker of amusement in her eyes.

Chitrangada: (calmly) "Yes."

Chitragupta: (pressing on, intrigued) "And this light… speaks to you?"

She finally looked at him, her expression calm, and composed.

Chitrangada: (softly) "The light doesn't speak in words. It

reveals. It murmurs through the breeze, dances in the flame's glow, and lingers in the fading cry of war."

Walking a few paces ahead, Ahilya turned her head slightly, catching the conversation.

Maya: (raising an eyebrow) "Sounds poetic for something leading you into the heart of a warzone."

Chitrangada: (smiling slightly) "Where there is darkness, the light must follow."

Ayyappan exhaled, shaking his head with a slight grin.

Ayyappan: (grinning) "You always talk like that?"

Chitrangada met his gaze, a knowing glint in her eyes.

Chitrangada: (amused) "Only when people ask too many questions."

Ahilya chuckled, shaking her head.

Chitragupta: (serious, cutting in) "But you said you were led to Kalki. Why him?"

Chitrangada: (firmly) "Because he has answers."

Maya exchanged a look with Chitragupta.

Maya: (narrowing her eyes) "Answers about what?"

Chitrangada hesitated, then finally spoke, her voice steady.

Chitrangada: (softly, but with weight) "The truth about the war. The truth about the darkness. And… the truth about me."

A heavy silence stretched between them. The only sound was the distant rustling of dry leaves and the whisper of the cold wind against their cloaks.

Chitrangada merely nodded, but something flickered in her gaze – anticipation, doubt, maybe even fear.

Ayyappan, still feeling the weight of gratitude toward her, exhaled deeply.

Ayyappan: (grinning slightly) "Then you're in luck. We were

heading to him anyway. Come, Chitrangada. You fight like a Yodha – you might as well meet their leader."

As they set off toward Eldoria Academy, there was an unspoken sense of change in the air. The battle had been won, but something lingered – an unseen presence, a shadow in the distance.

And they were right to be wary.

Hidden in the ruins beyond the battlefield, three pairs of golden eyes glowed through the darkness.

Maricha stood at the edge of a crumbling archway, his monstrous form barely visible in the shifting shadows. Beside him, his loyal aides – Viradha and Kabandha – lurched forward, their grotesque figures hunched over like predators awaiting their prey.

Maricha's lips curled into a smirk.

Maricha: (murmuring, amused) "The fools. They celebrate their little victory, thinking they've outmatched the darkness. How adorable."

Viradha's elongated limbs twitched.

Viradha: (whispering, uncertain) "They fought fiercely, Master. That girl – Chitrangada – fights like she has faced the darkness before."

Maricha chuckled darkly, his golden eyes gleaming.

Maricha: (mockingly) "And yet, she leads us straight to their heart."

Kabandha's grotesque mouth twisted into a grin.

Kabandha: (growling) "Master, shall we strike now?"

Maricha turned to them, his voice dripping with satisfaction.

Maricha: (softly, almost reverently) "Not yet. Our Lord desires something hidden within their sanctuary. The secrets buried within Eldoria Academy – old, powerful, forgotten. Let them think they are safe… let them lead us right to it."

Viradha hesitated.

Viradha: (cautious) "And if they uncover our plan?"

Maricha's smirk widened.

Maricha: (low, confident) "By the time they realize… it will be far too late."

As the Yodhas revelled in their innocent, illusory victory, Maricha relished in his dark triumph.

Maricha: (gloating) "Watch closely, my shadows. The Academy is now within our grasp, thanks to these naive Yodhas. The cosmos must be laughing at their folly."

Kabandha: (inquisitively) "So, what's next, Master?"

Maricha: (darkly amused) "Now, we wait. I will single-handedly finish Eldoria and gift our realm to the Lord of Darkness. These Yodhas are mere playthings in our cosmic game. Darkness will prevail."

As the Yodhas and Chitrangada disappeared beyond the hills, Maricha tilted his head to the sky, his golden eyes gleaming with cruel anticipation.

Maricha: (darkly amused) "The grand finale awaits."

His laughter echoed through the ruins, swallowed by the night.

The Yodhas finally reached the towering gates of Eldoria Academy, the last beacon of hope in their war against the darkness. The massive doors carved with celestial runes groaned as the guards recognized their returning warriors. Torches burned in the high corridors, casting flickering golden light against the stone walls. Despite the safety within the Academy, the air carried a sense of urgency – everyone knew war was coming.

Ayyappan turned to Chitrangada.

Ayyappan: (grinning) "Welcome to Eldoria Academy. Home of the Yodhas, last hope for the realm, and arguably the only place where a meal feels like a reward after surviving an ambush."

Ayyappan paused, his gaze locking onto Chitrangada with a playful spark. "It tastes even better when you've just saved the most captivating warrior on the field." He ended with a wink, his grin effortlessly disarming.

Chitrangada exhaled softly, a spark of amusement flickering across her face. For an instant, an unfamiliar flutter stirred within her – like a swarm of butterflies taking flight – while her cheeks warmed with a sudden, unexpected glow. But as swiftly as the feeling arrived, the warrior within her reasserted its presence. With resolute determination, she dismissed the distraction, and resumed her vigilant survey of the Academy, her eyes meticulously scanning every nook and shadowed corner. And her gaze was frantically searching for the one person who could give her the answers she needed – the one whom the Astral Council guided her to meet.

Maya: (gesturing down the hallway) "Come. Kalki will want to meet you."

Whispers trailed in their wake as they passed through the echoing corridors. Warriors and scholars alike peered at Chitrangada with open curiosity. Who was this mysterious warrior? Why had she arrived now?

Chitrangada ignored the murmurs. She had only one goal.

They reached the doors to the council chambers, which were heavy, ancient, and pulsing with old magic. Maya pushed them open.

And there, standing at the centre of the room, was Kalki.

The leader of the Yodhas. The guardian of Eldoria.

The one person who held the answers Chitrangada had spent her life searching for.

Chitrangada paused, her certainty cracking for the first time since she'd arrived.

Forging Bonds and Unravelling Celestial Mysteries

The Yodhas and Chitrangada returned from the eastern province, their minds still haunted by the recent ambush. The road to Eldoria was lined with quiet victories and unspoken fears. Even as the warriors shared tales of their triumphs, a shadow of unease clung to them—the enemy had known their movements and anticipated their arrival.

Above them, the dark sky loomed vast and wordless, bearing quiet witness to their frantic journey back. Each step felt heavier, as though destiny itself was tightening its grip.

An unfamiliar sensation coursed through her veins as Chitrangada stepped through the towering gates of Eldoria Academy. The atmosphere inside the grand hall pulsed with a living energy – restless, watchful, and full of silent anticipation.

When she passed the doorway, a wave of whispers spread through the corridors. A presence had arrived. Students and scholars peered from their chambers, their gazes lingering on her. Some whispered, some nodded in recognition, and some merely stared.

A young scholar, draped in dark-brown, and yellow robes, whispered to his companion.

"She is the one, isn't she? The chosen one?"

An elder priest, his silver beard shimmering in the moonlight, folded his hands in silent prayer.

"The cosmos has sent her. The cycle begins anew."

Chitrangada's steps faltered for a brief moment. She had been a warrior all her life, yet she never felt such an overwhelming sense of significance. Was she truly destined for something greater, or was she merely walking into a storm that had already been foretold?

Even the Academy's celestial artefacts – the ancient murals, the suspended orbs of wisdom – seemed to respond to her presence, glowing ever so slightly. The cosmos had acknowledged her.

Inside the grand hall, Kalki stood waiting. His presence was steady, yet his fingers betrayed a flicker of anxiety. The moment his gaze landed on the approaching warriors, his tense shoulders relaxed.

"Welcome back, my warriors," he said, his voice carrying across the chamber. "I trust your journey was… enlightening."

He searched their faces, his keen eyes absorbing every cut, every bruise, every unspoken burden they carried.

Chitragupta stepped forward, his tone both triumphant, and grim.

"It was a hard-fought battle, Kalki. The darkness has grown bold. They ambushed us when we least expected it. Had it not been for Chitrangada…" He turned towards her. "She saved Ayyappan from the clutches of a twisted minion. Her arrival was no mere coincidence – it was fate."

A flicker of something raw and unguarded passed over Kalki's face – panic. He turned sharply to Ayyappan, his voice urgent.

"Ayyappan." Kalki strode forward, his movements brisk. "Are you all right?" His voice, though steady, carried an edge of urgency. "What happened? Were you hurt?"

Ayyappan, caught off guard, hesitated for a moment before shaking his head. "No, Kalki, I – "

Kalki grabbed his wrists, scanning him for any wounds, his grip almost too tight. "Did they touch you? Did they – " He turned sharply toward Maya. "You were with him, weren't you? Did the demons?"

The tension in the hall thickened. The Yodhas exchanged uncertain glances. Chitrangada, standing slightly apart, felt a strange unease creep into her bones. Kalki was a leader of unshakeable resolve, a warrior revered for his composure in the face of chaos. Yet, here he was, unravelling before their eyes.

Maya, ever perceptive, stepped forward. "We're fine, Kalki," she said firmly, her voice carrying an unspoken warning. "The battle was difficult, but we handled it."

Rudrama, standing silently at the corner of the room, immediately cleared her throat, stepping in to ease the tension. "Indeed, they were ambushed. The shadows moved faster than they anticipated." She turned to Chitrangada, a rare admiration in her voice. "But she fought with incredible skill. She arrived just in time to save Ayyappan."

At this, Kalki's grip on Ayyappan loosened, his expression shifting. His gaze flickered toward Chitrangada, his earlier panic quickly masked behind a composed exterior.

Kalki exhaled, collecting himself. "I mean, I hope you all are safe," he amended smoothly. "No one is harmed?"

Kalki caught himself. He exhaled and took a step back. His tone had shifted, calm and deliberate, every word measured precisely.

Maya's eyes narrowed slightly. Chitrangada, too, caught the shift, the deliberate attempt to correct his words. Something about the way he had reacted felt… off.

Ayyappan, however, seemed oblivious. He turned to Chitrangada, his face breaking into an earnest smile. "She didn't just fight, Kalki. She was magnificent."

Chitrangada felt the warmth of his gaze, but before she could respond, she caught the briefest flicker of something in Maya's expression – an unease, a shadow of concern.

Maya quickly masked it, offering a slight nod. "Yes, she fought well. We're lucky she was there."

But Chitrangada wasn't fooled. There was something beneath Maya's words, a guardedness that hinted at something unspoken.

Having fully regained his composure, Kalki studied Chitrangada with a new intensity. “You've proven yourself already,” he said. “The Astral Council has chosen you for a reason.”

Chitrangada felt the weight of their words and how they regarded her now, not just as an outsider but as one of them.

Kalki's expression softened. He studied Chitrangada for a long moment before nodding.

Kalki turned, his piercing gaze locking onto hers.

Kalki: (calm, observing) “So, you've finally arrived, Chitrangada.”

She inhaled sharply.

Chitrangada: (quietly, but with certainty) “And I am not leaving without the truth.”

A slow smile ghosted across Kalki's lips.

Kalki: (softly) “Then let us begin.”

“You carry something rare, Chitrangada. Strength and righteousness.” He gestured toward the Academy walls, where ancient symbols pulsed faintly. “The cosmos has guided you here for a reason. The Astral Council watches.”

His words were met with quiet reverence. The Yodhas exchanged glances, understanding the gravity of what had been said.

Chitrangada met Kalki's gaze, unwavering.

“Then tell me,” she said. “What am I meant to do? Why did the Astral Council choose me?”

Sensing the conflicts of emotions raging inside Chitrangada, Kalki looked at her with a comforting and assuring way, “I know you're in search of answers, Chitrangada, and your mind roils with a storm of doubts. Yet amid the chaos, one truth burns bright: deep in your soul, you've always known that you were destined for something extraordinary… something which others around you would never willingly opt to do. From the most inconspicuous challenges to the fiercest trials, you've forged balance with your indomitable spirit.

Can you not feel the call of destiny echoing through every fibre of your being?"

The other Yodhas respectfully withdrew, sensing that this conversation was not meant for all ears.

Kalki motioned for Chitrangada to follow. They walked silently through the Academy's sacred halls, past the murals of forgotten wars and celestial prophecies.

He finally stopped before a grand tapestry woven with golden threads. It depicted a lone warrior standing between the light and the abyss, arms outstretched, the cosmos bending at their will.

Kalki traced his fingers along the fabric. "The Astral Council chose you, Chitrangada, because you are the bridge."

She frowned. "The bridge? Between what?"

Kalki turned to her. "Between realms. Between fate and choice. You are not merely a warrior – you are a harbinger."

Chitrangada swallowed, the weight of his words settling in.

"But why me? What makes me worthy?"

Kalki's gaze didn't waver. "Because your soul carries something most others have lost – an unwavering belief in the cosmos. A righteousness that does not falter, even in the face of the unknown. You did not know Ayyappan, yet you risked your life for him. You fought without hesitation."

She exhaled sharply. "And the whispers? I was guided here by a voice, Parvati. Who is she?"

At the mention of the name, Kalki's expression changed. Reverence flickered across his face, and he instinctively touched the trident mark on his palm.

"Parvati, the Divine Mother," he murmured. "She sees where time holds no meaning, seeing what others cannot. If she called you here… then your path is truly woven into the fabric of destiny."

"If I were chosen to restore balance," she said, her voice low, "then what is it that threatens to destroy it?"

Kalki's expression darkened. The weight of his silence was more telling than any words.

Finally, he spoke. "The Lord of Darkness," he said gravely. "An entity driven to dismantle everything we've sworn to defend. His reach is growing, his shadows spreading. And now, he knows of you."

An unknown sensation ran through Chitrangada's spine.

Chitrangada's mind raced. The whispers, the visions, the pull toward Eldoria had all been orchestrated by something far beyond her comprehension.

She squared her shoulders. "Then I will not falter. Tell me what must be done."

Unbeknownst to them, far beyond the sacred walls of Eldoria, unseen eyes watched.

Maricha stood cloaked in darkness, his lips curling into a slow, calculating smile.

He had seen it all – the girl, the whispers, the vulnerabilities.

And more importantly… he had seen Kalki's weakness.

"Ayyappan," Maricha mused, his voice like rusted steel. "The guardian's heart lies with you. Intriguing."

Kabandha knelt before him. "Is this the moment, master? I ache for the thrill – I'm tired of lurking in the shadows. Please, master, let us strike now, and shatter this realm. Look at them – they tremble already, scrambling to amass every weapon and ounce of might against us, oblivious to the reality that we're already here, watching them, delving into their minds, and hearts. Overpowering them will be nothing more than a stroll."

Maricha's smile was slow and deliberate. "Not yet. Let her believe she is ready. Let them all believe. I know overpowering them will be nothing more than a cakewalk. But are we not the harbingers of darkness? Are we not meant to spice things up with thrill and mystery? How dull the world would be if we ceased our unpredictable exploits. Is it not our nature, our instinct, to let the enemy perish slowly, mercilessly? Does the sight of despair not ignite our greatest high?"

Maricha gloated with the thought of making others suffer, "It's the dark essence present in the DNA of every being that has the power to add the tastiest flavours to life – the most seductive of poisons, veiled in sweetness, wrapped in mystery. It's as if the cosmos itself has devised a master plan, ensuring that light prevails so that no one can savour the seductive taste of darkness. I can't imagine a world bathed in nothing but light… ugh!"

He turned towards his cohort with a sinister smile.

"And when the time is right… We take everything from them."

The Convergence of Powers

The air inside the 'Disciplina Arena' crackled with energy, the rhythmic clang of swords, the whoosh of arrows, and the hum of magic forming a symphony of disciplined chaos. The Yodhas were deep in training, each warrior pushing themselves to their limits, refining their skills in preparation for the battles ahead.

Kalki and Chitrangada entered through the towering archway, their presence casting an unspoken command over the room. The intensity of training faltered momentarily as all eyes turned toward them. The warriors of Eldoria were curious about Chitrangada, the celestial warrior chosen by destiny, and now she stood before them, a living force, her presence carrying both command and enigma.

Kalki stepped forward, his voice echoing with authority.

Kalki: "Yodhas, allow me to formally introduce our newest member, Chitrangada. She possesses celestial powers and has been chosen to join our ranks. Together, we shall embark on a journey to protect Eldoria and restore balance to the realms."

Chitrangada stepped beside Kalki, radiating confidence. She looked at her new teammates, acknowledging their dedication, and bravery.

Chitrangada: "I'm honoured to join this extraordinary team of Yodhas. Each of you has proven yourselves in battle and demonstrated unwavering commitment to our cause. Together, we shall face the encroaching darkness and emerge victorious."

Chitrangada's gaze swept across the room, absorbing the sight of her newfound comrades. Ayyappan, swift and nimble, leapt effortlessly between obstacles, his twin daggers flashing in the dim light. Maya, the sorceress, wove intricate spells, her fingers tracing glowing runes in the air. Ahilya, the master strategist, sparred with

Chitragupta, their blades clashing in a display of calculated ferocity. The atmosphere was charged, and each warrior was lost in pursuing perfection.

Ahilya lowered her sword, stepping forward with measured grace.

Ahilya: "So, the celestial warrior finally stands among us."

Her tone contained neither hostility nor warmth – only the weight of measured curiosity.

Chitrangada met her gaze without hesitation.

Chitrangada: "And I intend to prove I belong."

A hint of a smirk ghosted across Maya's lips.

Maya: "Good. Because we don't need legends – we need warriors."

Kalki stepped forward, his voice steady, and authoritative.

Kalki: "Yodhas, today we welcome Chitrangada into our ranks. She has been chosen, not just by fate, but by her merit. She holds the flame of the stars within her soul, and with that light, we'll stand against the shadow threatening to swallow Eldoria."

Chitragupta, ever the tactician, regarded Chitrangada with keen interest.

Chitragupta: "Celestial powers, you say? Then let's see what she can do. It's not speech that shapes a warrior, but the choices carved in battle."

Ayyappan had always sought the thrill of challenge, not for praise, but for the clarity it brought, the way it stripped away pretence and revealed the truth beneath. Yet, as he stood before Chitrangada, the familiar thrill was tainted with something unfamiliar – an ache he could not name. A quiet storm had been gathering within him since their paths crossed. It wasn't just admiration. It was a pull – strange, powerful, and inescapable.

She turned something in him, something he had never known.

So, under the pretext of combat, he gave that emotion room to breathe. He stepped forward, his gaze steady, his voice low but laced with intensity.

Ayyappan: "A test of skill, then? Nothing like a good spar to break the ice. Let's see how my saviour fares when blade replaces fate."

His words were a challenge, yes – but also a question—a yearning.

Chitrangada met his gaze without hesitation. Her expressions remained composed, yet within her, a ripple echoed. He looked at her as though he saw beyond the warrior's mask, into the shadows she carried, the fire she tried to hide. She wasn't the one to waver, yet in that moment, a quiet warmth stirred within her – gentle, unfamiliar, and profoundly disarming.

Was it curiosity? Perhaps. Or perhaps it was something more profound – a silent desire to understand him as much as he seemed to seek her. She reached for her weapon with calm purpose, her voice a silken thread woven with quiet power.

Chitrangada: "I was born ready. I'm the chosen one… remember?" she chuckled.

Bound by the unspoken bond only twins share, Maya felt it before she understood it. A subtle shift in her brother's energy – an emotion too new, raw, and flickering beneath the surface. Her sixth sense had never failed her, and now it whispered to her of something fragile beginning to take root in Ayyappan's heart.

In the silence that followed, Maya saw the truth with chilling clarity – this was no mere duel. It was a convergence, a moment written long before time had etched its scars upon them. Two warriors. Two storms. And between them, a stillness so charged it threatened to unveil everything they had carefully kept hidden.

A sudden unease gripped her. What if this moment cracked open the past they had buried so carefully? What if Chitrangada, despite her valour, was not who she appeared to be? What if she looked too closely and saw the truth – their truth? What if she used it?

The questions spiralled, sharp and relentless.

Unwilling to let the moment deepen, Maya stepped forward, her voice deliberate, slicing through the charged air like a blade drawn too swiftly.

Maya, forcing a calm smile: "Time is of the essence. I wish to learn much about the warrior who saved my brother. And though I'm truly grateful, curiosity has its urgency. Who is she?"

Maya's words were polite, even warm, but beneath them lay a calculated intent. A shield. A warning. A distraction. And perhaps, a silent plea to protect her brother, who didn't yet know what his heart was reaching for.

Chitrangada, attuned to the undercurrents around her, felt it – the quiet weight in Maya's gaze. It wasn't hostility, but something sharper—a guardedness cloaked in civility. For a fleeting moment, she wondered if it was distrust… or something deeper. And then she understood. It was love – fierce, protective, and unrelenting – the love of a sister.

She held Maya's gaze unflinchingly and spoke with calm clarity—her voice steady but carrying the grace of someone who knew the value of hard-earned trust.

Chitrangada: "Please ask what you must." Her eyes didn't waver. "I understand. To stand beside one another in battle, trust isn't a courtesy – it's a necessity. And if I'm to earn yours… I welcome your queries." Maya, her eyes alight with intrigue, stepped forward.

Maya: "I'm curious about celestial power. They say it is not just strength, but a force beyond the mortal realm. Tell me, Chitrangada, have you ever glimpsed the Astral Council?"

Chitrangada's eyes dimmed slightly at the mention of the Astral Council. A flicker of something indistinct passed across her face.

Chitrangada: "I have not only glimpsed them, Maya. I have stood before them. I have heard their voices in the void and visions etched in the stars."

The weight of her words settled over the group, replacing their light-hearted banter with something more profound.

Ahilya, always perceptive, studied Chitrangada closely.

Ahilya: "Then you understand the cost of power."

Chitrangada inclined her head.

Chitrangada: "More than you know."

The moment stretched, an unspoken understanding passing between them.

Ayyappan clapped his hands together, breaking the tension.

Ayyappan: "Enough philosophy. Let's see some action!"

Chitrangada turned to Kalki, silently awaiting his approval. He gave her a nod.

Kalki: "Show them why you were chosen."

Chitrangada stepped forward, rolling her shoulders as she sized up her opponents.

Chitrangada: "Who wants to test me first?"

Ayyappan moved forward, drawing his sword with a metallic hiss.

Ayyappan: "Let's see if celestial warriors live up to their reputation."

The other Yodhas formed a loose circle around them, murmuring in anticipation.

The air grew still as Ayyappan lunged.

His blade came fast – too fast for an ordinary warrior to parry – but Chitrangada was not ordinary. In the blink of an eye, she twisted, dodging his strike with the fluidity of a shadow. The moment his momentum carried him forward, she struck, her palm connecting with his chest in a burst of energy that sent him skidding back.

Ayyapan's eyes widened, not in fear, but in exhilaration.

Ayyappan: "Bravo."

Without missing a beat, he recovered, launching a flurry of precise strikes. Chitrangada met him move for move, her blade flashing as she deflected his attacks. The onlookers leaned forward, their excitement palpable.

Maya, watching intently, murmured to Kalki.

Maya: "She's reading him."

Kalki nodded, arms crossed over his chest.

Kalki: "Not just reading – she's adapting."

Ayyappan attempted a feint, but Chitrangada anticipated it, sidestepping smoothly, and pressing the tip of her blade against his throat before he could react.

A beat of silence.

Then, Ayyappan let out a chuckle.

Ayyappan: "I concede. She's good."

After the decisive duel, Ayyappan was now sure of one thing: Chitrangada was special – maybe because she had saved his life, maybe because of the quiet confidence she carried like an unshakeable flame, perhaps because she was a warrior unlike any he had ever seen before. Or maybe, just maybe, because his heart fluttered in a way it never had, and a genuine liking had begun to take root within him. He pushed the thought aside. This was not the time. While Ayyappan had been dealing with his feelings, Maya was worried about the question: what if, in trying to hold onto something new, he let go of what they had spent years buying?

The charged air inside the Disciplina Arena refused to settle. Though the battle between Ayyappan and Chitrangada had ended, the Yodhas could still feel the invisible sparks crackling between them. Trust was not given freely – it was earned, and Chitrangada had just taken her first step into their ranks.

The circle of warriors erupted into murmurs of approval. Ayyappan whistled. Seeing Ayyappan's growing admiration towards Chitrangada, somehow made Maya a little uncomfortable.

Ayyappan: "Alright, I like her."

Ahilya's eyes shimmered with newfound curiosity.

Ahilya: "Your power… It's not just celestial. There's something else there, something deeper."

Chitrangada withdrew her blade, but her expression remained unreadable.

Chitrangada: "Perhaps."

Before anyone could probe further, Kalki's voice cut through the chatter.

Kalki: "Enough for now. There are graver concerns that demand our attention now."

He stepped to the centre of the arena, his gaze sweeping across his team.

Kalki: "The trials ahead will test us beyond our limits. It will take more than skill to guide us – it will take our strength in unity. As declared by the divine Krishna…"

He closed his eyes for a moment, then recited with solemn reverence:

"Karmanya Vadhikaraste Ma Phaleshu Kadachana,

Ma Karma Phala Hetur Bhurmatey Sangostva Akarmani."

His voice rang with conviction.

Kalki: "We must perform our duty without attachment to the outcome. Our actions must be our only focus. We fight not for glory, but for the survival of Eldoria."

The Yodhas stood taller, their expressions hardening with resolve.

Kalki, watching from the sidelines, couldn't help but feel a surge of pride. He had witnessed their growth, determination, and unwavering spirit. He felt the weight of conviction—they were ready to face whatever darkness awaited them. Chitragupta stepped forward, his voice steady.

Chitragupta: "Then let us train… train like never before. If war is upon us, we shall meet it not as scattered warriors, but as one force-unbreakable, indivisible."

Kalki: "Let us take inspiration from the path walked by Lord Rama. May our actions reflect the virtues he embodied. Our ancestors fought in epic wars, displaying an indomitable spirit, and valour. Their legacy reminds us of the heights we can reach when we stand together, even against formidable odds. Our history bears witness to their unwavering spirit and courage."

The team absorbed each word, their hearts ignited with pride and a fierce determination. The notion of celestial beings offering guidance added an air of mystique and reassurance to their mission. They were not just fighting for Eldoria; they had become part of a cosmic struggle, where mortal, and celestial forces converged.

In that moment, Kalki's expression was dejected, his gaze shifting beyond the training grounds. The remnants of their last battle still haunted him, not just in memory but in the whispers of fate. He had seen the signs – fractures forming in the very fabric of Eldoria's balance.

He turned to face the Yodhas.

Kalki: "Our mission is no longer just a battle against those who seek to conquer. The darkness we face is older, deeper. It does not merely threaten Eldoria – it seeks to unravel it."

A weight fell upon the team. They had faced formidable enemies before, but something about Kalki's tone sent an unsettling vibe down their spines.

Maya, ever perceptive, narrowed her eyes.

Maya: "You're not just talking about the warlords or the corrupted. There's something else, isn't there?"

Kalki met her gaze, and for a moment, hesitation flickered in his eyes. Then, with quiet resolve, he spoke.

Kalki: "I have seen it."

Silence.

Kalki was not one to speak of visions lightly. If he had seen something, it was not a mere warning – it was a prophecy.

Ahilya broke the silence and stepped forward, her expression calculating.

Ahilya: "Tell us everything."

Kalki exhaled, bracing himself.

Kalki: "It was not a dream. It was a glimpse beyond the veil – beyond time itself. I stood in the ruins of Eldoria, the sky fractured like shattered glass. The rivers ran black. Long ago, when darkness first crept upon our ancestors, fate sealed a grim destiny. The realm teetered on the brink of oblivion without a trace. Once a land of breathtaking beauty, Eldoria was on the precipice of being swallowed by a void where the sun would never rise, and life itself would have become an illusion."

A cold wind swept through the arena, though there was no storm outside.

Kalki: "Our ancestors have felt its hunger."

Chitrangada stiffened.

Chitrangada: "Was it a mortal presence that threatened Eldoria before?"

Kalki's jaws tightened.

Kalki: "No."

A low murmur spread through the Yodhas. Maya, lost in her thoughts, her fingers clenched in quiet defiance.

Maya: "Something ancient, then. Something that should not have awoken."

Chitragupta, who had remained silent until now, finally spoke, his voice measured.

Chitragupta: "If what you saw was a future that awaits us, then we have two choices – either we succumb to it or forge a different path."

Kalki nodded.

Kalki: "That is why we must act now. The forces we face are gathering. The Astral Council has already sensed the shift in the balance. Time is not on our side; we cannot afford to wait."

Kalki raised his hand, beckoning the team to gather closer.

Kalki: "Before we embark on this journey, let us reaffirm our commitment to one another and the mission at hand. Repeat after me, 'We are the guardians of Eldoria, united in purpose, and bound by trust. Together, we shall prevail.'"

The team members echoed the words in unison, their voices blending into a mighty chorus of dedication and unity. The energy in the Disciplina Arena surged, crackling with a newfound sense of purpose and resolve.

Kalki: "Remember, my fellow Yodhas, we are each other's strength. Together, we form an unbreakable bond that transcends individual capabilities. *Even if we falter or the darkness threatens to consume us, we shall not lose hope or faith. For in our moments of weakness, we shall rise again, united with even greater intensity, and fight back with unwavering resolve until the very last.*"

His words resonated deep within the Yodhas' hearts, igniting a fire within them that burned with unyielding determination. They understood that they were not alone in this battle and that their unity would be the source of their power.

The circle of warriors tightened, their gazes locked in unspoken agreement. They had trained. They had fought. And now, with Chitrangada among them, they would rise to face the darkness together. As the echoes of battle cries filled the Disciplina Arena, a new chapter in Eldoria's history had begun.

Trials and Temptations

An unsettling, unseen force slithered in as Kalki and the Yodhas departed the Displina Arena.

The air in Eldoria had changed.

The walls of the great fortress, which had once felt like a sanctuary, now seemed like a cage, the shadows stretching unnaturally in the flickering torchlight.

Unaware of Maricha and his cohorts who had trailed behind them, the team felt an eerie and gloomy atmosphere as Maricha began to sow chaos and discord throughout Eldoria.

Doubts seeped into the minds of the once united team, as suspicions, and mistrust clouded their judgement. The tightly woven fabric of their camaraderie started to unravel, giving way to a fragile sense of distrust.

As the shadows continued their malevolent influence, they paved the way for the arrival of the Lord of Darkness, orchestrating the destruction of Eldoria. The once harmonious realm now faced imminent peril, its foundations shaken by the encroaching darkness.

Chitrangada tightened her grip on her blade. Something was wrong.

The Yodhas had fought together for months, yet now, a rift had begun to form – a chasm carved by suspicion, by whispers that slithered through the corridors at night. She saw it in Ahilya's tense stance, in Ayyappan's fleeting hesitation. Even Maya, always indecipherable, seemed more distant than before.

And worst of all?

Every person she met was cloaked in uncertainty, leaving her unsure of who truly stood by her side.

A sharp voice shattered the silence.

"Again!"

Kalki's command cracked through the air like a whip. He stood in the centre, his silver blade gleaming under the twilight sky. His piercing gaze swept over the Yodhas, not violent but undeniably harsh.

Ayyappan wiped a trickle of sweat from his brow, his muscles taut with exhaustion. "Acharya, we've been training since dawn. We need rest, or we'll fight as weak as the ones we train to defeat."

Kalki's eyes narrowed. "And when the enemy comes? When they bring the night upon you, will you also beg them for rest?" His tone resonated with frigid severity, as unyielding as the cold metal clenched in his clasp.

Ayyappan stiffened, but before he could argue, Kalki spoke again.

"Doubt is a disease. And right now, it is spreading through you like a plague."

A tense silence followed. Chitrangada glanced around – no one spoke, but the unspoken words filled the air.

Kalki's voice softened, though the edge remained. "If you waver now, you are already dead." He raised his sword. "Again."

Ayyappan exhaled sharply and raised his weapon. The others followed, but something in the air had changed.

Maya observed the conversation, her eyes alight with a subtle, knowing amusement. She caught Chitrangada staring and smirked. "You feel it too, don't you?" she murmured.

Chitrangada hesitated. "Feel what?"

Maya leaned in, her tone barely more than a breath. "The breaking. The unravelling. Don't you feel the pull of something mystical and hypnotic?"

Chitrangada's stomach tightened. Before she could respond:

A scream tore through the Academy.

An invisible, eerie presence was evident, but no one knew it.

The sound of shattering glass followed. Heavy footsteps—a rush of movement.

The shadows had breached the walls.

Rudrama reacted first. "The eastern corridor!"

Before Kalki could issue a command, a cold wind surged through the training ground. The walls trembled as dark tendrils slithered through the cracks. The scent of rot thickened, suffocating the air.

Kalki drew his celestial trident, its silver blade humming with divine energy. "Chitrangada! Divide the team into two units – deploy one group immediately to seize control of the inner sanctum! Ayyappan, Maya – protect the students and hold the outer walls! No one – " his voice darkened " – no one lets the darkness through."

Chitrangada didn't hesitate. "With me!" she ordered, then strode forward, guiding her team into the Academy's core. The shadows, which were nothing more than illusions created by Maricha, slithered, whispers rising in their wake.

And deep within, unseen, Maricha watched.

Maricha stood at the edge of Eldoria's protective barrier, blackish-golden eyes gleaming with cruel amusement. Shadows coiled around him, restless, eager.

A low chuckle escaped his lips. "Look at them."

Beside him, Viradha knelt. "Is this the right time to strike, my Lord?"

Maricha smirked. "Not yet, Viradha. Let them rot in their doubt. Fear is a much sweeter poison."

He gestured towards the Academy, where the Yodhas scrambled, already fractured.

"They will tear themselves apart long before we touch them."

Maricha, enjoying his sinister plan unfold, gloated to his aides, "The Astral Council has become too weak. Look! How easily can I control these mere beings of Eldoria? Even the so-called 'chosen one', Chitrangada, is an extremely vulnerable soul. I'm amazed to see that these naive so-called Yodhas of Eldoria even dared to face the power of our Lord."

Inside the Academy, the Yodhas were not just fighting shadows.

They were fighting themselves.

Chitrangada saw it—the flickers of hesitation, the uncertain glances. The battle had barely begun, yet cracks were already forming.

Then Chitragupta's voice cut through the chaos.

"How did they breach the walls?" His tone was sharp, accusatory. "The barriers should have held… unless someone let them in."

A dangerous silence of doubt fell.

Rudrama, understanding the gravity of the situation, turned sharply. "What are you suggesting?"

Chitragupta's eyes darkened. "I'm saying there's a traitor among us."

The accusation sent a ripple through the group. Suspicion crept into their eyes, coiling like a viper.

Ayyappan's grip tightened around his sword. "That's a grave accusation, Chitragupta."

Chitragupta didn't back down. "Then tell me how else the shadows slipped past divine protection? Someone opened the gates."

Chitrangada stepped forward, voice firm. "Enough. This is exactly what they want. We rise as one or crumble alone."

But even as she spoke, the doubt had already taken root.

And then – the whisper came again.

Not from the shadows. Not from the walls.

From within her mind.

"Foolish girl… do you truly think they trust you?"

A cold shudder ran down her spine.

"Do you honestly believe you belong among them?"

She gasped, breath coming in short, sharp bursts. No. No, I won't listen.

But the voice only laughed.

"You are alone, Chitrangada. Just like before. Just like always."

She looked around at the way Ayyappan's fingers grasped the sword's pommel, his fingers digging into the weapon like a vice, at Maya's unreadable gaze, at the flickers of uncertainty in every eye.

The shadows weren't just attacking Eldoria.

They were inside them now.

And if she didn't act fast, Eldoria wouldn't need an enemy to fall.

It would destroy itself.

Chitrangada moved carefully, every step calculated, her fingers gripping the hilt of her sword. The whispers hadn't stopped. If anything, they had grown stronger. They slithered through the air, curling around her ears like serpents, sinking venomous doubts into her mind.

You cannot trust them.

They are watching you.

They will betray you first.

Maricha found the perfect opportunity to feed on Chitrangada's emotional conflict as he started to sow doubts in her mind. Voices echoed in her mind, casting doubts on her worthiness and raising questions about her role and the motives of the Astral Council. But Chitrangada refused to succumb to weakness.

She could hear voices saying, "Chitrangada, you are such a fool. The Astral Council is playing you. You aren't the chosen one. You are one ordinary woman. You stand no chance in front of our mighty force. Even the weakest of our soldiers is better than you. Time is still there. Run back to your parents. This isn't even your realm. Why would you die for some strangers? Who would take care of your parents and your family?"

"Who would take care of your clan? You haven't even met anyone from the Astral Council. Do you know anything about who Kalki is and what he is hiding? Run and we shall spare your life."

But Chitrangada wasn't that weak. She remained steadfast, drawing strength from the support of her team and the unwavering belief in her purpose. Eldoria had started to grow on her, and she had become fond of this place. She knew succumbing to the darkness would mean the end of Eldoria and the realm itself. She refused to let her doubts consume her, choosing instead to embrace her destiny and the power within her.

As Chitrangada led her team into the heart of battle against the encroaching darkness, she encountered moments of doubt and despair among her comrades. Sensing their faltering resolve, she rallied them with words of courage and conviction.

Chitrangada: "Yodhas, remember why we fight. We are the guardians of Eldoria, and together, we possess the strength to overcome any obstacle. We have faced our fears, confronted our inner demons, and emerged stronger. May our unity shake the very heart of darkness!"

Chitragupta, the seasoned warrior, spoke up, his voice laced with uncertainty.

Chitragupta: "Chitrangada, what if we are not strong enough? What if the darkness engulfs us, one by one?"

Chitrangada: "Chitragupta, I understand your fears, but we must not allow the shadows to undermine our confidence. What makes us strong isn't just the power we hold – it's the unbreakable bond we share. We're more than allies; we're a family. And no force can break through us when we stand as one."

As the battle raged on, Chitrangada noticed the growing affection between Ayyappan and herself. Ayyappan's eyes often lingered on her, filled with admiration, and something more. However, Chitrangada couldn't fully embrace these feelings, knowing the delicate balance they were striving to maintain amidst the chaos.

Maya, always watchful, observed the interactions between Chitrangada and Ayyappan, her thoughts consumed by the potential consequences of their burgeoning emotions.

Maya: (whispering to herself) "Ayyappan's growing affection for Chitrangada could disrupt our desperately needed balance. Love can uplift us to great heights and expose our deepest vulnerabilities. The chaos thrives on vulnerability. We must tread carefully."

Meanwhile, Chitrangada couldn't shake the strange unease she felt towards Maya. Maya's concealed nature and cryptic presence stirred a deep suspicion within her.

Chitrangada: (to herself) "There's something about Maya that doesn't sit right with me. Her mysterious demeanour and hidden past raise doubts in my mind. Can I truly trust her? Or does she have her own agenda amidst this chaos?"

Despite her reservations, Chitrangada knew that their mission required unity and focus. She kept her unease to herself, prioritizing the collective goal over her concerns. Amid battles and discussions, Chitrangada continued to inspire and motivate her team. Her unwavering belief in their abilities and her relentless pursuit of justice became a guiding force for the Yodhas, pushing them beyond their limits.

Kalki, on the other hand, was taken aback when he realized that the force corrupting Eldoria was the same that had crumbled his lineage—the Rakshasas. Fear gripped him as he contemplated battling his clan, which had surrendered to the shadows. A storm brewed within his mind, questioning his fitness for the impending battle and whether his inner demon would become a liability for his students.

However, relief washed over him as he heard the soothing

voice of Rudrama, a trusted ally who understood his inner struggle. Rudrama reassured him, acknowledging his strength in the face of his inner demon. She reminded him of his resilience and that he had transformed a part of the shadow into an Eldorian over the years.

Rudrama's unwavering support uplifted Kalki's spirits, reaffirming his determination to overcome his past and protect his newfound love for Eldoria. They shared a connection that defied explanation.

Kalki: (taken aback) "This is the same force, the same reason that corrupted my lineage, the Rakshasas. I can't believe I might have to face my clan, those who surrendered themselves to these shadows. This battle will be the toughest for me, especially with the siblings, Maya, and Ayyappan, around."

Kalki's mind raced with doubt and fear, questioning his fitness for the impending battle.

Kalki: (trembling) "Am I even fit for this battle? Will my inner demon become a liability for my team? I don't know how powerful it is, and if my willpower will be enough to tame it."

Rudrama: (calmly) "Don't worry, Kalki. You are much stronger than your inner demon. Trust yourself. This certainly isn't your first battle against darkness. Over the ages, you have seasoned as a mature mentor. You have been Eldoria's guardian for a long time now. Place your trust in the light that resides within you; in moments of turmoil, the emblem of the trident will guide you back to your true path. And as far as the siblings are concerned, they shall face their destiny."

Kalki: (relieved) "I've been losing confidence in myself. It feels like I'm reliving the painful events that crumbled my family. I don't want to lose my commitment and love for Eldoria to the shadows. I don't want to lose any of you. I want my Eldoria to be free from the sinister clutches of the darkness, but I don't know whether I'm ready for another battle."

Rudrama: "You won't, Kalki. I can sense it. This time, you're an experienced soldier, and know the enemy. Buckle up, trust yourself, and fight like it's your last chance. Fight and fight harder this time to save the realm. You're not a demon, Kalki. You possess worth and integrity beyond what you perceive. It's time to avenge your clan and save the realm."

Kalki's mark glowed. With Rudrama's words of consolation, Kalki fought to compose himself and get a grip back.

Kalki: "Thank you, Rudrama. You've always had my back. You're my only family left."

Rudrama: "You know I trust you, Kalki. I'll always have your back and do whatever it takes. I have always believed in your intentions and have sensed that you will lead Eldoria back to the path of light whenever the clutches of darkness threaten it. Do not forget that even the cosmos aids those who fight for the truth and light."

Kalki: "I know, and I trust only you. You know what to do if things don't work out as planned. It's your responsibility, Rudrama. You must do the needful."

Rudrama: "Let's not get carried away, Kalki. For now, stop these thoughts, and concentrate on winning the battle. I know you can do it. Believe in the highest strength of the light."

Unbeknownst to Kalki and Rudrama, Chitrangada overheard their conversation, her curiosity piqued by the mention of Kalki's inner demon, the Rakshasas, the siblings, and Rudrama's role in case the plan fails.

Sensing the opportune moment, the vicious Maricha, and his cohorts started enabling Chitrangada's doubts as humongous tides of vulnerability in her mind. Suddenly, her resolve began to shake, and a doubt arose about whether she was on the right path, whether what she thought the cosmos was guiding her to fight was the righteous path.

Whispers of the Forgotten Legacy - 'Unearthing the Past'

Darkness was creeping into her mind like a slow, inescapable tide. For the first time since arriving in Eldoria, meeting Kalki, and taking up the fight against Maricha and his forces, Chitrangada felt the weight of uncertainty clawing at her soul. She had fought against doubt before—shoved it aside, crushed it under her unwavering resolve. But now, it had lodged itself deep within her, whispering insidious thoughts that refused to be ignored.

She wasn't sure when it had started. Perhaps it had been the growing tension among the Yodhas; their once unbreakable unity seemed to fray at the edges. Maybe it had been the whispers she swore she could hear, laced in the wind, sowing suspicion in her mind. Or perhaps it had been that fateful night when she overheard Kalki and Rudrama speaking in hushed voices, voices laden with secrets that involved her.

That was the moment her faith had begun to waver.

What if I'm not the chosen one?

The question struck her like a physical blow. The mere thought of it made her stomach twist uncomfortably. Everything she had fought for, every battle, every sacrifice – was it all a lie? Had she been sent here on the foundation of a false prophecy?

She stood at the edge of the training arena, her gaze locked onto the abyss below – a dark, yawning gorge that stretched endlessly beneath the cliffside. The wind howled through the canyon, a haunting melody that only fuelled her unease.

Behind her, the Yodhas moved through their drills, their movements sharp yet lacking the fire they once held. Maricha's influence was spreading. The warriors of Eldoria, once bound by unshakeable trust, now seemed distant, hesitant, wary of one another. The cracks were visible in the way they spoke in hushed tones, in the way their gazes lingered on shadows that were not there. Darkness's war was not just of weapons and bloodshed—it was a war of the mind. And he was winning. Chitrangada clenched her fists. Her heart screamed at her to focus, to shake off the unease and return to the fight. But her mind, traitorous as it was, would not let go of the growing suspicion.

She turned sharply, her feet carrying her toward the one person who could give her answers. Kalki.

Kalki stood near the centre of the field, observing the Yodhas. His expression was indecipherable, but his eyes held an unmistakable weight, as though he carried burdens far greater than anyone knew.

Chitrangada's steps were firm but torn between anger and desperation. When she stopped before him, Kalki immediately sensed something was wrong. He needed to address her doubts and fears, to ease the turmoil within her.

"Is everything alright, Chitrangada?" His tone held firm, yet a trace of concern lingered beneath the surface.

Her jaw tightened. "No. Nothing is okay."

Kalki's expression darkened. "What happened?"

Chitrangada inhaled sharply. She wasn't one for riddles, for games. She had always been direct, and this moment would be no different.

"Who am I, Kalki?" The words came out heavier than she intended. "Who are you? And what are you hiding from me?"

Kalki's brows furrowed, his posture shifting slightly, as if bracing for impact. Chitrangada stepped closer, her whisper sharp with urgency, as if each word carried the weight of fate. "I overheard you speaking with Rudrama."

For the first time, she saw genuine surprise flicker across his face, followed by something else – hesitation.

Chitrangada's pulse quickened. There. That hesitation. That was all the proof she needed that something was wrong.

She pressed forward. "You spoke about me as if I were a tool. As if… as if I wasn't meant to know something. I've felt it for days now, this strange… unease. I've fought against it, told myself I was imagining things, but I can't ignore it anymore." She shook her head, frustration evident in her voice. "Tell me the truth, Kalki. What is it that you and the others refuse to say?"

A long silence followed.

"Tell me what's bothering you," Kalki urged gently. "Tell me exactly what you heard and how it's troubling you."

Tears welled up in Chitrangada's eyes as she poured out her heart to Kalki. She shared her fears of inadequacy and the excruciating pain of emotions that consumed her. The shadows whispered warnings, planting seeds of doubt, claiming she was not the chosen one.

As Chitrangada sought out Kalki amidst the commotion, her voice trembled with frustration and desperation. "Kalki, I can't ignore this any longer. The uneasiness, the doubts, it's suffocating me. I need to know the truth. What is it that everyone is hiding? Eldoria, the Astral Council, even you. Why is there such a pervasive sense of secrecy?"

Kalki's expression mirrored Chitrangada's distress, and he understood the gravity of her predicament. He took a deep breath, his eyes locked with hers, conveying profound empathy. "Chitrangada, I understand your frustration. The shadows of doubt have seeped into every crevice of Eldoria, leaving us all grappling with uncertainty. But the truth is complex and delicate, and I must guide you through the labyrinth of secrets."

Chitrangada's gaze hardened, determination etching itself onto her face. "I can handle the truth, Kalki. I need to know what's at stake. How can I fight for Eldoria if I'm left in the dark? Tell me, please."

Kalki exhaled, rubbing a hand over his face. "Chitrangada… It's not that simple."

Her heart pounded. "Then make it simple."

Kalki's gaze met hers, searching, deliberating. His voice turned grave, each word falling like the toll of a warning bell.

"The truth is… Eldoria is standing at the edge of Armageddon – once again."

Chitrangada's eyes narrowed, confusion laced with questions. A chill ran down her spine.

"Once again? What do you mean?"

Kalki nodded slowly, the weight of ancient memory darkening his tone. His heart grew heavier with the guilt that had haunted him since time immemorial—a guilt that refused to fade, no matter how many battles he fought or how many souls he tried to save. And as that guilt surged, the visions returned—merciless and raw—visions no living soul should endure.

He staggered for a breath, the weight of it all crushing against his ribs. Just as the agony reached its peak – when time felt like it might shatter him from within – the trident etched on his palm blazed with a fierce, divine light. It seared through the chaos, anchoring him back to the present. For the cosmos and Kalki, both knew, this wasn't the hour for grief or guilt. This was the hour for resolve. There was no time left to drown in feeling. Chitrangada froze as she saw Kalki stagger, the light in his eyes flickering beneath the weight of unseen torment. Fear gripped her chest as she rushed to his side, catching him before he could fall. Her voice trembled.

"Kalki… What's happening to you? Are you alright? And this mark… this trident on your palm… what is it?"

The mark still pulsed with a strange divine energy, casting a faint glow between them.

Kalki closed his eyes for a breath, drawing strength from somewhere deep, beyond pain, beyond memory. When he opened them, there was fire behind the weariness.

"You will know, Chitrangada," he said, voice low but undaunted.

"All of it. In time. But for now… hold your faith. Not in me, but in the grand plan that threads us all together – even when it feels like it's faltering."

He rose straighter, the glow in his palm dimming, yet something far brighter igniting his eyes.

"This mark… this burden… It's a reminder. Of what was. Of what's coming." He turned away, as if seeing through centuries.

"As I mentioned earlier, this isn't the first time Eldoria has heard the footsteps of the end. The Kalyuga has come before – silent at first, then savage."

He looked back at her, voice like thunder held beneath still waters.

"And this time… it may not leave anything behind."

Kalki continued, his voice tinged with sorrow and fury, "And just like before, there are those who believe in the illusion of darkness… who welcome it with open arms, mistaking its curse for a gift."

The words struck her with the force of a sudden storm.

Chitrangada took a step back, as if the mere idea of it was something tangible, something vile. "What?"

Kalki's expression was grim. "There are those among us who believe that the only way to defeat the Lord of the Darkness and his chief in command, Maricha, is to wield the very power he commands. They believe that the light alone is not enough."

Chitrangada's stomach churned. "And you? What do you believe?"

Kalki didn't hesitate this time. "I believe in balance. Darkness alone cannot devour a realm, Chitrangada. It needs willing hearts – souls seduced by its false promises. It thrives not by force, but by invitation. The true danger begins when the living beings are drawn to it… when they trade truth for power, and hope for the poisoned faith of the abyss."

His voice was steady, filled with conviction. "I have witnessed the ruin that follows when power runs wild and unchallenged. I have seen the destruction it can bring. We cannot fall into the same trap that ruined my clan."

The words hung heavily between them.

Chitrangada inhaled sharply. "Your clan?"

Kalki's voice was solemn. "My ancestors."

A flicker of pain crossed Kalki's face. For a moment, he looked like a man caught between past and present, between duty, and grief.

"Chitrangada," Kalki said with a mixture of gentleness and pain. "I've been in your shoes before. I know the weight of this dilemma and the toll it can take on one's soul. We cannot let Eldoria face the same fate as my clan, the Rakshasas. We cannot let history repeat itself."

Confusion etched across Chitrangada's face as she tried to comprehend Kalki's words. The mention of the Rakshasas stirred a deep curiosity within her. Kalki felt compelled to share his past with Chitrangada. Sensing her inner turmoil, Kalki decided not to delay any further. Taking Chitrangada by the hand, Kalki led her to a secret place, a hidden entrance that opened within the earth. As they descended into the depths, the surroundings shifted, and they found themselves in an old sanctuary.

Meanwhile, listening to Chitrangada, and Kalki's conversation, Maricha got intrigued, and followed them secretly like a shadow while Viradha and Kabandha continued their attack on Eldoria.

As Chitrangada stepped into the forgotten sanctuary, a hushed silence fell upon the air, and the weight of history pressed against her chest. The ancient stone columns rose tall, their carvings telling tales of heroism and despair etched in time. Soft rays of sunlight, filtered through the stained-glass windows, danced upon the floor in a captivating display of colours.

Her eyes widened in awe as she surveyed the grandeur of the sanctuary. It was as if she had stumbled upon a lost world, a chapter of history buried in the annals of time. Turning to Kalki, her voice quivered excitedly and confused, "Kalki, what is this place? How did you find it? It feels like stepping into the forgotten echoes of a great lineage."

Kalki's gaze swept across the majestic hall, reverence shining in his eyes. "This, Chitrangada, is the heart of our lineage. A sanctuary hidden from the world, preserving the secrets, and wisdom of our ancestors. Within these sacred walls, we shall uncover the truths that have eluded us, the answers that have been buried in the sands of time."

As they ventured deeper into the temple, the corridors grew dimly lit, revealing intricate carvings on the walls. Each stroke told a story, depicting the struggles, triumphs, and sacrifices of Kalki's ancestors. The air grew heavy with the weight of centuries, and the silence echoed with the whispers of forgotten tales.

The walls glimmered with gold and marble, resonating with the splendour of a bygone era. Scrolls, books, and artefacts filled the archives, chronicling the extraordinary journey of the Rakshasas. Chitrangada's fingers delicately traced the contours of the carvings, her mind flooded with questions.

"Kalki, these carvings tell of wars long buried – of a legacy swallowed by the silence of ages. Who were your ancestors? What happened to them? Why have they been consigned to oblivion?"

Kalki turned to face her fully. "Chitrangada, there is something you must understand. The history of Eldoria is not as simple as light versus darkness." He gestured around them. "Forgotten. Their legacy twisted into something monstrous."

The weight of his words settled over her like a suffocating fog.

She swallowed. "Then why bring me here? Why am I part of all this?"

Kalki's gaze bore into hers, his following words shifting the very foundation beneath her feet.

"Because you are the key to uncovering the truth."

An oppressive hush settled over the chamber, dense with long-buried truths. The air seemed to hum with the echoes of a past long buried beneath the sands of time. Chitrangada's heart pounded as she took in the grandeur of the sanctuary—this hidden temple, untouched by the world above.

Kalki's voice carried the weight of a solemn legacy, tinged with an unyielding determination. "Our ancestors were the Rakshasas, a once proud and powerful clan that held the weight of Eldoria's protection on their shoulders. They possessed extraordinary gifts, and their loyalty to our land and people was unfaltering. But their journey was one of sacrifice and resilience, cut short by the encroaching shadows and the demons that lurked within."

"You keep speaking of them as if they were different from you," she said, studying him carefully. "As if they were something… more."

Kalki's jaw tensed. "Because they were."

Chitrangada's breath hitched.

"These carvings," Kalki continued, gesturing to the walls around them, "tell the story of the Rakshasas – the first protectors of Eldoria. They were warriors of immense strength, gifted with power beyond imagination. But they were betrayed." His voice hardened. "Their legacy was stolen, their names rewritten in history as villains, monsters."

Chitrangada's fingers curled into fists. "Who did this?"

Kalki's eyes darkened. "The ones who claimed to fight for the light."

A cold dread settled in her stomach. She wanted to deny it, to argue that the Suras – the revered protectors of Eldoria – couldn't have done something so vile. But as she gazed at the carvings, at the pain etched into the stone, she couldn't ignore the evidence before her.

"The Suras rewrote history," she murmured, realization dawning upon her. "They twisted your ancestors into the reflections of the enemy they once stood against."

Kalki's silence was answer enough.

Chitrangada swallowed, her throat dry. "Then… what does that mean for us now? For Eldoria?"

Kalki turned to her, his expression unreadable. "It means we are fighting a war built on centuries of deception. And you, Chitrangada, are at the centre of it."

Her pulse thundered in her ears.

The flickering torchlight led them to a hidden chamber, a sanctuary within a sanctuary. Ancient scrolls and fragile manuscripts lined the shelves, their contents a treasure trove of forgotten knowledge. Chitrangada's eyes widened with anticipation as she approached, her voice filled with reverence and curiosity.

"These scrolls, the words they hold, must be priceless. What secrets will they reveal to us?"

Kalki carefully unfurled a time-worn scroll, its delicate pages telling tales of lost battles, forgotten rituals, and the struggles faced by their ancestors. "These words, Chitrangada, hold the essence of our heritage. They are a map to unlocking our true potential, guiding us towards fulfilling our destinies. I've been trying my best to establish the quintessence of these ethos and principles in our realm. Within these archives lies the key to preventing Eldoria from facing the same dark fate that befell our clan."

In this sacred space, frozen in time, Kalki shared his own experiences, his voice resonating with the echoes of lost battles, the weight of sacrifices, and the lessons he had learned. Within these ancient archives, Kalki hoped Chitrangada would find the answers she sought, and that her doubts would be shattered by the profound truths waiting to be discovered.

The Lost World of the Rakshasas

As Chitrangada and Kalki delved deeper into the temple, the truth of Kalki's heritage unfolded. The history revealed the trials and tribulations faced by the Rakshasas and the challenges that led to their downfall. It also shed light on the immense power they possessed and the knowledge they had accumulated over generations.

Kalki's voice resonated with a mixture of reverence and sorrow as he delved deeper into the history of their lineage. The tapestry seemed to come alive, its faded threads whispering tales of a bygone era.

"Chitrangada, the Rakshasas' glory reached its pinnacle during the reign of King Ravana." Kalki's words carried a sense of pride and longing. "Their powers were unmatched, their wisdom revered. They stood tall as celestial beings, guardians of the fabric that held the realms together. Eldoria flourished under their watchful gaze, a land of enchantment and boundless potential."

Chitrangada's eyes widened, captivated by the grandeur of the past. She could almost hear the echoes of the Rakshasas' footsteps as they walked the hallowed grounds of their sacred city.

"But amidst their prosperity, darkness cast its malevolent shadow," Kalki's voice turned sombre. "Satan, a figure shrouded in sinister intentions, rose to challenge the Rakshasas' reign. He was cunning, charismatic, and relentless in his pursuit of power. Satan preyed upon the weaknesses and desires of our kin, sowing seeds of doubt and discord among them."

As Chitrangada absorbed Kalki's words, she could feel the weight of tragedy settling upon her heart. The tapestry before her, once a symbol of grandeur, now depicted the ruins of a once-mighty city, a stark reminder of the Rakshasas' fall from grace.

"Betrayal, turmoil, and devastating battles followed," Kalki's voice quivered with raw emotion. "The Rakshasas, torn apart by internal strife, stood divided when they needed unity the most. Malakar exploited their vulnerabilities, exploiting their love, ambition, and thirst for power. The grand city crumbled, its splendour reduced to rubble and sorrow."

A sense of grief and injustice welled up within Chitrangada as she envisioned the tragedy that befell her ancestors. Once revered as celestial beings, the Rakshasas had succumbed to their own frailties and external adversaries. The magnitude of their fall echoed through the chambers of the temple, a haunting reminder of the consequences of pride and discord.

"But, Chitrangada," Kalki's voice gained strength, his eyes filled with determination, "we must not let the Rakshasas' legacy be forgotten. We must rise above the ashes of our past, learn from their mistakes, and reclaim our rightful place as guardians of Eldoria."

Chitrangada's gaze shifted from the tapestry to Kalki, her resolve ignited by his words. The weight of history pressed upon her, urging her to carry the burden of her lineage and seek redemption.

"Indeed, Kalki," Chitrangada spoke with conviction, her voice carrying the echoes of her ancestors. "The Rakshasas' fall shall not be in vain. We shall unearth the truth, restore honour to our name, and ensure Eldoria thrives under our protection again."

King Ravana, a figure of unparalleled majesty and wisdom, stood before his people, a beacon of strength, and inspiration.

King Ravana, a figure of awe-inspiring grandeur, possessed an appearance befitting his noble stature and regal lineage. His tall frame stood with a commanding presence, radiating an aura of authority that made the air quiver in reverence. As he walked, his footsteps carried a weight that echoed through the halls, announcing his arrival with every stride.

Adorned in majestic attire, King Ravana's garments spoke of both opulence and dignity. He draped himself in rich fabrics that flowed with grace, each fold and intricate design embodying the artistry of skilled artisans. His regal robe, crafted from the finest silk, enveloped him in a tapestry of vibrant hues, reflecting the splendour of the kingdom he governed.

Upon his head rested a crown of gold, encrusted with precious gemstones that glimmered like stars in the night sky. The crown was an emblem of his authority, a symbol of his rightful place as the guardian of Eldoria. The meticulously arranged jewels that adorned it mirrored the cosmic realm from which his power emanated.

King Ravana's countenance exuded a rare blend of strength and compassion. Like pools of liquid gold, his eyes held a profound depth of wisdom and discernment. They had witnessed the rise and fall of empires, gazed upon the mysteries of the universe, and seen both the light and the darkness within.

His features, chiselled elegantly, portrayed a visage that inspired fear and admiration. A strong jawline framed a regal face, while his well-groomed beard added an air of sophistication. Though his expression was often serene, it carried an underlying intensity, revealing the depths of his intellect and the weight of his responsibilities.

King Ravana's ebony skin, kissed by the sun's rays, radiated an ethereal glow. It bore the marks of his wisdom and experience, the battles fought, and the sacrifices made. Every line etched upon his face told a story, a testament to the strength and resilience that defined his reign.

The air seemed to change in King Ravana's presence, as if bowing before his majestic aura. The atmosphere grew with anticipation, and whispers hushed as all eyes turned towards him. Such was the impact of his presence that even the birds ceased their songs, acknowledging the arrival of their sovereign.

King Ravana's regal appearance, with his profound wisdom and unwavering leadership, instilled fear, and admiration in the hearts of his subjects. He was a beacon of strength and guidance, a ruler who commanded respect and inspired loyalty. In his very being, he embodied the essence of a noble king, transcending mortal limitations, and becoming an embodiment of the divine.

King Ravana, the noble guardian of Eldoria, wielded a weapon befitting his divine authority—the legendary trident. Crafted from a rare and celestial metal, the trident possessed an ethereal gleam that reflected power and righteousness.

The trident stood tall, reaching great heights, and exuding an aura of strength that echoed throughout the land. Its three prongs, each sharpened to perfection, symbolized the unity of mind, body, and spirit. It was believed that only the worthy, the chosen successor of Eldoria, could claim the trident as their own, and it served as a testament to their divine birthright.

The handle of the trident was adorned with intricate carvings depicting scenes from Eldoria's history and the triumphs of the Rakshasas. Each stroke of the artisan's hand brought to life the legends and heroes of the past, reminding all who beheld it, of the lineage from which King Ravana had descended.

At the base of the trident, a gleaming orb of lustrous crystal shimmered with an inner light. The gemstone, known as the 'Heart of Eldoria', was said to house the very essence of the land, its vitality, and resilience. It symbolized the divine connection between the ruler and the realm, a conduit through which the cosmic energies flowed.

When King Ravana wielded the trident, his every movement seemed to carry the weight of centuries of wisdom and the gods' might. With a flick of his wrist, he could summon storms to cleanse the land or calm the raging seas with a gentle touch. The trident became an extension of his will, a tool through which he enacted justice and protected the realm.

The trident's power was not to be taken lightly, for it held the potential to bring both salvation and destruction. It was a weapon that demanded respect, as it embodied the sacred duty bestowed upon the chosen successor of Eldoria. Generally, the firstborn, recognized as the rightful heir, had the privilege of wielding this regal artefact, a symbol of their divine lineage and the hope of the kingdom.

As King Ravana brandished the trident, his subjects and adversaries alike could not help but feel the weight of his authority and the magnitude of his responsibility. The trident served as a constant reminder that Eldoria's future was intertwined with the one who possessed it—a chosen leader destined to protect and guide the realm with unwavering devotion.

"In his possession," Kalki's voice carried a sense of reverence, "King Ravana held a symbol of his supreme power. A blue sapphire gemstone, intricately moulded into a golden ring, rested on his middle finger, its radiance reflecting his authority and connection to the cosmic forces."

Chitrangada's eyes sparkled with curiosity as she interrupted, unable to contain her excitement, "Where is the ring now, Kalki? Does it still exist?"

A shadow of melancholy crossed Kalki's face as he replied, "The fate of the ring remains a mystery, Chitrangada. Its power, an irresistible lure, drew the attention of the forces of darkness that coveted its immense strength. The Lord of Darkness himself yearned to possess it, seeking to harness its potency and become the ultimate ruler."

Chitrangada's gaze intensified, her eagerness unabated. "What transpired after that? Tell me, Kalki."

With a deep breath, Kalki delved into the tale, his voice rich with emotion and tinged with sorrow, "Guided by the wisdom of

King Ravana, the Rakshasas flourished in Eldoria, building a society that embraced their unique gifts and celebrated the diversity of their realm. The Rakshasas were not mere creatures of darkness; they were beings of immense power and profound knowledge. They wielded their abilities gracefully and used them to maintain the delicate balance between the realms."

As the words hung in the air, Chitrangada envisioned the harmonious society that had once thrived under King Ravana's reign. She could almost feel the vibrancy and unity that permeated the land, a testament to the Rakshasas' resilience and the wisdom of their great king.

"But," Kalki's voice grew solemn, "the peace they had forged was fragile. The forces of darkness, drawn by the ring's allure, grew relentless in their pursuit. The Rakshasas found themselves locked in a battle against the encroaching shadows, which would test their strength, unity, and very existence."

Chitrangada's heart raced with anticipation, her mind yearning for the continuation of the story. She knew the trials that awaited the Rakshasas would be formidable, and she was prepared to unravel the mysteries and confront the darkness threatening their world.

Chitrangada and Kalki stood on the precipice of destiny, determined to honour King Ravana's legacy and reclaim the power scattered across the realms.

In the kingdom of Eldoria, King Ravana's splendour was complemented by a cast of extraordinary individuals, each possessing unique qualities that added to the kingdom's grandeur. Among them stood Mandodari, the enchanting Queen of Eldoria and Ravana's beloved consort. She possessed a grace and elegance that rivalled the most beautiful moonlit nights, her presence commanding respect, and admiration. Her wisdom in diplomacy and the arts made her an invaluable adviser to the king, her counsel shaping the kingdom's fate.

Besides the royal couple, two sons graced the halls of the palace – Malakar and Kalkeyas. Malakar, the elder, fiercely ambitious Rakshasa, was a gallant warrior who revelled in the spoils of luxury. With a hunger for power and a penchant for indulgence, he sought to carve his path, guided by his insatiable thirst for greatness.

Kalkeyas, in stark contrast, was a solitary and introspective soul. With a love for solitude and a passion for teaching, he immersed himself in pursuing knowledge, seeking enlightenment, and understanding in the depths of his seclusion.

Amidst the royal lineage stood Vibhishana, Ravana's younger brother, whose unwavering loyalty and deep connection with nature were renowned throughout Eldoria. His emerald-green skin mirrored his affinity for the earth, and his ability to communicate with the animal world granted him an extraordinary gift.

Vibhishana played a pivotal role in preserving the harmonious balance between the Rakshasas and the natural world as a guardian of the realm's delicate ecosystems. His unwavering dedication made him a cherished ally.

And towering above them all was Kumbhakaran, a Rakshasa of immense strength and stature. Despite his imposing exterior, Kumbhakaran harboured a gentle, and compassionate soul, his love for his people transcending physical might. His voracious appetite, capable of devouring feasts that could feed an entire village, was matched only by his unyielding loyalty to Eldoria. With every powerful stride, he defended the kingdom from any threat that dared to endanger its peace, becoming a formidable force of protection and security.

United as a clan, the Rakshasas, alongside their revered king, and his esteemed family, governed Eldoria with benevolence, and wisdom. They revered the land's natural beauty, ensuring that its forests flourished and its rivers flowed with vitality. Embracing the diversity of creatures that called Eldoria home, they fostered a sanctuary where Rakshasas and other mystical beings found solace and safety. Eldoria, under the watchful eyes, and steadfast hearts of its noble protectors, stood as a beacon of harmony and a testament to the enduring spirit of its inhabitants.

Its cities rose like celestial marvels, boasting architectural wonders that whispered tales of ancient wisdom. Grand palaces, adorned with intricate carvings that seemed to breathe life into stone, stood as majestic monuments to the Rakshasas' mastery of craftsmanship. Vibrant marketplaces pulsed with the vibrant energy of commerce and culture, where the melodies of merchants and artisans intermingled with the laughter of the people. And amidst it all, temples adorned the land, their towering spires reaching towards the heavens, symbols of the Rakshasas' unwavering devotion to their gods.

But the Rakshasas' guardianship extended far beyond the physical realm. With unmatched prowess in martial skills and the arcane arts, their warriors formed an elite force that cast a formidable shadow upon those who dared challenge Eldoria's sovereignty. Clad in armour forged from the depths of fiery forges and wielding weapons that sang with the power of celestial storms, these noble warriors stood as a stalwart shield, unwavering in their duty to protect Eldoria from external threats.

The Rakshasas defended the kingdom's borders with unyielding loyalty from the treacherous mountains to the expansive plains. Their battle cries echo through the ages as a testament to their indomitable spirit.

In that golden age of the Rakshasas, Eldoria basked in a radiant tapestry of prosperity and harmony. The land thrived under the benevolent rule of King Ravana, whose wisdom flowed like an eternal river, guiding the kingdom towards greatness. The people, grateful for his just, and compassionate leadership, found solace in a world where dreams and aspirations were nurtured, and the pursuit of knowledge was cherished.

Eldoria stood as a beacon of hope, a testament to the unity and strength of its noble inhabitants. At that time, the essence of the Rakshasas' noble lineage permeated every corner of the kingdom, casting a radiant glow upon its people and forever etching their legacy in the annals of history.

Kalki welled up with nostalgia, pride, and shame. Chitrangada, awestruck in disbelief, held Kalki's hands with empathy and consoled him as they further inspected the place.

They started scrolling through the manuscripts and books when Chitrangada found Eldoria's preamble. The book containing the preamble exuded an air of timeless elegance and significance. Bound in rich, supple leather, the cover bore intricate embossed designs depicting scenes from Eldoria's natural landscapes and the Rakshasas' noble heritage.

The leather, aged with wisdom, and adorned with subtle golden accents, exuded a sense of regality and importance. The book's dimensions were generous, its pages crisp, and of the finest quality parchment. Each page was meticulously handcrafted, the edges adorned with delicate gold leaf, shimmering in light. With its smooth texture and slight ivory hue, the parchment evoked a sense of antiquity, reminiscent of ancient manuscripts carefully preserved through the ages.

The book's spine was expertly crafted, showcasing intricate gold filigree, forming ornate patterns that mirrored the design elements on the cover. As Chitrangada held the book, its weight conveyed a sense of gravitas, reflecting the significance of the words contained within. Opening its cover, the fragrance of aged paper mingled with the faint scent of ancient ink, transporting the reader to a bygone era of wisdom and enlightenment.

Chitrangada opened the book, which read:

In the realm of Eldoria, we, the Rakshasas, and the diverse beings who call this land home, come together under the radiant sun and the gentle moon to forge a harmonious and prosperous future. Guided by our ancestors' wisdom and our shared aspirations, we establish this constitution to uphold the sacred values that define us.

We, the beings of Eldoria, cherish every individual's intrinsic worth and inherent rights. With respect for the sacredness of life, we affirm the equality and dignity of all beings, transcending barriers of race, species, and origin. In our pursuit of justice, we strive to foster an inclusive society that celebrates the uniqueness of each soul and embraces the beauty of diversity.

Recognizing the interconnectedness of our realm, we pledge to be custodians of its bountiful natural wonders. We honour the rivers, forests, and mountains that nurture us, committing to their preservation, and sustainable use. With reverence, we seek harmony with the delicate ecosystems that flourish within Eldoria's embrace, ensuring a legacy of vitality and abundance for generations to come.

Eldoria stands as a sanctuary of knowledge and enlightenment. We affirm the fundamental right to seek truth, encourage free thought, and pursue wisdom. Through education, we empower ourselves, and future generations to unlock their fullest potential, nurturing a society built on enlightenment, innovation, and compassion.

As inheritors of a rich heritage, we heed the call of our ancestors to safeguard the peace and security of Eldoria. United in purpose, we stand as protectors against external threats that seek to disrupt our tranquillity. We defend our land and its inhabitants with strength and valour, upholding the noble principles that have guided our ancestors since time immemorial.

We, the people of Eldoria, with unwavering faith in our shared destiny, embark upon this journey together. Bound by the ties of unity, we commit to fostering understanding, empathy, and cooperation among all who call this land home. In times of joy and challenge, we embrace the spirit of solidarity, valuing the well-being, and welfare of our community above all.

In witness of our shared commitment, we set forth this constitution of Eldoria. This covenant binds us in mutual respect and collective responsibility. As we embark upon the path of progress, let our actions be guided by compassion, justice, and the pursuit of an enlightened and harmonious future for all. May the flame of hope forever burn bright, illuminating the way towards a more just, equitable, and prosperous Eldoria.

As Chitrangada gazed upon the beautifully crafted book, her eyes widened with awe, captivated by its intricate details and profound significance. She felt deeply reverent, as if the words resonated with her soul. The preamble of Eldoria spoke to her, igniting a sense of purpose and belonging she had never experienced before.

Standing beside Chitrangada, Kalki observed her reaction, a mixture of emotions. Nostalgia swept over him like a gentle breeze, and memories of his journey and the sacrifices made by his ancestors flooded his mind. He felt a lump forming in his throat, his eyes moistening with tears of remembrance.

Tears rolled down from both Kalki and Chitrangada's eyes, realizing that a prosperous time like this, that one had lived in its full glory, had lost its prints somewhere in history, and no one had even an iota of memory that a beautiful time like this prevailed in Eldoria. Kalki held the books in his arms as he clanged them to his chest. He closed his eyes, and a mixed feeling of euphoria and misery clouded his mind.

The Knock of the 'Kalyuga' (Armageddon)

Chitrangada's voice trembled with awe and sorrow as she contemplated the enigmatic downfall of the Rakshasas. "What a marvellous and rich governance the Rakshasas had. It was indeed a golden era. I wonder what happened to them that had been so grim that even history has deleted their existence," she mused, her eyes searching for answers in the depths of the forgotten temple.

Kalki's voice grew sombre as he continued the tragic tale of the Rakshasas. "In the grim and harrowing battle between light and darkness, the Rakshasas, once embodiments of nobility, and righteousness, faced their ultimate challenge. As the forces of corruption marshalled their greedy desires, the true nature of some of the Rakshasas was revealed – their dark power and sinister intentions, concealed beneath a deceptive veil of treacherous beauty."

Fate had a cruel twist in store for the Rakshasas. As if the clash of ideologies wasn't enough, a merciless wave of natural disasters descended upon their once glorious realm. The skies of Eldoria turned ominously dark as thunderstorms unleashed their unrelenting fury, torrential rains transforming the once lush lands into a watery abyss.

The tranquil rivers, once a source of life, turned into raging torrents, consuming everything in their path. Once teeming with abundance, the fertile soil became a desolate wasteland incapable of nurturing life. And the vibrant forests, once teeming with life's symphony, withered away, their majestic trees stripped bare, as if mourning the loss of their former glory.

With each passing day, the forces of nature grew more relentless, unleashing their wrath upon Eldoria. Blistering heat waves scorched the land, scorching fields, and causing droughts that choked the once-flourishing crops. Ferocious winds, fuelled by a vengeful fury, howled through the desolate landscapes, uprooting ancient trees and reducing the magnificent structures that once stood as testaments to Eldoria's grandeur to nothing but rubble and ruin. The elements seemed to conspire against the Rakshasas, unravelling their prosperity and reducing their kingdom to a desolate wasteland.

The weight of tragedy hung heavy in the air as Chitrangada and Kalki stood amidst the remnants of the forgotten temple. It was a poignant reminder of the immense challenges the Rakshasas had faced, their existence erased not only from history but from the very fabric of Eldoria itself. In that solemn moment, the questions lingered, and the quest for understanding grew more urgent, as they sought to uncover the truth behind the annihilation of a once magnificent clan.

Chitrangada's voice trembled with disbelief and apprehension as she connected the ancient tragedy of the Rakshasas to the present turmoil in Eldoria. "Good Lord, Kalki! If I'm not mistaken, this is happening in Eldoria again. The parallels are uncanny," she exclaimed, her heart heavy with a sense of foreboding. "I'm not getting a good feeling, Kalki. I hope the history of the Rakshasas holds hope for us in these dark times."

Kalki's eyes filled with determination as he reassured Chitrangada amidst the swirling uncertainty, "All I can promise you, Chitrangada, is that we will fight with unwavering sincerity. We will leave no stone unturned in our quest to find a different fate for Eldoria. I need you to delve deep into the intricate tapestry of the Rakshasas' war, seeking every shred of knowledge that may guide us to a different fate."

Chitrangada's gaze met Kalki's with resolute determination. "Let us face this peril together, Kalki. Bound by a shared purpose, we will navigate the treacherous path ahead, uncovering the forgotten secrets, and rewriting the destiny of Eldoria. Our strength lies in our unity; we shall prevail against the encroaching darkness together."

Amid the raging turmoil, the insidious grip of darkness tightened its hold on Malakar, consuming his essence. The once-noble and ambitious Rakshasa had succumbed to the alluring whispers of power, his heart twisted by greed and insatiable ambition. No longer content with the rightful influence he possessed, Malakar had transformed into a tyrant, his desires eclipsing the very principles and values that had once defined the Rakshasas.

With every passing moment, Malakar's insidious transformation became palpable. His eyes, once filled with a glimmer of hope and purpose, now burned with a sinister fire. His steps echoed with a haughty arrogance, as if he believed himself entitled to control and domination over Eldoria. The hunger for power had corrupted his soul, warping his once-noble intentions into a self-serving quest for supremacy.

Gone was the reverence he once held for the land and its inhabitants. The well-being of Eldoria and its people became mere inconveniences, obstacles to be crushed beneath his iron fist. Malakar's ambition knew no bounds as he schemed and plotted, his actions shrouded in darkness, indifferent to the suffering he caused. His lust for dominion tainted the very essence of the Rakshasas.

As Eldoria quivered under the weight of his oppressive rule, the loyal Rakshasas witnessed with heavy hearts the descent of their kin into darkness. The echoes of their cries reverberated through the land, their pleas for justice drowned out by Malakar's growing power. The fate of Eldoria hung precariously in the balance, threatened by the very Rakshasa who was meant to protect and nurture it.

Malakar, the firstborn son of the mighty King Ravana, possessed an awe-inspiring presence that commanded both fear and admiration. Standing tall and resolute, he bore the physical markings of a born warrior. His muscular frame exuded strength and prowess, a testament to his years of rigorous training and countless battles fought.

Clad in ornate armour adorned with intricate engravings, Malakar's attire reflected his status as a formidable warrior. A crimson cape billowed behind him, symbolizing the bloodshed and victories that marked his path. His obsidian-black hair cascaded down his broad shoulders, a stark contrast to his piercing golden eyes, which glinted with ruthless determination.

Malakar's prowess on the battlefield was legendary, as tales of his victories spread like wildfire across Eldoria. He possessed a mastery of various weapons, wielding them with lethal precision and unparalleled skill. With each swing of his sword, he carved a path of destruction, leaving his enemies in fear. The ground quaked beneath his feet as he charged into battle, a force to be reckoned with.

His relentless pursuit of victory had earned him the title of Eldoria's pride. He had repeatedly led the Rakshasa forces to triumph against formidable foes, defending the kingdom with unwavering resolve. Malakar's exploits became the stuff of legends, his name whispered in hushed tones by friend and foe alike.

Yet, beneath the valorous facade, a dark yearning lurked within Malakar's heart. Despite the glory he had achieved and the power he wielded, it was never enough. He craved absolute authority, a thirst for dominion that consumed his very being. The principles of good governance, cherished by his father and the Rakshasas, held no sway over him. For Malakar, ruling and being the most powerful became an all-consuming obsession.

His hunger for power knew no bounds, driving him to trample over the ideals that once guided the Rakshasas. He saw governance as a means to an end, a tool to secure his absolute authority. The welfare of the people and the principles of justice were cast aside in his ruthless pursuit of supremacy.

Eldoria, once proud of its valiant warrior, now found itself caught in the grip of a ruthless soldier whose lust for control knew no bounds.

Consumed by an insidious hunger for power, Malakar's descent into darkness was swift and merciless. His once-noble aspirations twisted into a malevolent obsession that eclipsed all reason and compassion. No longer content with mere riches, he craved absolute dominion over Eldoria, sparing no thought for the consequences of his actions.

Driven by envy and a twisted sense of entitlement, Malakar's heart turned black with malice. He resented the prosperity and joy that adorned the lives of Eldoria's inhabitants, convinced that he alone deserved such blessings. He wove a web of deceit with cunning and manipulation, spreading discord, and mistrust like a venomous serpent.

Malakar struck a sinister bargain with the shadows in his insatiable quest for wealth. He bartered the land, selling its sacred beauty, and untamed splendour to the highest bidder. The shadows, agents of darkness, descended upon Eldoria like a plague, exploiting its resources, and littering the once-pristine realm with their toxic presence.

Greed turned the wheels of industry, and the very veins of Eldoria ran thick with the pollution of progress. The once-pure rivers now flowed with poison, their once-clear waters stained with the sins of neglect. Industries that once championed sustainability and harmony with nature became engines of death, extracting every ounce of wealth at the expense of the land and its inhabitants.

Education, once a beacon of enlightenment, faltered under Malakar's rule. Knowledge became a luxury reserved for the privileged few, while innocent children were robbed of their innocence and forced into lives of toil and servitude. The echoes of their stolen laughter were drowned out by the machinery of exploitation, as the soul of Eldoria withered under Malakar's tyrannical grip.

As his reign of darkness unfolded, Eldoria mourned the loss of its noble heritage. The principles of justice and prosperity were discarded, trampled beneath the boots of a ruthless ruler who only saw power and conquest. The land that had once thrived with unity and harmony now lay broken and divided, its people oppressed, and its spirit shattered.

Witnessing the devastation wrought upon Eldoria by their blood, the members of Malakar's family, including the once-mighty King Ravana, stood united in disbelief and heartache. They could hardly fathom the depths to which their beloved land had descended, ravaged by the very one they once cherished as kin.

Driven by love and desperation, the family confronted Malakar, encircling him with hearts heavy with grief. They pleaded with him to cast aside the all-consuming darkness and rediscover the virtues that had once defined the Rakshasas: compassion, justice, and unity. Their voices swelled in a chorus of earnest entreaties, seeking to penetrate the fortress of his corrupted soul.

But Malakar, now a puppet of his insatiable ambitions, remained deaf to their pleas. His heart, once brimming with love for his family and devotion to Eldoria, had been eclipsed by the encroaching shadows. He scoffed at their words with a venomous smirk, deriding their ideals as feeble and naive. To him, power and dominance were the only currencies of worth, and he dismissed their concerns as mere sentimentality, unworthy of his attention.

In his relentless pursuit of strength, Malakar resorted to cunning, and manipulation. He enticed others to join his cause, weaving a web of promises and allurements. Wealth, power, and a coveted place by his side were dangled as baits to tempt the vulnerable. With each recruit, he grew more intoxicated with his delusions of grandeur, savouring their unquestioning loyalty, and adoration.

Seduced by the allure of darkness, his followers bowed before him in reverent worship. Blinded by their fervent belief, they blindly embraced Malakar's twisted vision, eager to bask in his reflected glory. The seeds of devotion that he had sown sprouted into an army of loyal disciples, bound by their shared devotion to their fallen prince and the all-consuming shadows that surrounded him.

As Eldoria trembled under the weight of Malakar's wicked reign, hope flickered like a fragile flame in the hearts of those who dared defy the darkness. Kalki, and the remnants of the Rakshasas were determined to confront the encroaching tyranny and rekindle the fading embers of hope. United in their resolve, they stood as the last bastions of resistance, ready to wage a battle that would determine the fate of Eldoria and the very soul of its people.

They confronted him, their voices quivering with grief and fury, desperately trying to rekindle the spark of goodness that once resided within him.

"How could you forsake the bonds of blood, Malakar? We believed in your potential for greatness, and you have squandered it for your selfish desires!" They cried out, their words echoing through the desolate landscape.

But Malakar, consumed by his insatiable hunger for power, remained an impenetrable fortress. His heart, encased in a fortress of greed and ambition, was impervious to their pleas. To him, his family's efforts were nothing more than feeble hindrances on his path to ascendancy. He scoffed at their attempts to reason with him, dismissing their love as mere hindrances to his insatiable thirst for dominance.

Threats dripped from Malakar's tongue as he confronted his

family, his eyes ablaze with a sinister, otherworldly light. Unyielding in his resolve, he unleashed wrath upon them, warning them of dire consequences should they dare to stand in his way.

Kalkeyas stepped forward, burdened with a heavy heart and driven by a sense of duty. His voice, filled with concern, and urgency, cut through the air like a sharpened blade.

Kalkeyas: "Brother, I implore you to reconsider your chosen path. The darkness that envelopes you closes your eyes to the true essence of our existence as Rakshasas. Our purpose lies not in exploiting Eldoria's treasures for personal gain but in safeguarding and nurturing them. We are the **Rakshaks**, the protectors of Eldoria, not the **Bhakshaks**, the devourers of its wealth."

A smirk etched across Malakar's face, his voice dripping with arrogance and scorn.

Malakar: "Ah, dear brother Kalkeyas, always the righteous one, aren't you? But tell me, what has righteousness brought us? Power and wealth are the true measures of strength. Eldoria is ripe for the taking, and I shall seize it with an unyielding grip. I shall rule over this land with an iron fist, unchallenged, and unrivalled."

Malakar's tone was eerie and arrogant as he questioned Kalkeyas.

Malakar: "Little brother, reveal to me what darkness and light are. How can you be sure your path is right and mine is wrong?"

Kalkeyas: "Darkness descends when a multitude suffers, while only a select few profit from others' misfortune. Light ensures every life is crucial, possessing equal rights. Picture yourself in the shoes of those affected by your actions."

Malakar: "Once again, those rehearsed lines of ancient wisdom. This is all a conspiracy blocking powerful individuals like me from realizing our true potential and attaining ultimate power. Do not obstruct my path, or I'll forget the bond of blood, my brother."

Kalkeyas: "Malakar, listen. True power lies in understanding the consequences of our actions. It's not a conspiracy; it's a call for responsibility."

Malakar: "Responsibility, you say? The world bows to strength, not feeble notions of responsibility. I won't let anything hinder my ascent to power."

Kalkeyas: "Power gained at the expense of others is a fragile throne. Consider the impact on lives and the world. There's strength in compassion, not just dominance."

Malakar: "Compassion won't grant me the supremacy I seek. The world respects those who seize control. I won't be held back by sentiment."

Kalkeyas: "But at what cost? Is it worth sacrificing everything, even the bonds of blood? There's a greater strength in unity and understanding."

Malakar: "Unity is a facade, a veil over the eyes of the weak. I'll forge my path, with, or without your understanding. Cross me, and you'll see the extent of my power."

Kalkeyas: "Malakar, I implore you to reconsider. True strength is tempered with wisdom, not blinded by ambition. The path you're on may lead to ruin, for yourself and others."

As Malakar's words echoed through the chambers, the family of Rakshasas stood united, their hearts heavy with both sorrow and despair.

The mighty King Ravana stepped forward with an air of authority, his voice resounding through the chamber like thunder. Disappointment etched upon his face, his eyes burned with sorrow and stern resolve.

Ravana: "Malakar, have you forgotten the invaluable teachings of our ancestors, the wisdom carefully passed down through the ages? Power without responsibility is an empty triumph, a fleeting illusion. Eldoria does not belong to one, but to all who inhabit its land. It is our sacred duty to ensure their well-being and nurture a realm of harmony."

Malakar's laughter filled the chamber, a mocking symphony reverberating off the walls.

Malakar: "Wisdom and teachings, dear father, are shackles that bind the weak and feeble-minded. I have transcended such trivial matters. Eldoria shall quiver beneath the weight of my dominion, and all shall kneel before me or face the wrath I unleash!"

Mandodari, her voice filled with sadness and desperation, approached her son, her eyes pleading for his redemption.

Mandodari: "Malakar, my beloved son, do you not remember the love and compassion that once bloomed in your heart? The darkness has clouded your judgement, but a glimmer of hope remains for your redemption. Return to the path of righteousness before it engulfs you."

Malakar sneered, his voice dripping with disdain.

Malakar: "Love and compassion are the virtues of the weak, Mother. I have transcended such trivial emotions. Eldoria shall bear witness to my reign of unyielding power, and you shall all rue the day you dared to stand against me."

Vibhishana, his voice soft yet firm, stepped forward, clutching a sacred scripture in his hands, its pages trembling with profound knowledge.

Vibhishana: "My dear nephew, the ancient scriptures speak of the sacred duty bestowed upon us as Rakshasas. They proclaim, 'With great power comes great responsibility.' To serve and protect is the path to true greatness. Release the chains of your arrogance and embrace your true purpose."

Malakar erupted in derisive laughter, his voice dripping with scorn and defiance.

Malakar: "Scriptures and ancient wisdom hold no weight in my eyes, Uncle. I am heralding a new era cloaked in darkness and absolute power. I had hoped you, with your supposedly profound intelligence and foresight, would see the truth. Join me or face the dire consequences of your foolishness."

Kumbhkaran, his towering presence filling the room, could no longer contain his anger. His voice thundered with authority, carrying a profound sadness that seemed to shake the foundations.

Kumbhkaran: "Nephew, you have strayed far from the righteous path, but there is still hope for your redemption. The immense strength within you can be channelled to protect and nurture Eldoria, not to unleash its destruction. The path to righteousness beckons, if only you would open your heart and heed its call."

Malakar's laughter pierced the chamber, a chilling echo infused with malevolence. His eyes glinted with a twisted delight.

Malakar: "Redemption? Ha! There is no redemption for one such as me, Uncle Kumbhkaran. Eldoria shall bear witness to its darkest days, and you shall all rue the consequences of obstructing my path to triumph. Submit to me now, for your feeble safety."

Ravana, his voice resonating with the weight of ancient wisdom, began reciting verses from the holy Bhagwat Gita. His voice carried the teachings of Lord Krishna, piercing through the darkness that had engulfed Malakar's heart.

Ravana: "One deluded by ego believes, 'I am the doer'. But the truly wise understand that it is the divine that guides our actions. Release yourself from the chains of arrogance and greed, Malakar, and reconnect with your true purpose."

For a moment, Malakar's laughter wavered as the verses reached his ears, but the grip of darkness swiftly reclaimed his noble side.

Malakar: "Divine will? I am the master of my destiny, father! Your naive words hold no sway over me. Eldoria shall crumble beneath my indomitable might, and you shall all bow in subservience or suffer the dire consequences."

Mandodari stepped forward, her voice trembling with sorrow and pleading desperation.

Mandodari: "Our ancient wisdom speaks of the eternal soul, the Atman, and the profound cycle of life and death. It reminds us that our actions carry far-reaching consequences. Do not allow darkness to blind you to the eternal truth."

Malakar's expression twisted into a sneer of disdain.

Malakar: "The Atman, the cycle of life and death, mere philosophical musings! I have transcended such trivialities. Eldoria shall witness the ascendance of a new ruler who knows no boundaries and fears no consequences."

Ravana, his voice filled with a solemn understanding, continued to impart his wisdom.

Ravana: "Even the mightiest rulers are bound by cosmic laws and principles. The holy Gita teaches us that we are mere instruments in the hands of fate, and our true power lies in serving a higher purpose. Return to the righteous path, my son, before it is too late."

Malakar's laughter grew louder and derisive, his eyes ablaze with defiant determination.

Malakar: "Fate and cosmic laws? I am the master of my fate, father! Eldoria shall bear witness to the unfathomable extent of my power, and with darkness as my ally, you shall all kneel before me or face the full force of my wrath and unrelenting devastation!"

As Malakar stormed out of the room, his rage breathed like a fiery dragon, leaving behind an atmosphere heavy with tension and the weight of imminent choices. The air seemed to hold its breath, as if foreboding the consequences that would unfold in the wake of Malakar's fury.

Satan's Call

As Malakar's malevolence intensified, Eldoria bore witness to the depths of his depravity. The once vibrant and prosperous realm transformed into a haunting reflection of its former glory. Once adorned with the graceful flight of colourful birds, the skies now hung heavy with a perpetual shroud of darkness. Once teeming with life, the lands succumbed to a desolation that mirrored the emptiness within Malakar's soul.

He remained resolute in his wickedness. Blinded by his insatiable greed, he callously ignored their pleas, drawing others into his dark embrace. With silver-tongued persuasion, he seduced the vulnerable and corrupted the virtuous, building an army of twisted souls who revelled in their newfound alliance with darkness.

"Join us," he whispered, his voice dripping with honeyed deceit. "Together, we shall conquer Eldoria, and claim its riches as our own. Morals and ethics are mere shackles, hindrances to our ascent," he sneered, mocking the concepts of honour and compassion. "Why settle for scraps when we can seize the entire feast? Let those who oppose us tremble beneath our rule. Eldoria is but a playground for our ambitions, a canvas upon which we shall paint our legacy," he boasted, intoxicated by his arrogance.

Under Malakar's command, this unholy alliance revelled in its newfound power, indulging in the darkest corners of its desires. It unleashed calamities upon Eldoria, distorting the natural order, and unleashing chaos. Floods ravaged the land, a consequence of the corrupt industries' carbon footprint on the planet.

Famine and disease spread like wildfire, ravaging the once-fertile fields. Darkness consumed the hearts of the people, leading to riots and bloodshed, with envy, anger, and greed reigning supreme. The inhabitants of Eldoria suffered mercilessly under this reign of terror, their lives shattered, and their hopes extinguished by the unyielding onslaught of darkness.

Then, the Lord of Darkness, known as Satan, took notice of Malakar. In him, Satan recognized a true potential, a loyal warrior who could further his sinister agenda. With a wicked grin, the Lord of Darkness set his sights on Malakar, intent on moulding him into an instrument of eternal darkness, forever bound to the infernal depths of their shared destiny.

In the depths of Eldoria's forbidding abyss, within a chamber steeped in malevolence, Malakar stood alone, his heart burdened by insatiable ambition and his mind consumed by an all-encompassing darkness. Retrieving his royal sword, bearing the sinister emblem of the Rakshasas, he drew it across his palm, allowing scarlet droplets of his life force to spill forth. In this macabre offering, he surrendered himself to Satan, the Lord of the Darkness, an ominous entity reigning over the realms of maleficence.

As the room became enshrouded in an atmosphere pregnant with anticipation, the Lord of Darkness materialized before Malakar, radiating an aura of terror and malevolence that sent icy shivers coursing through his very core. Towering and commanding, he swathed himself in billowing robes of shadow, seemingly alive as they writhed and twisted of their own accord. His skin, pallid and ashen like a forgotten cadaver, clashed with eyes ablaze in an unholy crimson glow, their intensity penetrating the darkest recesses of one's soul.

The Lord's countenance twisted into a grotesque fusion of skeletal features and contorted flesh, eternally locked in a grimace of malicious glee. From his twisted maw jutted jagged, serrated teeth, grinding, and gnashing with an insatiable hunger for the anguish of others. Sinister tendrils of energy coiled and slithered around him, akin to abyssal serpents, whispering wicked secrets, and weaving promises of boundless power to those audacious enough to listen.

Satan, the Lord of the Darkness, exuded an air of regal presence, though twisted, and perverted by the very essence of his existence. His elongated fingers culminated in razor-sharp claws, their wickedness gleaming with an otherworldly darkness that voraciously devoured all surrounding light. Each step he took resounded with an eerie resonance, a chilling symphony that echoed the anguished screams of the forsaken.

When his voice resonated from his lips, it carried a bone-chilling resonance that curdled the marrow within one's bones. It formed a haunting melody of whispered malevolence, a dissonant symphony of agony capable of unravelling the very fabric of the strongest-willed. This voice dripped with irresistible temptation, promising dominion and untold power while concealing the eternal suffering that lay in its wake.

In Satan's presence, the air grew dense and suffocating, as if life itself had been drained from the surroundings. Shadows deepened and contorted, distorting the perception of reality, for the Lord of Darkness possessed the power to warp the very fabric of existence.

To behold the Lord of the Darkness was to witness an abhorrent embodiment of all that was twisted and vile. He personified the darkest depths of the human psyche, the embodiment of fear, and an unrelenting pursuit of power. His visage seared itself into the minds of those unfortunate enough to gaze upon him, forever haunting their dreams, and tainting their thoughts with visions of unending darkness.

Within the depths of terror, Malakar discovered his malevolent master, willingly surrendering himself to the abyss of depravity and embracing a path that would forever shroud Eldoria in a suffocating veil of despair.

Bowing before Satan, Malakar's voice quivered with a mixture of admiration and desperation. "Mighty Lord of Darkness, I offer myself as your devoted servant. Bestow upon me the power to subjugate Eldoria, to unleash unbridled chaos, and inflict untold suffering upon this land. In exchange, I pledge my undying loyalty to you."

Satan, the Lord of Darkness, his voice a chilling echo, spoke with a beguiling allure, "You crave power, Malakar, and power I shall bestow upon you. But heed this warning—it comes at a steep price. Your soul shall forever be entangled with the shadows, consumed by an insatiable hunger for more."

In Malakar's eyes, a fervent flame ignited, his voice resolute with unholy conviction. "I am willing to pay any cost. Eldoria shall be my sacrificial offering, and together, we shall cast this land into eternal night. Make me an instrument of your wrath, my Lord, and I shall ensure your dominion over all."

A wicked smile curled upon Satan's lips, his voice dripping with both amusement and malice. "You are but a pawn in the grand tapestry of darkness, Malakar. Serve me faithfully, and I shall grant you powers that surpass your wildest dreams. Eldoria will become a mere plaything in our hands, its people crushed beneath the weight of their own desolation, as I bring forth the Kalyuga, the ultimate Armageddon."

Malakar pledged:

In the realm of shadows, where darkness dwells,
Where wickedness thrives and evil compels,
I, Malakar, a vessel of despair,
Pledge my loyalty to the Lord of Darkness's lair.
With bated breath and heart consumed by night,
I surrender my soul, embrace the blight,
No more shall light adorn my twisted path,

For I'm the harbinger of eternal wrath.
In verses dark, this oath I now proclaim,
A verse of loyalty, forever etched in flame,
Satan, I bend my knee,
Bound to your will, a servant I shall be.
Through veils of darkness, his power reigns,
Beneath your guidance, my ambition attains,
I cast away morals, embrace wicked desires,
Fuelling the fire of chaos, as darkness transpires.
Oh, Lord of Darkness, ruler of the abyss,
Grant me strength; let my every action hiss,
With your whispers of torment, I shall conspire,
To bring Eldoria down, engulfed in unholy fire.
No mercy shall I show, no conscience to restrain,
In your name, I shall sow discord and pain,
The land shall tremble, its people cower,
As I unleash upon them the darkest hour.
So heed my words, ye who still cling to the light,
For I, Malakar, have embraced eternal night,
In the abyss of shadows, my loyalty lies,
Forever bound to the Lord of Darkness, I rise.

As the pact was irrevocably forged, an infernal surge of malevolent energy engulfed Malakar, seeping through his veins like venomous tendrils. His eyes glowed with an unholy radiance, reflecting the corruption that now coursed within him. In that pivotal moment, he metamorphosed into the embodiment of Eldoria's destruction, the malignant force that would orchestrate its downfall.

In a voice dripping with fervent devotion, Malakar proclaimed, his words echoing through the shadows, "I bind myself to you, Lord of Darkness. Eldoria shall tremble beneath our combined might. No glimmer of light shall escape our relentless grasp, and this land shall be swallowed whole by the abyss of anguish and desolation."

Thus, Malakar's fate was forever sealed, his path intertwined with the Lord of Darkness in an unbreakable embrace of maleficence and doom.

Evil Needs Sacrifice

As Malakar's pledge echoed through the chamber, a perverse grin spread across Satan's face, his features contorted into a mask of wicked delight. His voice, like a chilling whisper in the wind, slithered through the air.

"Malakar, my faithful servant," Satan hissed, his words laced with a sinister edge. "Your loyalty has been proven, but there remains a seed of doubt within me. I've chosen you for a grand purpose, but somehow, I get an uneasy feeling whenever I look at you. There's something about you that makes me uncomfortable trusting you, and I find it extremely unsettling. To truly serve the darkness, you must offer yourself completely—mind, body, and soul. Are you prepared to surrender yourself entirely to the depths of my dominion?"

Malakar, his eyes burning with a zealous fervour, responded without hesitation, "My Lord, I willingly cast aside my former self. I surrender all that I am to your malevolence, an instrument of your will with unwavering devotion."

A wicked smile curled upon Satan's lips, his eyes gleaming with twisted satisfaction. "Very well, Malakar. To test the depths of your allegiance, I shall subject you to trials of unfathomable darkness. Only through these trials shall your loyalty be truly proven."

Malakar's voice resonated with unyielding resolve. "I embrace your challenge, my Lord. Test me with your darkest trials, for I have unwavering faith in your guidance. I shall emerge triumphant, a testament to my undying devotion."

Satan revelled in his wicked amusement, his voice a chilling symphony of malevolence. "Oh, tested you shall be, Malakar. Temptations shall lie before you, choices that are cruellest in their essence. Will you falter and succumb, or will you rise above as the epitome of darkness? For it is in complete surrender and unwavering faith, without a shred of doubt, when choices are made with unfaltering conviction, that one becomes the embodiment of true darkness."

A glimmer of excitement danced in Malakar's eyes as he spoke with absolute certainty, "I am your loyal servant, Lord Satan. I shall not waver. I shall conquer every trial, overcome every test. My loyalty to you and the path of darkness knows no bounds."

Satan's laughter resonated through the chamber, a cacophony that carried both delight and sinister anticipation. "So be it, Malakar. The path ahead shall be fraught with treachery and moral decay. Embrace it wholeheartedly, for your loyalty shall be forged in the crucible of temptation. Show me that you are worthy of being a vessel of true darkness."

The Lord of Darkness fixed his piercing crimson gaze upon Malakar, his voice resonating with an insidious command.

"Malakar, to prove your dedication to the darkness, I present you with your first challenge," Satan intoned. "At the heart of Eldoria lies a sacred religious sanctuary, a symbol of faith, and hope, a sanctuary you once protected and revered. Your task is to reduce it to ashes, to shatter the beliefs of the common people and extinguish the flame of determination within your own clan."

Malakar's heart skipped a beat, his mind recoiling at the magnitude of the task laid before him. The weight of the challenge settled upon his shoulders, and he struggled to suppress the remnants of empathy that still lingered within him. The atmosphere grew taut with stifling tension, as if the very fabric of reality awaited his decision.

With a clenched fist, Malakar lowered his gaze, bowing his head in reluctant submission. "As you command, my Lord. I shall bring devastation upon the sanctuary, turning a beacon of hope into ruins, for I am your loyal servant."

With those words, Malakar materialized within the sacred grounds, a place of solace and serenity for the devout souls of Eldoria. The air crackled with a palpable sense of reverence, and the soft murmur of prayers filled the atmosphere. It was a place where faith thrived, untainted by the shadows that had engulfed Malakar's heart.

As he beheld the grand edifice before him, adorned with intricate carvings and stained glass, his resolve wavered. Images of worshippers, who had once regarded Malakar as their prince, their faces radiant with devotion, flashed before his eyes, stirring a dormant conflict within his tormented soul.

"Malakar," a voice whispered into his thoughts, the voice of Satan, goading him relentlessly. "Bring ruin to their sanctuary. Let their prayers turn to ash, their faith crumble beneath the weight of your darkness."

The ambience transformed, the once gentle rays of sunlight casting haunting shadows upon the sacred walls. Malakar's inner turmoil surged, but the allure of power and his desperate desire to prove his loyalty propelled him forward.

As the sanctuary crumbled before him, Malakar stood amidst the wreckage, his eyes gleaming with a twisted satisfaction. The once-hallowed grounds now lay in ruins, a testament to his unwavering allegiance to darkness. The anguished cries of the common beings resonated through the air, pleading for mercy and salvation.

But Malakar, consumed by his allegiance to the darkness, turned a deaf ear to their pleas. The remnants of his former self withered away, replaced by a ruthless determination etched upon his features. His heart, once touched by compassion, had hardened into a vessel of unyielding cruelty.

A wicked smile played upon his lips as he surveyed the devastation he had wrought. The flames danced in his eyes, reflecting the malevolence that coursed through his veins. He revelled in the chaos, embracing the role of the merciless herald of destruction. The once-proud sanctuary now lay shattered, its sacred aura extinguished by the shadow of darkness. The land of Eldoria trembled, its inhabitants gripped by a despair that seemed to seep into the very fabric of their existence.

Malakar, now fully consumed by the darkness, basked in his newfound power. With every crumbling stone and shattered relic, his dominance over Eldoria grew, his influence spreading like a venomous plague.

Little did the common beings know that this was only the beginning. The path of darkness that Malakar had embarked upon was paved with further atrocities and untold suffering. As the dust settled upon the ruins of the sanctuary, an ominous silence descended, foreboding the calamities that would follow in its wake.

Eldoria, once a land of hope and harmony, now trembled under the tyrannical reign of its fallen prince. The echoes of anguish reverberated through its desecrated halls, a chilling reminder of the depths to which Malakar had descended. The future of Eldoria seemed shrouded in an unrelenting darkness, as the once-noble warrior became a harbinger of despair and destruction.

As the echoes of devastation subsided, a twisted smile played upon Malakar's lips, a grotesque reflection of the triumph and torment within him. Satan's laughter reverberated through the desolate grounds, a chilling symphony of victory for the forces of darkness. The very air seemed to tremble in response, carrying the weight of Eldoria's despair and mourning, as the once-sacred sanctuary, a bastion of light, hope, and happiness, lay in ruins.

In that haunting moment, Malakar felt a surge of satisfaction, knowing that he had passed Satan's first test, proving his unwavering devotion to the path of darkness. The anguished cries of the shattered souls echoed in his ears, but their pleas fell upon deaf ears as he pressed forward, ready to embrace the next sinister chapter of his corrupted destiny.

With each trial that awaited him, Malakar delved deeper into the abyss of his loyalty. The Lord of Darkness whispered insidious commands and temptations, pushing him to the edge of his being. But with every challenge conquered, his allegiance grew stronger, binding him irreversibly to the dark forces that beckoned him.

There was no turning back for Malakar now. The allure of power and the promise of eternal darkness had consumed him completely. He had willingly surrendered his kindness, forsaking any trace of light that had once flickered within his soul. With every step, he embraced the darkest depths of his being, relishing in the malevolence that coursed through his veins, for he was now a vessel of darkness, bound to fulfil the darkest desires of his maleficent master.

Secrets Unfurling

In the midst of the story, Kalki paused and asked Chitrangada, trying to slowly understand the curiosities and doubts that played in her mind.

Kalki: "Tell me, Chitrangada, what do you think about our team?"

Chitrangada: "I believe in them, and I believe in the Astral Council. We're the chosen ones for safeguarding Eldoria and restoring the balance of the realms. I trust my team members and I trust you."

Kalki: "Is there anyone in particular among us whom you find a little mysterious? Is there anyone whom, when you see, a tinge of doubt crosses your mind? Be honest with me as I need to know how and what our team thinks of each other, before we fight the war."

Chitrangada: "If I were to be completely honest, then I would say Maya intrigues me. There's something different about her, and if rumours are to be believed, both the siblings, Maya and Ayyappan, have guarded their origins from everyone."

Kalki: "But still, it is only Maya that brings doubts to your mind. Is there any particular reason?"

Kalki's eyes bore into Chitrangada, a glimmer of uncertainty flickering within them. The weight of their mission pressed upon his shoulders as he delved deeper into the enigma surrounding Maya and Ayyappan, their mysterious teammates. Chitrangada's words hung in the air, hinting at the lingering doubts and unease that shrouded her perceptions of Maya.

In the midst of their critical discussion, the room seemed to grow colder, the air thick with tension. Chitrangada's voice trembled slightly as she sought clarity from Kalki. "Why are Maya and Ayyappan shrouded in such secrecy? Why do I feel that you and

Rudrama know something that none of us are aware of? What does this mean for our team and the fate of Eldoria?"

Kalki paused for a moment, his gaze unfaltering. "Chitrangada, there are forces at play that extend beyond our understanding. The realms are on the precipice of chaos, and Maya's true nature may hold the key to the balance we seek. I cannot reveal everything now, but trust me when I say that my every action is guided by the welfare of the realms."

Chitrangada's determination wavered, her trust in Kalki momentarily tested. The weight of uncertainty loomed over their team, casting a shadow upon their unity. Yet, deep down, she knew that Kalki's words held a deeper truth, one that would be unveiled in due time.

With a resolve steeled by their shared purpose, Chitrangada nodded, her eyes reflecting a mix of determination and apprehension. "I will trust you, Kalki. For the sake of Eldoria and the Astral Council, I will stand by your side and face whatever challenges lie ahead. May our actions be the beacon that restores the balance and vanquishes the darkness."

Kalki's countenance softened, a flicker of gratitude in his eyes. "Thank you, Chitrangada. Together, we will uncover the truth and shape the destiny of the realms. Our journey has just begun, and it is in the face of uncertainty that our bond will be tested. Let us march forward, united in purpose and unwavering in our pursuit of justice."

Their words lingered in the air, a testament to their unyielding determination. Little did they know that the path they had chosen would lead them to revellations beyond their imagination, unravelling secrets that would shake the very foundation of their beliefs. The fate of Eldoria hung in the balance, and their team would soon face challenges that would test their loyalty, their trust, and their resolve.

Malakar was married to Chhaya, who possessed an allure that was as mysterious as her origins. Little did the world know, that there was a greater purpose hidden in Chhaya's destiny. Concealing her true essence beneath the cloak of illusion, she emerged as a goddess veiled in secrecy, leaving no trace of her origins for the world to decipher. Yet, unbeknownst to all, a profound purpose lay concealed within the depths of Chhaya's destiny.

Chhaya, adorned with cascading locks of raven hue, possessed eyes that shimmered like moonlit reflections upon tranquil waters. Her beauty was an exquisite paradox, captivating, and haunting in equal measure. She exuded a quiet confidence, carrying herself with poise, and an unwavering determination. Though shadows danced within the depths of her gaze, her heart burned with a compassion that yearned for the well-being of her family and the preservation of light within their lives.

Within Chhaya resided a mystical essence, an enigmatic energy that intertwined with the very fabric of reality. She possessed a profound gift—the innate ability to manipulate perceptions and craft illusions that could ensnare even the sharpest of minds. It was a power that defied the boundaries of possibility, rendering her a mistress of deception.

Her command over illusions was a testament to her strength, a formidable weapon wielded with both grace and precision. Yet, amidst her extraordinary abilities, it was her boundless love for her family and unwavering loyalty to Eldoria that truly set her apart, inspiring awe and reverence in all who witnessed her devotion.

Chhaya, a vessel of mystery and magic, stood as the mother of three remarkable souls. – Alaya, Aryan and Aks. Though Alaya and Aryan were twins, Alaya had arrived a minute earlier, claiming her place as the eldest. Alaya inherited the grace and wisdom that flowed through her lineage, poised to carry the torch of hope into the darkest of days. Aryan, her valiant son, possessed an unyielding spirit aflame with righteousness, destined to stand as a beacon of justice in a world shrouded in shadows. And little Aks, the youngest and most vulnerable, was cradled within the tender embrace of his mother's love, a symbol of innocence amidst the tumultuous realm they inhabited.

Each child, a treasured reflection of her essence, held a unique place within Chhaya's embrace. Alaya, the eldest, mirrored her mother's compassion and tender spirit, their bond fortified through whispered secrets and shared dreams. In Alaya, Chhaya found solace, a kindred soul who nurtured her mother's light and fiercely protected the sanctity of their familial love. As the firstborn, Alaya basked in the adoration of her mother, her father, and the entire Rakshasa clan, their pride a testament to her radiant presence.

Aryan possessed an insatiable thirst for adventure, his spirit echoing Chhaya's daring nature. Together, they embarked on countless escapades, their laughter cascading like echoes of joy through their abode. Chhaya found solace in Aryan's unwavering trust, his belief in her indomitable strength becoming a source of courage that fuelled her determination. With Aryan by her side, the goddess of illusion felt invincible, knowing that her child's faith would fortify her resolve.

And then there was Aks, the youngest of Chhaya's brood, a flash of innocence and curiosity. In his wide-eyed wonder, Chhaya discovered a respite from the encroaching shadows, for his pure heart reminded her that goodness still flourished amidst the prevailing darkness. Together, they traversed realms of enchantment, as Chhaya wove tales of magic and wonder, nurturing the flame of imagination that burned bright within Aks' tender soul. Their interactions were a dance of love and discovery, embracing the extraordinary that unfolded even in the most daunting times.

As the matriarch of her family, Chhaya pledged her unfaltering commitment to safeguard her children from the encroaching malice that sought to devour their world. She would not hesitate to lay her life on the line, wielding her mastery of illusions as an impenetrable shield against the forces that sought to dismantle their unity.

Her love was a fortress, fortified with an unyielding resolve, standing as a bastion of protection amidst the tempestuous journey ahead. For Chhaya, the goddess of illusion, the bonds of familial love transcended the bounds of reality, and she would face any darkness with unyielding courage and a heart aflame with unhesitating devotion.

Within the depths of their humble abode, bathed in the ethereal flicker of candlelight, Chhaya would tenderly tuck her beloved children into their beds, banishing their worries and fears with delicate kisses and whispered words of solace. Like a sorceress of dreams, she wove illusions of serenity around them, transforming their restless minds into realms of enchantment, where the shackles of nightmares held no dominion.

Through laughter, tears, triumphs, and defeats, Chhaya nurtured an unbreakable bond with her children, their hearts entwined in an unspoken language of love and understanding. With unwavering devotion, she guided them along the labyrinthine paths of life, her touch a soothing balm to their weary souls.

Yet, within the sacred confines of their haven, an air of sombreness settled heavily, as Malakar, a vessel consumed by the encroaching darkness, approached Chhaya. His voice, laden with urgency, and temptation, reverberated through the room, while his eyes burned with a volatile mix of desire and desperation, the atmosphere pulsating with a tangible tension.

Malakar: "Chhaya, my love, join me on this perilous odyssey into the abyss. Together, we shall seize unimaginable power and rise as indomitable entities. The entirety of the cosmos will bow before our might. We shall not merely govern Eldoria but ascend to become its ultimate deities.

"I have beckoned my father, mother, uncles, and Kalkeyas, urging them to join us in unlocking our true potential, to comprehend the truth that we, the Rakshasas, surpass all others. May wisdom prevail among them, and may they realize that I am not their adversary, but rather the harbinger of their ultimate success."

Chhaya recoiled in anguish, her heart aching with disbelief and sorrow. The echoes of Malakar's destructive exploits had reached her ears, tales of chaos unleashed upon Eldoria and the desecration of the sanctuary of faith. She could scarcely fathom the torment inflicted upon those whom he had vowed to protect.

The inhabitants of Eldoria, once fervently loyal to their favourite prince, their hero, the chosen successor to the mighty King Ravana, now found themselves engulfed in an all-consuming disbelief. The very figure they had looked up to, their saviour and guardian, had revealed himself to be the architect of their impending destruction.

"Malakar, my love, what has befallen you?" Chhaya's voice quivered with a cocktail of anguish and bewilderment. "I have heard whispers of your unleashing chaos upon Eldoria and the destruction of the sanctuary of faith. How could you torment those whom you vowed to shield from harm? I struggle to comprehend the anguish that grips the inhabitants of Eldoria. They stand in disarray, unable to reconcile the dissonance between their adoration for their beloved prince and the harrowing reality that you seek to annihilate them."

Chhaya's voice trembled with a delicate mixture of sorrow and unwavering determination as she pleaded with Malakar, her eyes mirroring the weight of their shared agony. Deep within her, a secret burdened her heart, known only to her and Parvati from the Astral Council, a secret that held the key to their family's destiny.

Chhaya: "Malakar, my love, my soul weeps for the darkness that has ensnared you. I have witnessed the depths to which it can descend, its insatiable hunger that devours all in its path. I cannot forsake the flickering light within me, within our beloved children. There is too much at stake that hangs in the balance.

"Return to us, my love, before it is too late. Consider our children, especially our precious Alaya, who cherishes the belief that her father is a beacon of nobility. I implore you! Return to our embrace. We need you, Eldoria, your parents, and your brother need you."

Her words, infused with the raw tenderness of a mother's love, hung in the air like a fragile plea, desperately seeking a glimmer of hope amidst the encroaching darkness. Malakar's voice reverberated with a desperate tone, teetering on the edge of frustration and urgency as he made his final plea to Chhaya, determined to sway her to his side, oblivious to the depths of her hidden truth.

Malakar: "I am your husband, Chhaya, the mighty warrior of the Rakshasas, and I shall remain steadfast in my path. The power I now possess is beyond comprehension, making me invincible. The sanctuary fell because it symbolized the old order, the obsolete chains that bound Eldoria. I bring chaos to eliminate those who hinder progress. Under my rule, Eldoria will ascend to greatness, with us as its unquestionable masters. I am weary of the hollow promises of equality and democracy. Together, we can shape this world according to our desires, bending reality to our will. Why cling to feeble light when true power awaits within the embrace of darkness?"

Chhaya's eyes shimmered with a delicate fusion of sadness and longing, her resolve solidifying as she prepared to reveal the haunting truth concealed in her existence, and the time had come for her to unveil the shadowed chapters of her past, even if it meant shattering their fragile bond.

Chhaya: "Malakar, you have known me as your wife and partner, but there is a part of my past, a secret shrouded in darkness, that I have withheld from you. Listen closely, for I comprehend the very essence of darkness and its pervasive grip."

Malakar's curiosity piqued, his voice laced with intrigue as he pressed for answers. Drawn to the enigmatic aura that enveloped Chhaya, he unknowingly mirrors his attraction to the Lord of Darkness.

Malakar: "You have always been a mysterious enigma to me, Chhaya. An otherworldly presence surrounds you, an undeniable power emanating from the depths of your being. It captivates me in a manner akin to my allure to the Lord of Darkness. Who are you truly, my beloved?"

Chhaya's voice trembled with pain and determination as she unveiled the truth, her words cutting through the silence like a blade through the darkness.

Chhaya: "I am the daughter of Satan, a child born into the clutches of darkness, fleeing its malevolence to find sanctuary under the watchful gaze of Parvati, the guardian of the Astral Council. I bear witness to the unspeakable horrors that darkness can inflict. My father, Satan, sacrificed his son, and claimed the life of his beloved wife as offerings to the insatiable hunger of darkness.

"Tell me, Malakar, has he started testing you? Has my cruel father demanded the blue sapphire ring that belongs to your father? And has he revealed the ultimate test, the sacrifice that will define your destiny?"

Malakar's eyes widened in astonishment, the realization dawning upon him like a lightning bolt. It seemed that his union with Chhaya, Satan's daughter, had destined him to become the Lord of Darkness's most formidable warrior.

Malakar: "You, a daughter of darkness? It all falls into place now, the mysteries that surround you. But why keep this truth hidden from me, from our children? What purpose does it serve?"

Chhaya's voice trembled with a mixture of sorrow and determination, her words carrying the weight of an impossible choice.

Chhaya: "Malakar, I held this secret to shield you, to protect our children, and Eldoria from the abyss that awaits those who succumb to darkness. I have witnessed the devastation it unleashes, the lives it consumes. It offers the illusion of power, convincing you that you control it, but darkness controls you. I could not bear to expose our beloved family to a malevolent fate. I could not willingly let darkness claim us."

Malakar's face contorted with shock and disbelief, his grip tightening with anger coursing through his veins.

Malakar: "How dare you keep such a secret from me? How dare you defy my wishes, betray our love? Your ties to darkness run deeper than I ever fathomed. You have kept me in the dark for far too long."

Chhaya stood her ground, her voice unwavering despite the pain in her words.

Chhaya: "It is precisely because of my connection to darkness that I fight against it. I have witnessed its havoc, its insatiable hunger. I cannot allow our children to be consumed by its grasp. We must find a way back to the light, for their sake and the salvation of Eldoria."

Malakar's expression was contorted, and fascination, and anger were etched upon his face.

Malakar: "You speak of darkness with conviction, yet you resist its embrace. Why cling to the light when true power lies within the shadows?"

Chhaya's eyes flashed with a fire that matched her resolve, her voice entwined with a fierce determination.

Chhaya: "Malakar, true power does not lie in the depths of

darkness. It resides in the balance, in the harmony of light and shadow. I fight against the darkness because I know its alluring grasp, its insidious whispers. In its cruel game, I will not allow our family to become pawns."

Their words hung in the air, the weight of their choices heavy upon them. The realization that their paths had diverged, perhaps irreversibly, filled the room with an unspoken grief. The revellation of Chhaya's true nature had deepened the chasm between them, leaving their love in tatters. The mysteries that enshrouded her past added a layer of intrigue and uncertainty as they stood on the brink of a fateful decision.

Burdened by her secret and love for her family, Chhaya knew that she must remain resolute in her fight against the darkness, even if it meant standing against the one she held dearest, for she was just a mother who would go to any lengths to protect her children.

The Ultimate Sacrifice

Driven by an all-consuming anguish and a relentless thirst for vengeance, Malakar embarked on a perilous journey to seek an audience with the Lord of Darkness. The path before him was fraught with ominous shadows that writhed and twisted in anticipation, as if aware of the gravity of his purpose.

With measured steps, Malakar approached the dark chamber where Satan, the embodiment of malevolence, awaited. The air seemed to thicken with maleficence, lending an eerie atmosphere to the encounter about to unfold.

Malakar's voice, dripping with a potent blend of bitterness and cunning, resonated through the chamber. He was poised to unleash the hidden secrets that lay within the depths of his wife's enigmatic past.

Malakar: "My Lord, I bring forth a revellation that will shatter the very foundation of our existence. Chhaya, my beloved wife, is your daughter, who once slipped through your fingers, seeking sanctuary under the watchful gaze of Parvati. I present this knowledge as a token of my unwavering loyalty to you.

"Let us guide Chhaya back onto the path of darkness, compelling her to atone for her perceived sins. In this revellation, it is now that the pieces fall into place, revealing why I, Malakar, am inexorably drawn to your dark allure, my Lord. Our destinies are entwined, and together, we shall wield unimaginable power, transcending the boundaries of this cosmos. United, we shall become invincible!"

In the depths of the accursed realm, where shadows danced with malicious glee, Malakar stood before the imposing figure of Satan. The air seemed charged with an otherworldly energy, crackling with a malevolence that sent shivers down his spine. His heart pounded in his chest, a blend of trepidation and exhilaration coursing through his veins.

Satan, the embodiment of darkness, regarded Malakar with an unsettling gaze, his eyes piercing through the depths of his very soul. His voice echoed with a chilling mix of amusement and contempt, a twisted melody that sent a chill down Malakar's spine.

Satan: "Ah, Malakar, the puzzle pieces fall into place. Your presence has stirred within me an unsettling recognition. The scent of Chhaya, my flesh and blood, clings to you like a putrid reminder of her defiance."

Malakar's eyes narrowed, a twisted smirk tugging at the corners of his lips. He revelled in Satan's acknowledgement, relishing the power it bestowed upon him.

Malakar: "Indeed, my Lord, the ties that bind Chhaya and me run deeper than the abyss. She, bearing your blood, embraced the feeble light while harbouring the essence of darkness within her veins. The irony of her betrayal is both wicked and sublime."

In the heart of the infernal realm, Satan, the embodiment of malevolence, seethed with a volatile mix of anger and betrayal. His voice echoed with a sinister edge, the essence of darkness entwined within his words.

Satan: "Chhaya, my flesh, and blood, daring to defy me, and seeking solace within the embrace of light? She shall not elude the consequences of her treachery. And you, Malakar, the cunning serpent who captured her heart, weaving a web of deceit around her. The stench of darkness that clings to you, commingling with her being, is an affront to my existence."

Malakar's demeanour turned colder, a venomous smirk dancing upon his lips as he relished Satan's discomfort.

Malakar: "Abomination or not, my Lord, Chhaya made her choice. She escaped your suffocating grip, your all-consuming darkness, and sought sanctuary in the radiance of light. She bore our children, a testament to her unwavering defiance."

Satan's eyes flickered with a volatile blend of fascination and fury, his voice a venomous hiss that resonated through the abyss.

Satan: "I am Satan, the Lord of Darkness. Even the feeble light trembles before my might. This little girl, my creation, believed she could betray me? How naive she is. She thought she could evade my grasp, hide behind her veil of illusions. But illusions can be shattered, and she shall face the wrath of her actions. The darkness will find her, no matter how far she flees."

Malakar's voice resounded with a sadistic glee, revelling in Chhaya's impending doom, as he continued his merciless taunts. The air grew heavy with a palpable tension, charged with malevolent energy.

Malakar: "Yes, my Lord, her illusions may have shielded her momentarily, but they will crumble beneath the weight of her betrayal. The burden of guilt she carries will consume her from within, a relentless torment that will leave her broken and defenceless."

Satan's grin widened, his eyes ablaze with vindictive pleasure, relishing the prospect of Chhaya's suffering.

Satan: "Chhaya will taste the bitter fruit of her transgressions, her defiance laid bare before the might of darkness. The full force of my power will descend upon her like a ravenous predator, tearing through her illusions, and leaving her exposed and vulnerable. Her torment will serve as a gruesome example, striking fear into the hearts of all who dare defy the darkness."

Malakar's voice dripped with a sinister satisfaction, his words laced with a twisted delight.

Malakar: "Indeed, my Lord. Chhaya bears the weight of her guilt and remorse, forever haunted by the darkness that resides within her. She may have momentarily evaded your wrath, slipping into the hidden recesses of the astral realm, but her crimes will forever haunt her, consuming her soul without respite."

Malakar's voice dripped with contemptuous amusement as he belittled Chhaya's misguided beliefs, his words laced with a twisted sense of superiority. The air crackled with a malevolent energy, anticipation hanging in the atmosphere.

Malakar: "Oh, how naive she is, thinking she sacrifices herself for some illusory 'greater good'. She deludes herself into believing her purpose is to protect the realms from your wrath. Her mind, clouded by the deceit of the light, owes its confusion to Parvati's influence."

A sinister grin played upon Malakar's lips as he revelled in his cunning, his voice dripping with calculated intent.

Malakar: "But, if it pleases the Lord, I have devised a plan to magnify your power and serve as a chilling example to the cosmos. Those tainted by darkness, those who bear the blood of darkness, will forever be barred from the embrace of light. Even the Astral Council, with its naive notions of second chances, will be forced to abandon their moral illusions."

The room seemed to hold its breath, the weight of Malakar's proposition hanging heavy in the air. The promise of unparalleled power and the shattering of ingrained beliefs added a layer of intrigue and uncertainty to the fateful decision ahead.

Satan's perplexed expression transformed into a mix of curiosity and caution as he addressed Malakar, his tone laced with a hint of warning.

Satan: "Speak, but do not test my patience. What is it that you have in mind?"

A wicked satisfaction coursed through Malakar's veins, his smile growing colder and more sinister with each passing moment.

Malakar: "My Lord, we must guide her back onto the path of

darkness, for she possesses your blood, and I have witnessed her prowess as a warrior. Chhaya is a formidable force to behold, and her skill in combat is mesmerizing. We shall be unstoppable with her by our side, my Lord."

Satan's gaze shifted, fascination and disappointment flickering in his eyes. His voice carried a hint of begrudging admiration.

Satan: "You possess a viciousness that surpasses expectations. It seems you were born as a gift to darkness. Chhaya had always intrigued me. I believed she would be the successor of darkness, but that insolent brat defied me and my plans. I will permit you to return her to the darkness if you can achieve your proposal. However, should she refuse, my wrath shall consume her."

In that chamber, cloaked in darkness, a newfound understanding unfolded between Satan, the Lord of Darkness, and Malakar, his newly anointed loyal pawn.

Satan: "Malakar, I see the fire burning within you, the embodiment of a true warrior of darkness. You have proven your loyalty and your unwavering commitment to embrace the shadows. I now place my trust in you, more than ever."

Malakar's eyes gleamed with a dark intensity, a surge of pride surging through him as he grasped the immense significance of Satan's words. Malakar's voice trembled with reverence, his words resonating with unwavering dedication.

Malakar: "My Lord, your trust humbles me. I have forsaken all else in my life to serve your cause, to embrace the boundless depths of darkness. I stand before you, ready to face any trial you lay upon my path."

Satan's expression twisted into a smug grin, his voice a tantalizing mix of excitement and foreboding.

Satan: "Very well, Malakar. The time has come to proceed. Two final challenges lie before you, trials that will shape the destiny of

Eldoria and plunge it into eternal darkness. The first test demands your strength and cunning. You must confront Ravana, the mighty king, and seize the blue sapphire ring he possesses—a symbol of light's fleeting power. The ring itself can potentially sway the tides of the impending battle for Eldoria."

Malakar's eyes widened with a potent blend of exhilaration and apprehension. The prospect of facing such an indomitable adversary thrilled him to his very core.

Malakar: "Ravana, my father, the embodiment of unrivalled might, has always kept that mesmerizing ring hidden from me. Its allure has haunted my dreams, whispering of its true destiny. It was never meant for my father; it was meant for a higher purpose. I can now fathom the connection I have felt throughout my life as the protector of Eldoria. I shall journey into the depths of this realm, confront my blood if necessary, and seize the blue sapphire ring as you command, my Lord."

Satan's voice reverberated with an intoxicating blend of authority and anticipation, resonating through the chamber.

Satan: "Retrieve the ring, Malakar, and deliver it to me. Let its power flow through us, a force to be harnessed and perverted in service of our insatiable darkness. Once you possess it, we shall unleash its boundless potential and consume every flicker of light that dares to defy us."

Malakar nodded, a newfound determination coursing through his veins, fuelling his sense of purpose.

Yet, as the weight of their unholy alliance settled in the air, Malakar couldn't escape a flicker of apprehension. His mind became a battleground, torn between loyalty to darkness and the lingering whispers of doubt. In a moment of vulnerability, he turned to Satan, his voice laced with uncertainty.

Malakar: "My Lord, I have proven my unwavering loyalty,

facing the challenges you've set. But what is the ultimate sacrifice you demand of me? What depths of darkness must I plunge into to fulfil my role?"

Satan's eyes narrowed, a sinister glimmer of wicked delight dancing within them. He leaned closer, his voice a seductive whisper that sent a shiver down Malakar's spine. Satan's voice echoed with a chilling mixture of authority and sorrow, enveloping the chamber in an aura of darkness.

Satan: "Ah, the ultimate sacrifice, my faithful servant. The crucible separates the devoted from the weak, the worthy from the unworthy. You must offer a sacrifice that cuts deep into your soul to prove your unyielding loyalty. Your children, they must become an offering to the insatiable hunger of darkness."

Malakar's heart froze in his chest, his mind spiralling into a tempest of conflicting emotions. His love for his innocent children clashed violently with his insatiable thirst for power and recognition.

Malakar: "My Lord, my children, they are my blood, my very essence. How can I bear to bring myself to sacrifice them? It tears at the very fabric of my being, wrenching my soul apart."

Satan's voice hardened, tinged with a potent blend of sorrow and bitter wisdom, born from his own experiences of loss and sacrifice.

Satan: "I, too, comprehend the torment accompanying such a sacrifice. I sacrificed my son, and I extinguished the life of my beloved wife. Through that ultimate act of darkness, Chhaya, your wife, and my wayward offspring, slipped through my grasp. The path to true power is paved with such agonizing choices."

A suffocating silence descended upon the chamber, the air thick with the weight of Malakar's excruciating dilemma. His heart pounded, the turmoil within him threatening to consume his essence. The image of his children's innocent faces haunted his thoughts, a painful reminder of the love he held so dear.

Malakar: "To sacrifice my flesh and blood. It is an abhorrent act, a perversion of nature itself. Yet, the allure of untamed power, the seduction of absolute dominion, grips my soul with an unrelenting force. My Lord, how can I reconcile these opposing desires that tear me apart? I beseech you, have mercy! Is there no alternative? Spare my children from this gruesome fate!"

Satan's eyes flickered with an unsettling blend of comprehension and malevolence. His voice, laden with a twisted wisdom born from aeons of darkness, pierced through Malakar's inner turmoil.

Satan: "The choice, Malakar, lies solely within the recesses of your tormented soul. The ultimate sacrifice is not one to be taken lightly. It demands your unyielding loyalty, your unwavering devotion to the realm of shadows. Ponder the boundless power that awaits you, the authority to wield life and death. Will you forsake the sacred bonds of love, severing the ties that bind you to your offspring, all in exchange for the limitless potential that darkness can bestow upon you?"

An Insidious Secret

A chilling silence settled upon the chamber, the air thick with anticipation and the weight of impending doom. Malakar's mind spun with a whirlwind of conflicting emotions, his heart torn between love for his children and the insidious lure of immortality. He struggled to comprehend the depths of Satan's manipulation, the extent of the sacrifice demanded of him.

Satan, the manifestation of darkness, concealed a sinister truth beneath his persuasive words. He knew that the blood running through Malakar's children held a unique blend of darkness and light, a powerful essence that could potentially bring about his demise. With a calculated air of manipulation, Satan sought to convince Malakar of the necessity of the ultimate sacrifice.

Malakar's voice trembled with disbelief and desperation, his words a desperate plea for clarity amidst the swirling darkness.

Malakar: "My Lord, are you suggesting that my children, their very existence, holds the key to immortality? Can their blood, a blend of light and darkness, grant us eternal life? This revellation overwhelms me. But what price must be paid for such a profound gift? What horrors await them, my innocent children, in this twisted path of immortality?"

Satan's eyes gleamed with a predatory gleam, and his voice dripped with an intoxicating blend of power and deceit.

Satan: "Ah, Malakar, the price is steep, but the rewards are beyond measure. Your children's sacrifice will secure our immortality and unleash a cataclysmic shift in the balance of power. Their blood, a vessel of immense potential, can grant us dominion over all realms. Through their sacrifice, darkness will consume the light, and we shall reign as eternal conquerors. Think, Malakar, of the legacy we will leave behind, the legends that will be whispered in awe for millennia to come."

Malakar: "You speak of the blood of darkness and light within my children. Are you saying their sacrifice would prevent your demise, my Lord?"

Satan's grin widened, a sinister twist that sent shivers down Malakar's spine. The truth unravelled before him like a ghastly revellation, the puzzle pieces falling into place with chilling clarity.

Satan: "Yes, Malakar, you finally understand. Their sacrifice, the merging of their blood, will rejuvenate me, breathe new life into my existence. Their essence, a potent elixir of darkness and light, will stave off the encroaching shadows that threaten to consume me. With their sacrifice, I shall transcend mortality, ascending to a realm of eternal power and dominance."

Satan's voice reverberated through the chamber, a chilling symphony of malevolence and triumph. His words pierced the air, laced with a dark revellation that sent shivers down Malakar's spine.

Satan: "Yes, my son, through the annihilation of this potent bloodline, the eternal dominion of darkness shall be secured. With the sacrifice of your children, the threat of our demise shall vanish, and we shall ascend as an unstoppable force, reigning over all realms. Destiny brought Chhaya to your side; her defiance was merely a means to further my plans. She, my favourite little rebel, unknowingly played her part, for I foresaw the union of darkness in your bloodlines, paving the way for our ultimate legacy.

"And as far as children are concerned, you and Chhaya will together give birth to the real children of darkness, and that can happen only when you fulfil the ultimate challenge of sacrifice and embrace darkness completely. But remember, for us to be immortal, you must sacrifice all three of your children."

Malakar's soul quivered under the weight of his conflicting

emotions. His love for his children waged war against the insidious whisper of ambition that echoed within him. The power and immortality promised by Satan seemed tantalisingly close, yet the cost it demanded threatened to consume his very essence.

Malakar's voice trembled, laced with anguish and indecision.

Malakar: "The thought of sacrificing my flesh and blood, my innocent children, fills me with unimaginable sorrow. How can I bear the weight of their lives on my conscience? To extinguish their light for the sake of my desires. It is a darkness I dare not tread."

Satan's words slithered like serpents, entwining themselves around Malakar's wavering resolve.

Satan: "You hesitate, Malakar, blinded by your affection for these mortal beings. But in the pursuit of ultimate power, sacrifices must be made. Their lives are but a stepping-stone on the path to our dominion. Embrace the darkness within you, let it consume your doubts. Only then shall true power be yours."

In the suffocating grip of his conflicting emotions, Malakar teetered on the edge of an abyss, the weight of his choices threatening to consume him. Love for his children tugged at his heart, a flame of fierce protection burning within, while the seductive whispers of power and immortality whispered tantalisingly in his ears.

The room seemed to close in, shadows lengthening and suffocating the last vestiges of hope within Malakar's heart. The weight of his decision pressed upon him, threatening to crush his soul.

With each passing moment, the world around Malakar seemed to hold its breath, the very fabric of existence trembling under the weight of his decision. His mind became a battlefield, where loyalty clashed with ambition and devotion clashed with the allure of darkness.

Malakar's resolve wavered as the seconds ticked, his thoughts fragmented and scattered like shards of shattered glass. He could feel the weight of his destiny pressing upon him, the magnitude of his choice threatening to unravel the very fabric of his soul.

In this crucible of fate, Malakar stood as a solitary figure, his heart torn asunder by the forces that contended for his allegiance. The echoes of his decision reverberated through eternity, for in that pivotal moment, the course of his life and the lives of his children hung in a precarious balance.

Kalkeyas

Unbeknownst to the Lord of Darkness and his brother, Malakar, a silent observer had been watching their every move. Kalkeyas, a figure shrouded in tranquillity and deep contemplation, had surreptitiously followed Malakar to the foreboding chamber, drawn by an unexplainable sense of unease.

As he stood at the threshold of darkness, his senses overwhelmed by the sinister conversation that unfolded before him, Kalkeyas felt his world shatter. A surge of anguish and disbelief coursed through his veins, threatening to engulf him in an abyss of despair. His heart pounded with a desperate rhythm, echoing the weight of the truth that bore down upon him.

Unlike his tempestuous brother, Kalkeyas embodied an aura of calm resilience, a pillar of strength in the face of adversity. His regal stature commanded respect, and his eyes glistened with an innate wisdom that transcended the ordinary. The features of the Rakshasas clan graced his countenance, sharp and discerning yet softened by an underlying compassion that touched the souls of those who crossed his path.

Clad in robes of humble earth tones, Kalkeyas blended seamlessly with the natural world he revered. He sought solace amidst the whispering trees and the gentle embrace of the wind, finding solace in the serenity of nature's embrace. Every movement he made was deliberate and measured, a testament to the depth of his introspection and the profound grace with which he carried himself.

Renowned for his role as a revered teacher, Kalkeyas possessed an insatiable thirst for knowledge, much like his illustrious father, the mighty King Ravana. Guided by his unyielding passion, he generously shared his wisdom with all who sought his counsel, imparting clarity, and understanding in a world plagued by turmoil. Many regarded him as a shining beacon of enlightenment amidst the encroaching darkness.

Though his serene nature yearned for tranquillity, Kalkeyas harboured a deep admiration for his elder brother, Malakar. He acknowledged Malakar's innate leadership qualities and the fervour with which he embraced his responsibilities as their father's rightful heir. Kalkeyas recognized the necessity of Malakar's audacity and unwavering determination, even if it clashed with his ideals. While some accused Malakar of boundless ambition and insatiable greed, Kalkeyas understood the primal drive behind his brother's actions, seeing it as a vital aspect for the survival of their clan.

Embedded within Kalkeyas' heart resided an unbreakable bond of love and reverence for Malakar. Their brotherly connection surpassed any conflicts or divergent paths they tread. Kalkeyas held a steadfast belief that, if directed towards virtuous ends, Malakar's strength could be a formidable force for righteousness. It pained him to witness his once-noble and virtuous brother succumb to the seductive promises of darkness, a descent he could not comprehend nor accept.

Kalkeyas' voice trembled with anguish and disbelief, his murmurs barely audible amidst the weight of his shattered convictions.

Kalkeyas: "No. Malakar, my brother, my role model. How could you forsake our shared principles? How could you entertain such malevolence, plotting the destruction of Eldoria and even contemplating the unthinkable sacrifice of your innocent children? This cannot be the path you have chosen."

Tears welled in Kalkeyas' eyes, each drop carrying the weight of their shattered bond. His mind raced, desperately searching for a glimmer of hope, for a way to comprehend the unfathomable truth. Deep within his soul, he yearned for his brother's awakening, a resurgence of the light that once radiated from his very being.

Determined to seek the truth and confront Malakar, Kalkeyas steeled himself and began plotting his next move. He knew he had to tread carefully, for their bond as brothers had always been unbreakable, and he refused to believe that it had been irreparably severed.

Kalkeyas: "I must find a way to reach Malakar, to make him see the depths of the darkness he's descending into. But first, I must gather more information and unveil the hidden secrets. If Chhaya truly is Satan's daughter, then her escape and refuge under Parvati must hold the key to understanding the true nature of this unholy alliance."

With a heavy heart and a resolute spirit, Kalkeyas mustered his family together, their eyes reflecting a mix of fear and determination. Each member carried the weight of their apprehensions, yet they stood united in the face of the encroaching darkness.

Kalkeyas: "We have come to a pivotal moment in our lives, where our choices will shape our destiny and the fate of Eldoria. The time for secrets and silence has passed. We must face the truth and confront the forces that seek to destroy us. Our bond as a family will be our strength, our love, and unwavering support guiding us through the treacherous path that lies ahead."

The air crackled with anticipation as Kalkeyas continued. Kalkeyas stood tall, his voice resonating with authority and sorrow as he addressed his family. Their faces reflected a mix of anticipation and apprehension. The weight of his words hung heavy in the air, each syllable piercing their hearts like a dagger.

"Father, Mother, and esteemed uncles, I bear news that will shake the very foundation of our souls. The encroaching darkness of Kalyuga has infiltrated our beloved Eldoria, casting its malevolent shadow upon our sacred land. And alas, it is not an external force that threatens us, but one of our own, our revered hero, Malakar, who has succumbed to the seductive allure of darkness. His path has veered into the abyss, from which there seems no return."

His family let out a collective gasp, their eyes widening in disbelief and anguish. The magnitude of the revellation left them reeling, their minds struggling to comprehend the unfathomable betrayal that had unfolded.

Ravana's voice quivered with apprehension and urgency as he implored Kalkeyas for clarity. The tension in the room was palpable, as every gaze fixated on Kalkeyas, awaiting his response.

"Kalkeyas, do not speak in riddles," Ravana demanded, his tone laced with unease. "Tell us, without hesitation, what you have discovered."

Kalkeyas took a deep breath, his voice steady yet heavy with the weight of his revellation. His eyes met Ravana's, filled with sorrow and determination.

"Father, I shall be blunt in my words, for the gravity of the situation demands no less," Kalkeyas began, his voice resonating through the chamber. "Satan, the Lord of Darkness, seeks to exploit Chhaya's lineage, her connection to our bloodline. He covets your powerful sapphire ring, the embodiment of light, to fuel his unholy powers and cast a shadow over Eldoria. But his insidious demands do not end there, for he demands the ultimate sacrifice from Malakar. Our innocent children, father, they are to be offered as pawns in Satan's twisted game, their lives extinguished to ensure his wretched survival."

A collective gasp filled the room, filled with disbelief and anguish. The enormity of Satan's malevolence reverberated through their souls, shaking the foundations of their resolve. Ravana's face contorted with anguish, his eyes brimming with tears as he grappled with the monstrous truth. His voice quivered as he spoke, the weight of his words echoing through the silence.

"Our children, our precious innocents," Ravana murmured, his voice filled with heartache. "To be sacrificed for the sake of darkness. This is a nightmare, a cruel twist of fate that threatens to devour us all."

The room fell solemnly silent, the weight of their predicament suffocating. Kalkeyas ignited a fire, a fierce determination that blazed within his eyes, undeterred by the despair surrounding them.

"But, dear family, let not despair consume our hearts," Kalkeyas declared, his voice resolute, and unwavering. "We are the protectors of Eldoria, the guardians of righteousness. We shall not yield to the darkness that seeks to corrupt us. United in love and unwavering in our purpose, we shall confront Malakar and unmask the depths of his deception.

"Together, we will stand against Satan's insidious plans, for the fate of our children and the destiny of our land hang in the balance. Let our collective strength be our shield and our unwavering determination be our sword. Our love and resilience shall prevail, even in the darkest times."

Ravana's face contorted with anguish and denial as he struggled to comprehend the magnitude of Kalkeyas' words. His voice trembled with hope and desperation, as if pleading for a different truth to emerge.

"Kalkeyas, you speak of a connection between Chhaya and Satan, but I cannot fathom such a bond. My son, Malakar, the beacon of hope for Eldoria, cannot possibly entertain such dark and heinous plans," Ravana protested, his voice filled with a father's disbelief.

Kalkeyas, his voice heavy with sorrow, looked deeply into Ravana's eyes, unwavering in his conviction.

"Father, I wish it were a misunderstanding, but the truth cannot be denied," Kalkeyas replied, his voice tinged with sadness.

"I overheard their sinister plans, their intentions to sacrifice your beloved grandchildren. And Chhaya, she carries the blood of Satan within her, a daughter who fled the suffocating grasp of darkness to seek solace in the light under Parvati's protection. The ties that bind her to the Lord of Darkness are undeniable."

Ravana's breath hitched, his mind reeling with the unbearable weight of the revellations. The image of his son, Malakar, once the embodiment of honour and nobility, now stained by the sinister alliance, shattered his heart. Tears welled in Ravana's eyes as he fought against the tide of disbelief, a glimmer of anguish breaking through his facade of denial.

"No, my son. How could you have strayed so far from the path of righteousness?" Ravana murmured, his voice trembling with a mixture of grief and fury. "To even consider sacrificing our innocent grandchildren. It is beyond comprehension."

Kalkeyas's voice filled with unwavering determination, he stepped forward, his eyes burning with a steely resolve.

"Father, we must face the truth head-on, no matter how agonizing it may be," Kalkeyas urged, his voice carrying a resolute tone. "We cannot afford to deny the reality that stares us in the face. Our beloved Eldoria is in peril, and we must protect it, even if it means confronting the darkest corners of our family."

Ravana, his gaze meeting Kalkeyas', nodded slowly, his heart heavy with grief and determination.

"You speak the truth, Kalkeyas. We cannot let this darkness consume us," Ravana agreed, his voice laced with a newfound resolve. "We shall gather our strength and uncover the full extent of this treachery. Our family and the people of Eldoria deserve justice, and we shall not rest until we have reclaimed the honour that has been tarnished."

Mandodari gasped, her hands trembling with disbelief and fear.

"Chhaya, the daughter of Satan? How could this be? What diabolical scheme does Satan have in store for our family?" Her voice quivered with a mix of anguish and desperation.

The weight of the revellation crashed upon their hearts like a thunderbolt. The thought of their innocent children being entangled in such darkness tore at their souls.

Kumbhakaran, known for his wrathful nature, bellowed in fury, his voice echoing through the chamber. "Satan dares to defile our bloodline, to use our flesh and blood for his sinister purposes? This madness ends now! We shall not allow our family to be manipulated like pawns in his wicked game."

Silence descended upon the room, heavy and suffocating, as the gravity of their predicament sank in. Ravana, the once-mighty king, locked eyes with Kalkeyas, a glimmer of hope flickering in his gaze.

"Kalkeyas, I implore you, assure me once more of this truth," Ravana pleaded, his voice laden with desperation. "Could it be that Chhaya, our daughter-in-law, the woman we welcomed into our hearts, is the catalyst for this darkness that has engulfed Malakar?"

Kalkeyas, his voice filled with sorrow, nodded solemnly. "Father, I have observed Chhaya closely, seeking any sign of darkness within her. But her love for our family, her unwavering dedication to Eldoria, remains pure. It is Malakar, consumed by the alluring promises of power and darkness, who has fallen under Satan's spell. I witnessed it with my own eyes, the depths to which he has descended."

Tears welled up in Ravana's eyes as he grappled with the harsh reality before him. The notion that the forces of darkness could sway his son shattered his heart.

"Our family, our legacy, is at stake," Ravana declared, his voice a mixture of determination and grief. "We shall not stand idle while Satan and Malakar lay waste to everything we hold dear. We must gather our strength, rally our allies, and unveil the truth to the people of Eldoria. The battle for our souls and the fate of our land begins now."

Mandodari's voice choked with anguish, she clung to Kalkeyas' arm as tears streamed down her face. "How can this be? Malakar, our blood, the hero who has defended Eldoria with unwavering loyalty. Are we to abandon him now? Can we not believe in his innocence?"

Kumbhakaran, his frustration evident in his voice, interjected with a stern tone, "We cannot let our emotions cloud our judgement, Mandodari. The truth stands before us, and we must confront it. Malakar may have succumbed to his desires, leading him down a treacherous path."

Vibhishana, the voice of reason, spoke calmly yet determinedly, "Let us not rush to condemn Chhaya, who has shown us nothing but loyalty and love. We must tread carefully and explore all possibilities. However, we cannot deny that darkness has tainted Malakar's actions."

Mandodari's heart ached. "Ravana, we cannot let Satan use our children as pawns in his wicked game. We must shield them from this impending doom."

Ravana nodded, his gaze resolute. "You are right, my love. We will do whatever it takes to protect our children and thwart Satan's plan. The sapphire ring, the embodiment of light's power, must be hidden away to preserve the delicate balance of our world."

Vibhishana, his expression a mix of contemplation and determination, spoke with unwavering conviction, "Brother, we cannot allow darkness to triumph over the bonds of love and the innocence of our children. We must confront Malakar, expose Satan's true intentions, and reclaim the light that has been obscured. Only then can we hope to save our family and Eldoria from this impending doom that looms over us."

His mind tormented by conflicting emotions, Ravana clenched his fists in anguish. "We must not lose sight of the looming threat that Satan poses. Chhaya's connection to him is undeniable, and we cannot ignore the danger it presents. Whether Malakar is innocent or not, our duty lies in safeguarding our family and Eldoria from the impending catastrophe."

Mandodari, trembling with fear and compassion, whispered, "But can we condemn Chhaya, who has shown us nothing but love and loyalty? Her refuge in the light, her desire for redemption, cannot be dismissed. We must tread carefully in our judgements."

Ravana, his heart heavy with responsibility, locked eyes with Mandodari. "My love, our decisions may cause pain, but we must prioritize protecting our children and our realm. While we search for the truth, let us not lose sight of the bigger picture. We must preserve what we hold dear."

The chamber pulsated with a palpable tension, an amalgamation of love, doubt, and the burden of their roles. They knew the path ahead would be treacherous, filled with sacrifice and uncertainty. With resolute determination, they pledged to unveil the truth and extinguish the encroaching darkness that threatened to consume their family and their cherished land.

Approaching Chhaya, a whirlwind of conflicting emotions churned within Ravana, Mandodari, Kalkeyas, Kumbhakaran, and Vibhishana. Doubts cast shadows upon their hearts, testing their faith and loyalty. But as their gaze met hers, all uncertainties dissolved, replaced by a profound understanding.

Chhaya stood before them, an ethereal figure emanating a gentle radiance that touched their troubled souls. Her eyes, once clouded with anguish, now sparkled with hope, as if she had been waiting for them to see the truth deep within her.

Blood Determines One's Destiny?

A tableau of love and torment unfolded as they entered Chhaya's abode. Her ethereal beauty veiled by a cloud of worry, she clutched her children tightly, shielding them from the encroaching darkness. Her eyes, pools of unspoken anguish, silently beseeched for empathy and understanding.

Chhaya's chamber exuded warmth and comfort, a haven amidst the chaos. Soft hues adorned the walls, while plush furniture beckoned with open arms—framed paintings captured stolen moments of joy with her children, adorning the room like precious treasures. Sunbeams pierced through the curtains, casting a gentle glow that bathed the space in serenity.

Seated upon the carpeted floor, Chhaya engaged in a spirited game of peek-a-boo with her youngest child, their laughter filling the air like ethereal music. Her face was illuminated with a radiant smile, a testament to the sheer delight that motherhood had brought her. In these fleeting moments of respite, she savoured the pure bliss that seemed so distant amid their turbulent existence.

Fully present in the embrace of motherhood, Chhaya crafted a world of security and nurture for her children. Her eyes shimmered with an endless wellspring of love and tenderness as she guided their exploration and embraced their innocent curiosity. Each interaction forged an unbreakable bond, a testament to their unwavering connection.

In this haven of light and love, the truth became ever more elusive; for how could such a beacon of compassion and devotion be intertwined with the darkness that loomed outside?

In that sacred space, the room seemed to transcend reality itself.

Chhaya, a living embodiment of purity and love, emanated a maternal aura that embraced her children with unwavering tenderness and care. It was a haven where their souls found solace, shielded from the harsh realities that loomed beyond its walls. The air brimmed with her children's innocent laughter, as if the very sound resonated with the essence of joy and contentment.

As they stood before Chhaya, a profound revellation coursed through their veins, dispelling the shadows of doubt and misconception. The veil of prejudice had been lifted, and they saw her for who she truly was—a beacon of light amidst the encroaching darkness. Blood no longer held dominion over destiny, and lineage could no longer define one's path.

A palpable tension enveloped the room, anticipation crackling like static electricity. Their gazes locked, suspended in a moment that held the weight of redemption and forgiveness. Ravana, his voice heavy with regret and realization, broke the silence.

Ravana: "Chhaya, we stand before you burdened by our doubts and misguided judgements. We questioned your loyalty, but now, as I peer into your eyes, I see nought but love, compassion, and the unwavering devotion of a mother."

Chhaya's eyes were filled with a mix of confusion and vulnerability. She looked at her family, searching for answers within their conflicted expressions.

Chhaya: "Father, I am at a loss. Doubts, judgements, allegiance. I do not comprehend what has transpired within these walls."

In a room consumed by an oppressive atmosphere, Kalkeyas summoned every ounce of his courage, his voice quivering with the weight of impending doom, as he unleashed the devastating truth that would tear at the very fabric of their existence.

Kalkeyas: "Chhaya, my sister-in-law, I bring forth news that will rend your heart asunder. Satan, the malevolent force, the embodiment of darkness itself, has resurfaced from the depths of his infernal realm. He seeks to ensnare Malakar, our brother, and orchestrate a diabolical scheme that involves the sacrifice of your innocent children. Eldoria stands on the precipice of annihilation, caught in the clutches of this impending catastrophe. We cannot ignore this grave truth; we must confront it together and defy him!"

Chhaya, her eyes widening in a potent mix of disbelief, pain, and sheer horror, instinctively clutched her children closer to her, a desperate shield against the encroaching darkness that threatened to consume them all.

Chhaya: "No. No, this cannot be true! How is it possible? I thought I had escaped his clutches, fleeing from the nightmare of my past, leaving behind the shattered remnants of my innocence. His wickedness tore apart my little brother, my mother, and their lives. How can he return now to haunt us once more? I cannot bear to endure their loss again, to witness the desolation he brings upon us!"

Chhaya's tears mingled with a fierce determination that blazed within her, an unyielding fire fuelled by a mother's love and the sheer strength born from the depths of her shattered past. With every word that escaped her lips, her resolve grew stronger, her voice echoing with defiance and unwavering determination.

Chhaya: "My beloved children, bearers of both light and darkness, I curse the cruel hand of fate that threatens to harm you. But listen closely, for in this moment, I vow as your mother to shield you from the horrors that await. I will not allow you to be mere pawns in his insatiable quest for power. My love for you is boundless, and my protective instinct knows no bounds!"

Rising to her full height, a radiant force of resilience and defiance, Chhaya's voice pierced through the suffocating air, resounding with the unwavering strength of a warrior.

Chhaya: "Once, I was a trembling child, fleeing from the clutches of darkness. But now, I am a warrior, a guardian fiercely shielding my children and this land. I will confront every challenge that dares to threaten you, drawing upon the depths of my being to ensure your safety. Neither my father's legacy nor the demons that haunt my husband shall lay claim to your lives. I will fight, for darkness shall not devour my children's innocence!"

In that moment, as her family stood before her, their hearts reverberated with a newfound understanding. They cast aside the fallacy that blood and lineage held ultimate sway, recognizing that the strength of love and the indomitable spirit of a mother could defy even the darkest of destinies.

Ravana's voice resonated with a mix of regret and enlightenment, his words cutting through the weight of their past misconceptions.

Ravana: "Chhaya, my daughter-in-law, we have been blind to the truth, shackled by the illusions of bloodline and destiny. Darkness does not define one's essence, nor does light belong exclusively to a chosen few. It is a conscious choice forged deep within one's soul. Your love for your children, untainted by the shadows that cloud Malakar, shines as a beacon of hope."

Mandodari, her heart heavy with a blend of sorrow and pride, reached out to embrace Chhaya, her touch conveying a depth of emotion that words could not encompass.

Mandodari: "Chhaya, my cherished daughter-in-law, you have shattered the chains that bound our minds. You have revealed the fallacy that plagued us, illuminating the truth that goodness can thrive even in the darkest recesses. Your love, your unwavering devotion to your children, is a testament to the strength of your character. Never doubt the power of your choices, for they can shape destinies."

Kalkeyas, resonating with newfound wisdom, gently clasped Chhaya's hand in his own, the connection between them imbued with shared understanding.

Kalkeyas: "Chhaya, my sister-in-law, you have imparted upon us a profound lesson. Our lineage does not define us; our choices in adversity mould our true selves. Darkness may have once coursed through your veins, but you have embraced the light within. You have shown us the transformative power of love and compassion, even after betrayal. We stand united with you, prepared to defend what is right and just."

Chhaya stood before them, her eyes filled with vulnerability and strength, her voice steady yet trembling with emotion.

Chhaya: "Father, Mother, my dear family, I appreciate your words and your understanding. It is true that darkness seeks to consume our world and that Malakar has strayed from the light. But I refuse to let despair consume us. We must rise as beacons of hope and unwavering love in darkness. Our children, innocent and pure, deserve a future free from the clutches of evil. It is up to us to protect them, to fight for their lives and the fate of Eldoria itself."

Kalkeyas's voice resonating with determination, stepped forward, his eyes ablaze with a newfound purpose.

Kalkeyas: "Chhaya, our sister, you have shown us the true meaning of strength. In your love for your children and your unwavering commitment to goodness, you have ignited a fire within us all. We will stand together, shoulder to shoulder, against the forces threatening our family and land. Darkness may have touched our lives, but it will never extinguish the light that burns within our souls. Let our unity be a testament to our resilience and unyielding resolve."

Chhaya's heart wrenched with a deep, agonizing pain as she received the devastating news that her monstrous father, Satan, had lured her beloved husband, Malakar, into his clutches. The realization that Satan had asked Malakar for the unthinkable, the ultimate sacrifice of killing their innocent children to embrace darkness completely, was a horrifying blow to Chhaya's soul. In that moment, a wave of nostalgia washed over Chhaya, bringing back haunting memories of her brother and mother being executed by her father, Satan. The weight of their loss pressed heavily on her chest, suffocating her with grief and despair. She couldn't fathom the possibility of history repeating itself, with her husband now being manipulated by the same malevolent forces.

Chhaya's voice trembled as she struggled to find the strength to speak, her words laced with anguish and desperation.

Chhaya: "No. No, this can't be happening. How could he do this? How could my father be so cruel? Haven't we suffered enough already?"

Tears cascaded down Chhaya's face, mingling with her anguished whispers. The weight of her desperation hung heavy in the air, as if the room itself mourned alongside her. Chhaya, her voice quivering with a mixture of sorrow and determination, pleaded to the depths of her husband's soul.

Chhaya: "Malakar, please. Hear my cries, feel the love that binds us together. Our children, innocent and pure, must not suffer the same fate as my brother and mother. We cannot allow Satan's darkness to claim their lives. We must find the strength to break free from his malevolent grasp and fight for their safety and future."

Her words carried a raw, fervent plea, reaching into the depths of her husband's consciousness, where the battle between light and darkness raged.

Chhaya: "I cannot bear the thought of losing them, the echoes of our lost loved ones still haunt my heart. Together, we can defy the shadows that threaten to snuff out their lives. Let the love we share be our guiding light in this treacherous darkness. We must protect our family, Malakar. We must reclaim the light that still flickers within you."

Chhaya clung to a glimmer of hope, her prayers echoing in the depths of her soul, desperately reaching out to her husband's heart. The weight of their love, the memories they shared, and the light still flickering within Malakar fuelled her determination to wage a battle against the encroaching darkness.

Kalkeyas, burdened by the magnitude of Chhaya's pain, knelt beside her, his hand gently clasping hers. In that tender touch, he conveyed a profound empathy and a silent vow to stand by her side through the trials ahead.

Kalkeyas: "Chhaya, my sister, I cannot fathom the depths of your anguish. To be torn between the love for your children and the loyalty to a husband who has strayed from the path of light is a torment that no one should endure. But know this: we stand together now, united in our untiring commitment to protecting you and safeguarding the future of Eldoria. Your pain is our pain, and we will not falter in the face of darkness."

Their voices intertwined, forming a chorus of unwavering support, as the family encircled Chhaya. They formed a shield of familial love, their collective strength shielding her from the consuming shadows that threatened to devour her world. In that sacred moment, they vowed to be her rock, her guiding light, her unwavering support in the battle against the forces that sought to tear their family apart.

Her eyes ablaze with a steely resolve, Chhaya gazed at her family with gratitude and unwavering determination. She felt a newfound strength surge through her veins, propelling her forward in the face of unimaginable challenges. The weight of her responsibility as a mother and the protector of her family fuelled her determination to confront the darkness that threatened to engulf them.

Chhaya's spirit grew stronger with each tear she wiped away, her resolve unwavering. She stood tall, her presence commanding, ready to face the trials that awaited her. In her heart, she knew that her love for her children and the need to safeguard her family required her to confront her beloved husband, Malakar, who had fallen under the sway of the malevolent forces.

Chhaya's voice echoed with resolute determination. She was the embodiment of a warrior-mother prepared to make unimaginable sacrifices for her family.

Chhaya: "I refuse to let the shadows consume my children's innocence. I will not stand idly by as my family is torn apart by the same evil that haunted my past. I will rise, fight, and challenge even my love if it means protecting the ones I hold dear from the clutches of darkness."

Her words reverberated with a fierce maternal instinct, a declaration that no power in the world could extinguish her love and devotion. With unwavering conviction, she solemnly vowed to herself and her children that their bond was unbreakable.

Chhaya: "I am a mother, and my love knows no boundaries. I will traverse the treacherous paths of my dreaded past, confront the sinister presence of my father, Satan, and defy any darkness that dares to threaten our family. The light within us shall never be extinguished; it will guide us through the darkest nights."

Chhaya's gaze transformed into a steely determination, her eyes blazing with an unwavering resolve fuelled by her love for her children and the memories in her heart. She could feel the weight of her ancestors' suffering, their spirits whispering in her ear, urging her to rise against the malevolence that plagued their lineage.

With each purposeful step, Chhaya embraced her role as a guardian, a shield against the encroaching darkness. She knew that her happiness must take a backseat to the safety and well-being of her children. The sacrifices she would make were a testament to the strength of her love.

Chhaya's voice resonated with an absolute resolve; the echo of a warrior-mother ready to face any adversary.

Chhaya: "My beloved family, your presence ignites a fire within me, a flame that cannot be extinguished. I refuse to let darkness taint our hearts, to sow the seeds of despair within our souls. I will stand unshakably, like a bastion of hope, for the sake of our children and the future of Eldoria."

Her words rang out, charged with a fierce determination that transcended her existence. She was resolute in her pursuit to break the cycle of pain and suffering that had haunted her family for generations. Love would be her guiding light, leading her through the labyrinth of darkness, as she vowed to emerge triumphant.

Chhaya: "History shall not repeat itself under my watch. I will shatter the chains that bind us, extinguishing the flames of anguish that have tormented our bloodline. Guided by the power of my love for you, my cherished family, we will rise above the malevolence that seeks to devour us. Together, we will carve a new destiny, where light triumphs over darkness, and our love prevails."

In that chamber, a symphony of determination and love echoed through the air, intertwining their spirits into an unbreakable tapestry. They stood united, forged by the fire of their shared purpose, ready to face the trials that awaited them with absolute resolve.

With a flame of unfaltering devotion burning within their hearts, they pledged to shield Chhaya and the precious world she held dear. No longer would she bear the burden alone; she was encircled by a fortress of love, an unyielding force that would defy the encroaching darkness. They would confront the looming abyss, drawing strength from the resolute support that bound their family.

And within the crucible of adversity, they would unearth the depths of their resilience and the indomitable power of kinship to conquer the shadow's malevolence.

Ravana, his regal visage etched with a mix of sorrow and fury, clenched his fists with unyielding determination. The weight of a father's heartache propelled him forward as he swore to reclaim his son from the clutches of ambition and avarice.

Ravana: "Malakar may have strayed, lured by the siren song of his desires, but we will not forsake him. Together, we shall stand firm against the encroaching darkness, unravel the web of deceit that ensnares him, and ignite the flame of his true self. With love as our guiding beacon, we shall restore him to the path of righteousness, no matter the cost."

Their voices melded into a resolute chorus in that hallowed chamber, their words echoing with unwavering determination. The air crackled with the weight of their collective resolve as they forged an unbreakable pact, a covenant to stand against the encroaching darkness that threatened to end their lineage and Eldoria itself. Their hearts burned with an undying flame, prepared to embark on a treacherous journey that would test their spirits to the very core.

With clenched fists and steely gazes, they vowed to defy the shadows that encroached upon their world, fuelled by a love that knew no bounds. Hand in hand, they would confront the blackened abyss, their courage an unyielding shield against the terrors that lurked within. Together, they declared:

In the depths of darkness, we shall ignite a radiant light,
With unyielding courage, we shall vanquish the night.
Bound by unbreakable hearts, united we shall stand,
In the face of the abyss, united hand in hand.
Through grim trials, our spirits shall soar,
For in our valiant fight, darkness shall be no more.

As their voices reverberated through the chamber, a solemn unity settled over the Rakshasa clan. They were resolute in their mission to save their reputation, their cherished family, Eldoria, and the realm itself. The weight of war loomed heavily upon Eldoria's doorstep, and the darkness they had once dismissed was now closer than ever.

Yet, armed with unyielding determination and fortified by the strength of their bond, they braced themselves for the impending battle that would define their legacy and determine the fate of their world.

The Battle of Light and Darkness

As the bugle of war resounded across the land, an electric tension gripped the battlefield, foretelling the clash of opposing forces. Amidst the chaos, Malakar stood at the forefront, a tragic figure consumed by the darkness that coursed through his veins. Gripping the wicked obsidian blade, his eyes glinted with a sinister resolve. Behind him, a legion of malevolent creatures loomed, their presence casting an eerie pall over the battlefield, poised to unleash devastation upon Eldoria.

In stark contrast, a resolute alliance rallied against the encroaching darkness. Chhaya, an embodiment of indefatigable determination, stood at the helm, her radiant spirit illuminating the gathering storm. Encircled by the united Rakshasa clan, their fierce loyalty was a shield against the encroaching shadows. They faced the imminent threat head-on. But they were not alone, for the people of Eldoria had heeded the call, joining their ranks to defend their beloved homeland.

As twilight descended, an ethereal veil settled over the battlefield, intensifying the clash of opposing energies. Dark clouds swirled overhead, crackling with malevolence, as thunder punctuated the symphony of chaos. The air quivered with anticipation as warriors from both sides clashed with ferocity, their weapons clashing in a cacophony that drowned out the anguished cries that pierced the night.

Chhaya emerged as a beacon of light amidst the encroaching shadows in the maelstrom's heart. Adorned in armour forged from the purest radiance, she moved with a grace that belied the weight of her purpose. Her sword gleamed with ethereal brilliance, and every swing was a testament to her unswerving love for her children and her unyielding dedication to protect Eldoria. Alongside her, the bow and arrow, infused with supernatural powers, weaved illusions that disarmed and bewildered the dark forces, leaving them vulnerable to the onslaught of righteous fury.

Amidst the chaos, Chhaya's every movement exuded a radiant strength, a testament to the indomitable spirit that burned within her. She carved a path through the darkness with each strike, her sword cutting through the shadows like a beacon of hope. Her presence rallied those who fought beside her, inspiring them to unleash their valour and push back against the encroaching tide of malevolence. Together, they stood as a bastion of light, unwavering in their resolve to defend Eldoria and extinguish the darkness that threatened to consume their world.

In the heart of the battleground, Malakar, now a vessel for the forces of darkness, surged forward with a sinister purpose. Once filled with warmth, his eyes now glowed with a malefic intent as he sought to obtain his father's coveted blue sapphire ring. This sacred artefact, a conduit of untold power, could unravel the fabric of Eldoria's existence, plunging the realm into eternal darkness.

But Chhaya, fuelled by an unwavering love that defied the odds, refused to abandon hope. Amidst the chaos and destruction, she fought with every fibre of her being, her heart torn between her love for Malakar and her duty to protect their children and Eldoria. With each strike, she infused her blows with a plea, hoping that her actions would break through the veil of darkness that shrouded Malakar's soul.

The clash of opposing forces ignited the battlefield, setting the air ablaze. Arcs of lightning crackled across the sky, illuminating the chaos that unfolded below. The warriors of the Rakshasa clan, fuelled by their indomitable spirit, unleashed their uncanny strength, their roars reverberating through the tumultuous landscape. Each clash of their weapons sent shockwaves through the ground, a testament to their unwavering resolve to protect their homeland.

In a heart-wrenching moment, amidst the swirling maelstrom of battle, Chhaya's eyes locked with Malakar's, tears streaming down her face. Through the chaos, she pleaded, her voice trembling with a mix of desperation and love. Her words echoed in the din of war, reaching the depths of Malakar's tormented soul.

"Malakar, remember who you are! The darkness that engulfs you seeks to consume you and our children. Fight against its grip! Embrace the love that still burns within you!"

Chhaya's gaze bore into Malakar's, her eyes brimming with a glimmer of hope. In that moment, she tapped into the depths of her being, harnessing the power of her love to reach out to him. With unwavering determination, she sought to bridge the gap between them, to remind him of their unbreakable bond and the person he once was before darkness ensnared his heart.

In that treacherous moment, Satan's venomous whispers infiltrated Malakar's mind, coiling around his thoughts with insidious intent. Doubt seeped into every fibre of his being as the Lord of Darkness played upon his insecurities, spinning a web of manipulation and deceit.

"Look, Malakar," Satan hissed, his voice dripping with malice. "Your own family doubts your worth, questioning your capabilities. They belittle your strength and mock your ambitions. Chhaya, your beloved wife, seeks to control you, to diminish your power. Ravana, your father, fears your rise to supremacy, threatened by the prospect of you surpassing him.

"And even your insignificant little brother dares to challenge you, a mere speck compared to your warrior prowess. What a pathetic display! It seems I was mistaken in believing you had the potential to become my worthy successor."

The words struck Malakar like poisoned arrows, with truths

and twisted half-truths that wormed their way into his psyche. Doubts gnawed at his resolve as he questioned his worthiness, his place among his family and in the world. The foundations of his belief began to crumble under the weight of Satan's manipulations, leaving him vulnerable to the darkness that threatened to consume him entirely.

With each poisonous word, Satan sought to sever the last vestiges of hope and love that tethered Malakar to his true self. The battle within Malakar's mind raged, a tempest of conflicting emotions and loyalties. In that critical moment, he stood at the precipice, torn between the desires that burned within him and the love that still lingered in his heart.

The seeds of doubt planted by Satan's treacherous whispers took root, intertwining with the memories of his past. Darkness clouded his judgement as he questioned the authenticity of Chhaya's love and the intentions of his own family.

The images Chhaya projected into his consciousness fought valiantly against the insidious lies, weaving a tapestry of cherished moments and shared happiness. But the seductive promises of power whispered by Satan clawed at Malakar's vulnerable heart, feeding his insecurities and desires.

As Chhaya's telepathic plea reached the core of his being, a flicker of recognition ignited within his eyes. The ember of his true self struggled to break free from the suffocating grip of darkness. The love and compassion that once thrived within him fought to reclaim their rightful place.

But Satan, sensing his hold on Malakar slipping, intensified his efforts. With calculated precision, he wielded the arsenal of doubt and manipulation, exploiting every weakness and fear within Malakar's wavering resolve. The Lord of Darkness spun a web of lies, tarnishing the image of Chhaya and casting doubt upon her intentions.

"Chhaya's love is a mere illusion, a ploy to control you," Satan hissed, his words like venom injected into Malakar's mind. "She betrayed her father, the master of darkness, and now she seeks to use you and your children as weapons to fulfil her ambitions. Her marriage to you was part of a grand conspiracy, a plan to bring about my downfall and secure her immortality. Embrace the power I offer, my son, and true freedom shall be yours."

Malakar teetered on the precipice of his choices, the battle within his soul raging. The love he once held for his family was twisted and tainted by doubt. The allure of power pulsed through his veins, promising liberation from his insecurities and a chance to shape his destiny.

In this fateful moment, the fate of Malakar, and the future of Eldoria hung in the balance. Would he succumb to the seductive whispers of darkness, abandoning love and loyalty in pursuit of power? Or would he find the strength to resist, to trust in the love that still flickered within his heart? The weight of his decision threatened to tip the scales of destiny and seal the fate of all those he held dear.

Malakar, consumed by confusion, and torment, found himself trapped in a twisted web of deception. The promises of immortality and dominion seduced his weary soul, blurring the lines between truth and the alluring whispers of darkness.

Chhaya's heart sank with desperation as she intensified her telepathic plea. She poured every ounce of her unwavering faith into her projections, desperately clinging to the memories of their love, their children, and the unbreakable bond they had forged. She fought to awaken the dormant spark within Malakar, urging him to resist the enticement of the shadows.

But darkness seized hold of Malakar, his soul swathed in Satan's venomous murmurings. The Lord of Darkness sneered in triumph as Malakar, now under his influence, lunged at Chhaya. Their swords clashed in a dazzling display of skill and desperation, their once harmonious connection shattered by the chasm of their opposing beliefs.

The battle raged with unforgiving intensity, each side locked in a dance of death and defiance. The ground quaked with the weight of their clashes, the air filled with the acrid scent of blood and the echoes of fallen warriors. Eldoria trembled under the weight of the struggle, on the precipice of its destruction.

As Satan's insidious whispers poisoned Malakar's judgement, a sinister determination gripped him. He now believed that his children were mere pawns in Chhaya's grand plan to eliminate her powerful father, Satan, and ascend to ultimate rulership. Malakar, blinded by hatred and consumed by the lies spun by darkness, accepted his role as an instrument of their destruction.

His heart was aflame with vengeance, and Malakar viewed his family and Chhaya through a distorted lens. He saw them as envious adversaries, each with their hidden agendas, conspiring to eliminate him and Satan. The tendrils of hatred coiled around his soul, fuelling his resolve to execute his children in the name of immortality and power.

In this climactic moment, hope seemed a distant memory, overshadowed by the overwhelming influence of darkness. The fate of Eldoria hung in the balance, its future teetering on the precipice of annihilation as the battle continued to unfold.

Satan revelled in his victory, his malevolent grin widening as he witnessed the triumph of darkness over weakness. In that moment, Chhaya's heart plummeted into an abyss of grief and determination. The devastating truth became clear: her beloved husband was lost to the allure of ultimate power, forever entangled in the web of greed and deceit spun by Satan.

In the heart of the raging tempest, Chhaya's gaze pierced through the haze of battle. Her eyes widened with a mixture of horror and anguish as she beheld the harrowing sight before her. The once-beloved figure of Malakar stood amidst the chaos, his eyes ablaze with a malevolent zeal.

Time seemed to slow as the weight of his intentions settled upon her, a suffocating darkness that threatened to snuff out any semblance of hope. The realization struck Chhaya like a thunderbolt—her husband, consumed by the twisted allure of power, was willing to offer their innocent children as sacrificial pawns in his quest for ultimate control.

Her heart shattered into a thousand fragments, each shard a testament to the love she had once held for Malakar. The torrent of emotions surged within her, a storm of grief, rage, and disbelief. She fought to steady herself amidst the chaos, her voice breaking through the cacophony of clashing weapons.

With a heavy burden resting upon her shoulders, Chhaya realized that the fate of their children and the world itself hinged on the grave choices she must make. The bloodline of her innocent offspring held the key, a weapon capable of piercing through the impenetrable veil of darkness and toppling the reign of evil.

She finally understood why the cosmos had conspired to lead her away from Satan, why Parvati had provided her refuge, why she had crossed paths with Malakar, and why she had brought their children into this world. The seemingly ordinary moments of familial love she had longed for had served a greater purpose.

Echoes of wisdom resonated in Chhaya's mind, as did the counsel she had received from Parvati and the sacred verses of the holy Bhagwat Gita. She recalled the profound words etched within her soul, guiding her in this darkest hour.

The sacred verses of the Bhagwat Gita echoed within Chhaya's soul, resurfacing in this dire moment of reckoning. Parvati's counsel reverberated through her being, guiding her to righteousness. She recited the profound words, their power coursing through her veins, lending her strength, and resolve in the face of overwhelming darkness.

Yada yada hi dharmasya glanir bhavati Bharata,
Abhyutthanam adharmasya tadatmanam srijamyaham.
Paritranaya sadhunam vinashaya cha dushkritam,
Dharma-sansthapanarthaya sambhavami yuge yuge.

These verses spoke of the eternal cosmic order, of the divine promise that whenever righteousness falters and darkness ascends, Lord Vishnu, the protector of the world, would descend to vanquish the wicked and restore balance. Millennia after millennia, he would manifest himself to deliver the virtuous and annihilate the malevolent forces that threatened to plunge the realms into chaos.

Chhaya's heart throbbed with a mixture of fear and determination as she contemplated the true extent of her father's depravity. The memories of his monstrous acts, the pain he had inflicted upon her mother and brother, surged forth like a tempest, fuelling her resolve to protect all that she held dear.

The weight of her lineage and her ancestors' legacy bore down upon her as she contemplated the unimaginable task before her. Fear clutched at her heart, the fear that her father would unleash destruction upon everything she held dear, just as he had extinguished the lives of her beloved mother and brother.

In this defining moment, Chhaya embraced her role as the harbinger of light in the face of overwhelming darkness. She steeled her resolve, drawing strength from the knowledge that she was chosen to fulfil a sacred duty: to safeguard the innocent and restore balance to the world. With the flickering flame of hope burning within her, she prepared to wage a battle to determine the fate of existence itself.

Bonds of Sacrifice - A Tale of Mother's Love

Amidst the remnants of shattered hopes and smouldering despair, Chhaya's spirit blazed with an unyielding determination. Her very being seemed to pulsate with an otherworldly energy, fuelled by her unwavering love for her children and the searing fire of her survival.

In the solitude of her sanctuary, Chhaya had immersed herself in ancient tomes, their pages laden with the wisdom of ages past. She had unravelled the intricate tapestry of light, delving into the esoteric knowledge passed down through generations of her lineage. Each revelation, each arcane incantation, added another piece to the puzzle that would aid her in her quest.

With resolute steps, Chhaya emerged from her introspection a beacon of radiant power. She embraced her dormant abilities, her essence becoming a conduit for the purest light that coursed through her veins. Sparks of ethereal energy danced around her, weaving a protective shield against the encroaching darkness.

Her mind became a battlefield of strategic brilliance, each move calculated with precision. She charted a course that would lead her through treacherous terrain and into the heart of darkness itself. Her allies rallied around her, their unwavering faith in her purpose bolstering her resolve.

A newfound aura of authority enveloped her as she donned her armour, forged from the celestial essence of righteousness. The weight of her responsibility mingled with the fierce determination etched upon her face, symbolizing her unwavering commitment to safeguard her children, Eldoria, and the very fabric of existence itself.

For she knew that within her resided the power to forge a

different destiny, to defy Satan's sinister designs and protect the innocents who depended on her. The clash of her footsteps echoed through the chambers of her mind, reverberating with a resounding proclamation: She would not falter, she would not fail. She would rise as a warrior of light, a defender against the encroaching darkness.

As she stepped forth, her radiant aura casting a luminous glow upon the path ahead, Chhaya embarked on a journey to test her spirit, her mettle, and the depths of her love. Armed with the brilliance of her power and the unwavering conviction of a mother who would stop at nothing to protect her children, she was prepared to face the relentless trials that awaited her.

Amid the chaos and turmoil, Chhaya's voice rang out, commanding her family's attention. Her words reverberated through the air, carrying a weight of determination and desperation. The clashing swords and thunderous roars of battle seemed to yield to the gravity of her words momentarily.

As they gathered amidst the battlefield's temporary respite, Chhaya's eyes blazed with sadness and unwavering resolve. Every line etched on her face spoke of the immense burden she carried upon her shoulders, the weight of a mother's love and the determination to safeguard her children from the encroaching darkness.

Though her voice trembled with the situation's urgency, it held an underlying strength that could not be shaken. Each word she spoke cut through the tumultuous air, stirring the hearts of her family members, who stood united in this dire moment.

With a heavy sigh, Chhaya turned her gaze towards Mandodari, her mother-in-law and the matriarch of their family. In that fleeting exchange of eyes, a silent understanding passed between them, a bond forged by the shared love and concern for the innocent lives at stake.

"Mother," Chhaya spoke, her voice filled with a mixture of pain and determination, "our children, the very essence of our existence, are in imminent danger. Malakar has succumbed to the darkness that envelops him, becoming a vessel for evil forces. We must protect them from his grasp, shield them from the monstrous intentions that seek their destruction."

Tears welled up in Chhaya's eyes, threatening to spill over, as she continued, her voice quivering with a profound sense of responsibility, "I implore you, dear mother, find a sanctuary, a place of refuge where our children can be hidden away from this ravaging storm. Your love, your grandmotherly instinct, can shield them from the darkness that looms over us."

Chhaya's tears flowed unabated, mingling with the sorrow, and determination etched on her face. In desperation and surrender, she reached out, her trembling hands finding solace within the grasp of Mandodari, the embodiment of maternal strength and love.

With a voice choked with emotion, Chhaya entrusted the safety of her precious children to Mandodari, her mother-in-law, whose love had always been a steadfast presence in their lives. The weight of the responsibility she placed upon Mandodari's shoulders was immense, and she knew that only a heart as resilient as Mandodari's could carry the burden with absolute devotion.

"Queen Mother," Chhaya's voice quivered with sadness and hope. "As the mother of Eldoria and the grandmother of our beloved children, I beseech you to be their guardian in this time of darkness. Your strength has always been an unwavering beacon and I trust that you will shield them from the horrors that await us. Let them know of our love and sacrifices, even if they may never see me nor comprehend the depths of this turmoil."

Chhaya's grip tightened, as if she sought to transfer her resolve and determination into Mandodari's trembling hands. "They are our legacy, the embodiment of our hopes and dreams. Shield them from the horrors that lie ahead, and let our love guide their paths. May they find solace and comfort in your embrace, understanding the sacrifices made for their well-being."

Her voice quivered with a mix of sorrow and determination, as Chhaya continued, her words laden with the weight of a mother's love, "Even if they never comprehend the depths of this darkness, let them carry within their hearts the knowledge that they were cherished beyond measure. You, Mother, are their guiding light, their protector. I trust in your unwavering devotion and the strength of your maternal embrace to shield them from the perils surrounding us."

Chhaya's grip tightened, as if she sought to infuse Mandodari with her determination. "I cannot bear the thought of their innocent souls being endangered by the very father they adore. But in you, Mother, I find solace and trust. May they find refuge in your embrace, shielded from the atrocities that lie ahead. Only you, with your unyielding love, can guide them through this treacherous path."

Chhaya released Mandodari's hands, a profound sense of surrender mingling with the pain on her face. In that moment, she entrusted her beloved children to Mandodari's loving care, knowing that the bond of a grandmother's love would shield them in her absence.

As the tears streamed down Chhaya's cheeks, a flicker of hope glimmered within her heart. She prayed that her children would grow up knowing the depths of their parents' love, even if they could never fully understand the sacrifices made for their protection.

At that moment, their shared sacrifice and unfaltering love hung heavy. Chhaya understood the magnitude of her plea, knowing that Mandodari's maternal instincts would be their children's most excellent shield. With one final, tearful glance, Chhaya released Mandodari's hands, entrusting her with a sacred duty that surpassed all others.

Mandodari's eyes shimmered with unshed tears, reflecting a potent mixture of anguish and determination. Slowly, she nodded, her voice quivering with profound emotion.

"Chhaya, my cherished child, our journey has brought us to this harrowing crossroad, where unimaginable circumstances confront us. Yet, as mothers, we share a bond that defies even the most daunting of challenges."

Her voice trembled with a blend of sorrow and resolve as she continued, her words laced with an unwavering determination, "Chhaya, we have known the boundless love and immeasurable joy of motherhood. And now, we stand on the precipice of our greatest trial. But fear not, my dear child, for I, your mother and the grandmother of Alaya, Aryan, and Aks, will protect them with every fibre of my being. Under my unwavering watch, darkness shall not lay a finger upon them. I am Mandodari, the mother of Eldoria, and I shall shield my precious grandchildren from the clutches of darkness."

With a gaze filled with maternal strength and untiring love, Mandodari continued, her voice carrying the weight of her commitment, "While you venture forth with our family, our Rakshasa clan, and the brave Eldorians to confront the encroaching darkness, I will remain steadfast in my duty to safeguard our beloved children. They shall remain untouched by the shadows that surround us.

"I will eagerly await your triumphant return, when we shall reunite as a family, forging a brighter future for Eldoria. Together, we shall weather this tempest, for the sake of our children and the destiny of our cherished realm. Let our victory over darkness be a cause for celebration. 'Vijayi Bhawa'—may you emerge victorious!"

As Mandodari's final words lingered in the air, a profound sense of purpose ignited within her. She stood tall, a bastion of unshakeable love and protection, ready to fulfil her role as the guardian of Alaya,

Aryan, and Aks. In that moment, she vowed to shield them from the encroaching darkness, determined to ensure their safety and preserve the light that flickered within their innocent hearts.

In their embrace, the weight of their shared destiny bore down upon them, intertwining their spirits in a bond that transcended the confines of their mortal existence. Mandodari and Chhaya stood resolute, their hearts aflame with a fierce determination to protect their children and safeguard the very essence of Eldoria itself.

As tears rose in Chhaya's eyes, her voice trembled with a raw emotion that echoed through the chamber. She clung tightly to her three children, their innocent faces reflecting the gravity of the impending battle. Every second became a bittersweet eternity, as Chhaya etched their precious features into her memory, unsure if this would be their last embrace.

Chhaya's voice, though filled with a mixture of love and sorrow, carried a resolute strength that echoed through the room, imprinting itself upon the souls of her children.

"My dearest Alaya, Aryan, and Aks, you embody my love, and the light guiding my existence. Know that no matter what transpires on this perilous journey, my love for you will forever burn within your courageous hearts. Embrace your strength, my valiant warriors, and remain steadfast in your pursuit of righteousness.

"Let no doubt cast its shadow upon your noble souls. Understand that each of you holds a purpose greater than yourselves, a purpose that can pierce the veil of darkness and usher in an era of eternal light. You are the chosen ones, destined to eradicate the very essence of darkness itself. In your hands, the fate of the realms rests, and your collective prayer shall beckon the light.

"With you as its leaders, the world shall find sanctuary, untouched by the insidious grasp of darkness. And above all else, never forget that you will always be my three precious, beloved children."

Chhaya held Alaya close, her voice quivering with love and sorrow, enveloping her in a tender embrace. The air was heavy with the weight of the impending battle, and Alaya's tears flowed uncontrollably, mirroring the anguish in her mother's eyes.

Chhaya's voice trembled as she spoke, each word laden with a mother's unwavering devotion. Her fingers gently brushed away Alaya's tears as she imparted her final words of guidance and love.

"Alaya, my beloved daughter, you are the beacon of strength and wisdom among your brothers. As their elder sister, I entrust you with a sacred duty. You have fought by my side, displaying a valour beyond your years. Your father and I have always been in awe of your indomitable spirit. We knew then that you and your brothers were destined for something extraordinary, but little did we comprehend the magnitude of your calling."

Chhaya's voice wavered with pride and solemnity, her eyes searching Alaya's for understanding.

"In you, Alaya, many have seen glimpses of my essence and they were right to do so. But trust me when I say you possess a power far greater than that of the entire Rakshasa clan. You are destined for greatness, my daughter. You are the epitome of strength and compassion. As you have fought by my side, it is your turn to guide your brothers on the path of righteousness."

Chhaya's voice grew softer, filled with a mother's tenderness as she addressed Alaya's role as their protector.

"Take care of your brothers, especially young Aks, who have yet to comprehend our plight's gravity. Teach them the lessons we have imparted upon you and Aryan. Stand united, support one another, and never waver in your trust and love. Together, you three form an unbreakable bond, a force that can send shivers down the spine of even the Lord of Darkness himself.

"If I am not to return, my darling, avenge your father and me.

Know that you were loved with a depth that moved the heavens and stirred the cosmos. Eldoria and the entire universe will rally behind you. You are never alone, my precious children."

Chhaya's voice was choked with emotion, and her final words lingered as a testament to a mother's love that transcended time and space.

"I love you, my children. Let that love guide you in the darkest of moments. Carry our legacy forward and fulfil your destinies. May the light of Eldoria forever shine through you."

Alaya's voice trembled, her plea echoing through the air, as she implored her mother to reconsider.

"Mother, we love you, and understand the depth of your care and concern. But we cannot stand idly by as you face this war alone. We have trained as warriors, and we have fought alongside you before. Please, allow us to stand beside you now. We can be a formidable force, an asset to the battle. We refuse to turn our backs and run. Let us fight together, Mother, for the sake of our family and Eldoria."

Chhaya's eyes softened, her heart aching at the sight of her brave children yearning to fight by her side. Yet, she remained resolute, knowing the greater purpose that awaited them.

"Not today, my darlings," Chhaya's voice held a mix of love and sorrow. "Today is not the day for you to face this battle. Your time will come; we will face a greater war together when it does. But for now, we must ensure your safety and protect the future within each of you. The cosmos has already set your paths and we must trust in its wisdom."

Aryan, his eyes filled with determination, stepped forward, his voice joining his sister's plea.

"But Mother, let us join you today. We can fight together, defeat our enemies, and train for the battles that await us. Let us prove our strength, loyalty, and dedication to our family and realm."

Chhaya gazed at her son, her heart torn between her desire to keep them safe and their unwavering resolve. She took a deep breath, her voice resolute yet filled with love.

"My dear Aryan, the time for you to shine will come, and when it does, you will stand beside me with pride. But today, I must face this battle on my own. Protecting you, Alaya, and Aks is my sacred duty. Trust in my love for you, my children. Have faith that the future holds great challenges and victories for each of you. Today, I fight for our family's survival. Tomorrow, we will face the world together, stronger, and more united than ever."

Chhaya's words hung in the air, a bittersweet melody of love and sacrifice, as the weight of their destiny rested upon their shoulders.

Chhaya gazed into her children's tear-filled eyes, her heart aching with pride and sorrow. She knew the weight of their destiny rested on their young shoulders, and the path ahead would be fraught with challenges and sacrifices. But she also saw the strength and determination burning within them, a flame that gave her hope for the future.

Chhaya's voice quivered with emotion as she imparted her final words of guidance and love.

"If only it were that simple, my beloved Alaya and Aryan. But the battles that lie before you are of cosmic proportions, ones that will shape the destiny of worlds. Your lives are too precious and vital to existence's grand tapestry. Promise me this, my darlings; no matter what may come, you will always stand together and protect and support each other unwaveringly. Let your bond be unbreakable, for it is through unity that you will find strength in the darkest of times."

Alaya and Aryan clung to their mother, their tears mingling with hers as they whispered in unison, their voices filled with both pain and determination.

"We promise you, Mother," they sobbed, "we will always stand together, side by side, through every trial and tribulation. We will cherish and protect one another, just as you have taught us. We will be the embodiment of your love, your courage, and your unwavering light. When you return to us, we will be ready, eager to learn from your wisdom and carry forth your legacy. You will forever be our guiding star, and we will make you proud."

Their embrace tightened, a tangible bond of love, resilience, and shared destiny. They found solace and strength in this solemn moment, knowing their united spirits would conquer the darkness and bring light to the cosmos. Chhaya's voice choked, heavy with emotion, as she addressed her children with strength and vulnerability.

"Alaya, Aryan, and Aks, my beloved warriors, listen closely. As your mother, I entrust you with the legacy of our love and the light that guides us. Mandodari, my dear mother, I beseech you to be their guiding force, their pillar of strength in my absence. Raise them to be fierce and righteous warriors, shaping their hearts with love, compassion, justice, faith, and unfaltering hope. Remind them that I will always be with them, even if my physical presence is no longer beside them."

Her voice quivered, yet it carried the weight of a mother's unwavering faith.

"Let them know that my love will forever burn brightly in their hearts, illuminating their path and strengthening their resolve. As you raise them, teach them about their heritage, the sacrifices of their ancestors, and the unbreakable family bond. Mandodari, my mother, I trust your wisdom, love, and unyielding spirit to guide them through the awaiting trials. Together, we will forge a future worthy of their boundless potential."

Chhaya's words hung in the air, etching into her children's and mother's souls. Their hearts swelled with a profound sense of purpose, ready to carry the flame of their mother's love and fight for the righteousness she embodied.

Mandodari's voice quivered with grief and determination as she made her solemn vow.

"Chhaya, my dear daughter, I accept this sacred responsibility with a heavy heart, for I have felt the pain inflicted by darkness within my son. But I promise you, with every fibre of my being, that I will devote myself to nurturing and guiding your children. I shall shield them from the shadows that threaten to consume their innocence. They shall grow up enveloped in the warmth of a grandmother's love, knowing the strength and depth of a mother's devotion."

Tears streamed down Mandodari's face, glistening with the weight of her promise.

"I vow to raise them with utmost love and care, imparting to them the values you hold dear. They will walk the path of courage and righteousness, embodying your spirit and the unwavering light within them. They shall carry the torch of compassion and justice, upholding the honour of our lineage. Every day, I will remind them of their true selves, heritage, and legacy as the children of Chhaya and the defenders of Eldoria."

Her voice resonated with sorrow and determination, carrying the weight of her commitment to her daughter.

"Chhaya, my dear daughter, rest assured that your children will know their worth, purpose, and the boundless love surrounding them. They will grow into warriors who wield their strength with grace and righteousness. I shall protect them fiercely, instilling within them the resilience to overcome any darkness that may come their way. Their spirits shall remain untainted, for I shall be their guardian and guide, their ever-present reminder of the love you bestowed upon them."

As Mandodari spoke these words, a sense of profound responsibility settled upon her, intertwining her fate with the destiny of the children she swore to protect.

As the battlefield pulsed with the rhythm of impending doom, Chhaya's love for her children burned like an inferno, wrapping them in an ethereal embrace of unwavering determination. She held them close, imprinting upon their souls the depth of her love and the unyielding strength that flowed through their bloodlines.

Chhaya bid her children farewell with a final kiss on their foreheads, knowing their paths diverged in this fateful moment. Her heart weighed heavily with a mix of pride and anguish, for she understood the magnitude of the battle that lay ahead.

Beside her stood Mandodari, a pillar of resilience forged in the crucible of adversity. Their shared pain had woven a bond that transcended the bounds of kinship, providing solace and strength as they confronted the trials that awaited them.

Hand in hand, Chhaya and Mandodari shared a solemn gaze, their eyes reflecting a myriad of emotions—determination, sorrow, and an unspoken understanding of the sacrifices that must be made for the greater good. In that fleeting moment, their connection radiated with profound power, a testament to the resilience of the Rakshasas' spirit in the face of unimaginable challenges.

With a nod of shared resolve, they parted ways, each stepping into their destined roles with a courage that defied the chaos around them. Chhaya, clad in armour adorned with symbols of her lineage, marched towards the battlefield, her every step resonating with the weight of her purpose.

Mandodari, filled with an indomitable spirit, embraced her role as the children's guardian, protecting their innocence in a world of darkness. She vowed to shield them from the horrors of war, to nurture their spirits with love and guidance, and to ensure that the flame of hope burned bright within their hearts.

As Chhaya and Mandodari ventured forth, their paths diverged, yet their destinies remained entwined in a tapestry of resilience and sacrifice. They carried with them the echoes of their shared purpose, the echo of a mother's love, and the unyielding belief that their actions would shape the fate of Eldoria and the lives entrusted to their care.

United We Stand for Eldoria's Soul

As the battle raged on, the air thick with the stench of blood and the deafening clamour of conflict, Chhaya, Ravana, Vibhishana, Kumbhakaran, and Kalkeyas convened in a hushed corner of the battlefield. The weight of their responsibilities bore down, etching lines of determination and weariness on their faces. Each knew their every decision and action held the power to shape Eldoria's destiny.

Amidst the chaos and the clash of weapons, their voices rose above the cacophony, blending with the symphony of war. Her eyes ablaze with an unyielding resolve, Chhaya spoke with a commanding presence that silenced even the chaos around them.

"We stand on the precipice of darkness, facing an adversary of unimaginable power and malice," Chhaya began, her voice carrying a steely determination. "But let us not forget the fire that burns within our hearts—the love for our children, our land, our values, and our very existence as the Rakshasas of Eldoria. We are not mere pawns in this battle. We are the protectors, the defenders, and the embodiment of light in this realm."

She paused, her gaze shifting from one face to another, seeking the unwavering commitment in their eyes. "Our enemy possesses great strength but lacks the passion that fuels our cause. History shall not remember us as monsters (Asuras), but as the deities (Suras) who fought valiantly to preserve the sanctity of our land. We carry the legacy of the Suras, the divine essence that shall guide us through the darkest of nights."

Chhaya's words hung in the air, a rallying cry that resonated deep within the souls of her companions. The gravity of their mission settled upon them, intertwining their fates and cementing their resolve.

"To triumph over darkness, we must strike with precision," Chhaya continued, her voice unwavering. "We must exploit any weakness we can find and guard ourselves against the allure of darkness. It thrives on weakness, greed, and insecurities. Our beloved Malakar, our fallen hero, serves as a grim reminder of the treacherous path that awaits those who succumb to their ambitions."

Her eyes gleamed with sadness and determination as she continued, "Heart-wrenching choices may lie ahead of us, but we must not waver. The darkness is seductive, promising power, and riches, but we must not lose sight of the true path. We fight not only for ourselves, but for the future of Eldoria and our children. Our lives, our honour, and the very essence of light are at stake."

Ravana, his imposing figure emanating authority and wisdom, absorbed Chhaya's words, his eyes narrowing with intensity. He acknowledged the weight of their adversary's power and the imminent threat posed by Malakar's allegiance to darkness.

"You speak words of truth, Chhaya," Ravana responded, his voice resonating with determination. "Our enemy may possess raw power and believe they have us figured out, but we shall prove them wrong. We shall dance with shadows, weaving a tapestry of deception and unpredictability. Our strategy must be cunning, born from the depths of our collective intellect and wisdom."

Ravana cast his piercing gaze upon Vibhishana, awaiting his counsel. The weight of their impending battle hung in the air, as each warrior sensed the magnitude of the challenges they would face.

Vibhishana, a beacon of wisdom and discernment, stepped forward, his voice steady and resolute. "Brother Ravana, our path forward is treacherous, but not insurmountable. We must embrace the unpredictability of this conflict and outmanoeuvre our adversary at every turn. Malakar, fuelled by darkness, has become a formidable force, his determination matched only by the Lord of the Darkness himself."

He paused; his words punctuated by the intensity of their situation. "To triumph, we must delve into the depths of our strengths and seek unconventional strategies. Our enemy will expect us to adhere to our well-known tactics, but we must shatter their assumptions. We must become the architects of surprise, striking where they least anticipate our blows."

Vibhishana's eyes blazed with conviction as he continued, "Let us exploit the chinks in their armour, the vulnerabilities that lie beneath their facade of invincibility. We shall sow doubt and discord within their ranks, capitalizing on their overconfidence and hubris. Like a serpent striking from the shadows, we shall dismantle their control over the dark forces."

His voice resonated with a mixture of caution and determination. "But remember, comrades, this is not a battle to be won by sheer force alone. It is a test of intellect and cunning. We must analyze every move, anticipate their counterattacks, and remain one step ahead. We must dance upon the edge of chaos, turning their darkness against them."

Vibhishana locked eyes with Ravana, their unspoken understanding reinforcing their bond as brothers and leaders. "Together, Ravana, let us inspire our warriors to rise above the ordinary, to embrace the extraordinary. The fate of Eldoria rests upon our shoulders, and we shall not falter. Our actions today shall echo through the annals of time, defining the legacy of the Rakshasas and the destiny of our land."

A fire ignited in Ravana's eyes as he continued, "Malakar and Satan may underestimate our resolve, but we shall exploit their overconfidence and strike at the heart of their control over the dark forces. We shall devise moves that defy their expectations, catching them off guard, and shattering their illusions of invincibility."

Ravana's voice boomed with authority as he addressed his comrades, "Each of you holds a crucial role in this battle. Kumbhakaran, your sheer strength and resilience will become a formidable weapon against our foes. Kalkeyas, your expertise in stealth and agility will enable us to infiltrate their strongholds undetected. Together, we shall dismantle their alliance, exposing the fractures within their ranks."

He cast a solemn gaze upon Chhaya, his eyes brimming with paternal concern. "And you, my beloved daughter, your unwavering love and determination will be a beacon of hope for us all. You possess a strength that transcends the physical, a power that can ignite the flames of righteousness in our warriors' hearts."

Ravana's voice lowered, laden with a mixture of pride and solemnity. "Remember, this battle is not just for our survival. It is for the future of Eldoria, for the light that flickers within every soul who calls this land home. We fight to protect our loved ones and uphold the very essence of righteousness and justice."

Chhaya looked at Ravana with inquisitiveness. "Father, but what about the powerful blue sapphire ring? Satan, the Lord of the Darkness, intends to have it under his control to become invincible. If the ring falls into his hands, it will end the realm."

Chhaya's eyes widened with relief and curiosity as she listened to her father's reassurances. The weight of the blue sapphire ring and its immense power had burdened her thoughts, fearing the catastrophic consequences if it were to fall into the hands of the Lord of the Darkness.

Ravana, a soothing balm amidst the chaos, spoke with the wisdom of ages, "My dear Chhaya, you need not fear for the safety of the blue sapphire ring. Since it came into my possession, I have been aware of the Lord of the Darkness' covetous gaze upon its power. I knew that a war would come, but little did I anticipate that it would be our son who would succumb to Satan's deceiving promises."

He paused, a mixture of sadness and determination etched upon his regal face. "Rest assured, my child, the blue sapphire ring is safeguarded in the cosmic realms, far beyond the reach of any malevolent force. Its true power can only be unleashed by its rightful bearer, a warrior who embodies righteousness and pure intentions. The ring will resurface when the time is ripe, when the cosmos aligns to anoint the chosen one."

Ravana's eyes glimmered with a timeless wisdom as he continued, "Today's battle, my daughter, is not waged to claim ownership of the blue sapphire ring. It is a fight to protect our grandchildren, the destined warriors who carry the burden of eradicating darkness from the world. The cosmic forces choose them, their very existence a testament to the triumph of light over shadows."

Kumbhkaran, his thunderous voice reverberating through the battlefield, bellowed with unwavering determination, "Enough talk! Let my fists be the thunderclaps that shatter their defences! I shall crush their armies to dust, leaving only remnants of their delusions of invincibility!"

Her eyes gleaming with admiration, Chhaya turned to Kumbhkaran, acknowledging his immense strength. "Uncle, your sheer might will be a formidable force in this battle. But let us not underestimate the power of finesse and trickery. As the goddess of illusion, I shall weave webs of confusion among the enemy lines. We aim to sow chaos and discord, fracturing their unity and exposing their vulnerabilities to our strikes."

Kalkeyas, his enigmatic presence casting an aura of intrigue, spoke with an air of mystery, "Behold, we shall envelop the battlefield in a shroud of shadows and enigma. Our mastery of arcane arts shall dance with darkness, obfuscating our movements and leaving our adversaries bewildered. For in the intertwining realms of darkness and light, our essence holds the key to tipping the scales in our favour."

Their voices harmonized, resonating with a potent mix of strength, illusion, and mystique. Their hearts ablaze with a fiery resolve, the warriors of Eldoria readied themselves for the imminent collision of cosmic forces. The stakes were higher than ever, for this battle had transcended the realms of mere conquest and power. It had become deeply personal.

Chhaya, Ravana, Vibhishana, Kumbhakaran, Kalkeyas, and the warriors of Eldoria stood together, their eyes reflecting the flickering flames of their shared purpose. Each step they took was laced with a profound sense of duty and a burning desire to shield their beloved land and children from darkness.

As they braced themselves for the impending clash, a surge of energy coursed through their veins, amplifying their resolve, and heightening their senses. They had witnessed the depths to which their kin had fallen, and now, united by an unbreakable bond, they were prepared to unleash a storm of retribution upon the forces that threatened their very existence.

Their weapons gleamed with an ethereal light, mirroring the determination in their eyes. With every heartbeat, their souls resonated with an unwavering commitment to protect the light that still burned within them, even in the face of overwhelming darkness.

The battlefield trembled beneath their feet as they advanced, the ground echoing their battle cry. They were warriors fuelled by love, vengeance, and an unyielding spirit that refused to be extinguished. Every step brought them closer to the heart of the conflict, where the clash of darkness and light would determine the fate of Eldoria.

In that pivotal moment, the line between ally and adversary blurred, for the true enemy was the darkness that had ensnared their loved ones. With unwavering determination, they would fight for victory and redemption, hoping to free those lost to the shadows and restore the balance of light.

The air crackled with tension as their fates converged on the battlefield, their destinies intertwined with the cosmic forces that governed their world. Eldoria trembled, poised on the precipice of oblivion, as the clash of darkness and light loomed on the horizon.

Their hearts beat as one, pulsating with the rhythm of a battle cry that echoed through the ages. With every breath, they summoned the strength of their ancestors, drawing from the wellsprings of courage that flowed within their veins.

In that moment, they were not just warriors but the embodiment of hope, the harbingers of a new dawn. The power of their unity, their love for Eldoria, and their unyielding spirit would guide them through the darkest of trials.

As the sun dipped below the horizon, casting its final rays upon the battlefield, they charged forward, an unstoppable force against the encroaching darkness. This battle would define their legacy, etching their names into the annals of history as saviours, warriors who had fought with unyielding valour to protect their land and the light that burned within it.

With every clash of steel and surge of magic, their resolve burned brighter, igniting a beacon of hope that pierced through the suffocating darkness. They were prepared to sacrifice everything, for their love knew no bounds and their dedication to Eldoria would endure for all eternity.

Amid the chaos, they remained unbroken, their spirits intertwined like the threads of a tapestry woven with unwavering loyalty and purpose. In this moment, they were not just warriors; they were the living embodiment of a legacy that would be whispered for generations to come, a testament to the indomitable strength of the human spirit and the triumph of light over darkness.

As the battlefield erupted in a symphony of clashes and cries, their battle cry resounded, echoing across the realms. They fought not only for victory but for the essence of their existence—the love, the honour, and the unyielding hope that defined them as the warriors of Eldoria.

The Perilous Journey - A Mother's Resolve and the Enchanted Vows

In the depths of despair and unwavering love, Mandodari guided her grandchildren—Alaya, Aryan, and Aks—through the treacherous depths of Eldoria. The hidden passage they tread upon was a labyrinth of ancient mysteries, shrouded in the enchantments of a forgotten era. It whispered haunting secrets, its winding tunnels leading them deeper into the heart of darkness.

As they ventured onward, the air grew thick with a malevolence that clung to their souls. Sinister whispers echoed through the shadows; their words laced with the venomous promises of Satan himself. The darkness seemed to claw at their heels, as if eager to consume their flickering light.

Yet, Mandodari's resolve burned brighter than the encroaching darkness. With every step, she shielded her grandchildren from the terrors that lurked, her love acting as a fortress against the looming evil. She bore the weight of their fear upon her shoulders, a heavy burden carried with unwavering determination.

The walls around them dripped with an unholy ink, tainted by the malefic presence that dwelt within. It oozed like liquid nightmares, threatening to drown their spirits in an abyss of despair. But Mandodari pressed on, her gaze fixed ahead, refusing to succumb to the sinister temptations that whispered through the corridors.

Their path intertwined with the very essence of darkness in the labyrinthine depths. Each turn and twist seemed designed to ensnare their hearts and shatter their resolve. Yet, Mandodari's love for her grandchildren blazed like a celestial beacon, illuminating their way through the stygian gloom.

As the walls closed in, suffocating their hopes, and dreams, Mandodari's unwavering faith radiated a protective aura around them. She invoked the ancient incantations of her ancestors, calling upon the forces of light to shield them from the grasp of the infernal abyss.

Malakar, now a vessel of darkness, unleashed wrath upon the fleeing group in the shadowed depths of the labyrinthine passage. His once-noble heart twisted and contorted, fuelled by Satan's false promises. No longer recognizing the love that bound him to his children, he became a relentless predator, hunting them with ruthless determination.

His footsteps echoed like the tolling of a funeral bell, each resounding thud sending tremors through the fragile tunnels. Waves of malevolent energy surged from his fingertips, cracking the stone walls and casting a sinister hue upon the fading light.

Mandodari, the grieving mother torn between love and duty, stood as a bulwark of protection for her innocent grandchildren. Her magic flared with an intensity born of desperation, forming a shield of shimmering energy that deflected the encroaching darkness. She channelled her every ounce of strength to keep her beloved ones safe from the clutches of their father.

Sensing the imminent escape, Satan, the orchestrator of their torment, unleashed his vile minions upon the group. From the depths of the underworld, a horde of twisted creatures emerged, their twisted forms a grotesque manifestation of their malevolence. Fangs glistened with an insatiable hunger, and claws dripped with the essence of wickedness.

Undeterred, Mandodari summoned her inner power, her eyes blazing with determination. She conjured barriers of ethereal light, weaving intricate spells that repelled the onslaught of demonic forces. She carved a path through the chaos with each incantation, guiding her grandchildren towards salvation.

Yet, the passage itself seemed to conspire against their escape. Walls shifted and morphed, narrowing to constrict their movements. Floors crumbled beneath their feet, threatening to plunge them into an abyss of despair. But Mandodari's unwavering love and determination fuelled her every step, her grace a beacon of hope in the face of relentless adversity.

Through the treacherous trials, Mandodari shielded her grandchildren with a mother's unwavering love, her presence a fortress against the encroaching darkness. She pressed on, her every stride a testament to her resolve, her every breath a defiance against the malevolent forces that sought to tear them apart.

A battle raged between love and darkness in the depths of the shifting passage. Mandodari, with every ounce of her being, fought to preserve the light that flickered within her grandchildren. She wove her magic and navigated the treacherous twists and turns, for she knew their survival meant the salvation of hope.

In the suffocating grip of darkness, the children clung desperately to their grandmother's hand, their innocent eyes betraying a potent blend of fear and trust. They witnessed the sacrifices their mother, Chhaya, and the rest of their valiant family were making to shield them from harm. Fuelled by an unshakeable faith in the flickering light within their pure hearts, they embarked on their perilous journey, marching forward with unyielding bravery.

With each step, the labyrinthine passage plunged deeper into the heart of darkness, amplifying the ominous aura surrounding them. The presence of Satan and the treacherous Malakar loomed ever closer, their vile voices reverberating through the suffocating corridors. Their words, dripping with malevolence, painted a sinister portrait of power and dominance.

Mandodari's grip tightened around the children, and she touched a shield against the encroaching chill that threatened to extinguish their spirits. She wove a protective veil around them in whispered tones of reassurance and unwavering love, shielding their vulnerable hearts from the icy grasp of fear.

In the face of this daunting adversity, Mandodari, and the children clung to a flickering flame of hope. They were acutely aware of the magnitude of the darkness surrounding them, yet their spirits remained unyielding. With untiring determination, they embraced the belief that their collective strength and resilience would enable them to outsmart and outmanoeuvre the encroaching shadows. Their hearts, radiant with hope, found solace in the unwavering conviction that the light, no matter how faint, would ultimately prevail over the darkest recesses of their journey.

As they delved deeper into the abyss, the darkness seemed to pulse with malevolence, twisting and contorting to amplify their fears. But the children found strength in the unyielding grip of Mandodari's love. Hand in hand, they confronted the harrowing unknown, their courage a beacon that defied the overwhelming odds stacked against them. Guided by an indomitable spirit, they pressed onward, drawing upon the collective power of their faith and the bonds that united them.

Mandodari's heart thundered within her chest as she led her grandchildren, Alaya and Aryan, along with their precious young brother Aks, through the treacherous depths of the passage. Each step reverberated against the cold, unforgiving stone walls, amplifying the sense of foreboding that hung heavy in the air. The flickering torches, casting an eerie glow, seemed to taunt them with their dancing shadows, whispering secrets of the darkness that awaited.

Alaya's gaze shifted to Aryan, her voice laced with sorrow and unwavering determination. As her fingers gently brushed against Aks' cheek, she sought solace in her brother's presence. "Aryan, do you think father knows the darkness that consumes him? Does he truly comprehend the extent of his transformation?"

Aryan's expression hardened; his features etched with a profound sadness. His brows furrowed, reflecting the weight of their shattered illusions. "I wish I had an answer, Alaya. But the way he looked at us, his once-loving gaze was now vacant and hollow. It felt as though we were nothing more than mere pawns in his twisted game. The father we knew has become a stranger, entangled in a web of his ambitions."

The words hung heavy in the air, punctuated by the haunting echoes of their footsteps. The siblings exchanged glances, their unspoken bond resonating with a profound understanding. In their hearts, they carried the burden of their father's descent into darkness, a burden they had no choice but to bear.

Mandodari, her heart heavy with the weight of their anguish, clung to her grandchildren's hands with unwavering resolve. The encroaching darkness seemed to yield to her determination as she sought to instil strength and hope in their shaken souls.

"My beloved grandchildren," she began, her voice quivering with a deep anguish, "I know the path we tread is treacherous and filled with uncertainty, but we must find the strength within ourselves to endure. Remember your brave mother's sacrifices, the Rakshasa clan's unwavering loyalty, and the united force of the Eldorians fighting by our side. We are not alone in this battle. We have the love of your mother, the blessings of the realms, and each other. Together, we shall navigate through this darkness."

As they approached a narrow passage, the walls closing in, a tremor of fear ran through Alaya's voice. "Grandma, what if father catches up to us? What will he do?"

Mandodari's voice quivered with a blend of grief and determination. She squeezed their hands tighter, as if to provide a shield against the looming threat. "We cannot let that happen, my dear Alaya. Your father has strayed from the path of light. But I promise you, I will do everything I can to protect you three. We will find a way to overcome this darkness that has befallen him."

Aryan's voice cracked with anguish as he searched for answers. "Why did he turn against us, Grandma? What have we done to deserve this? How could he abandon his own family?"

Mandodari's eyes shimmered with unshed tears, her voice filled with sorrow and unfaltering love. "No, my beloved grandchildren, you have done nothing wrong. In your innocence and purity, you are beacons of light in this dark world. Sometimes, even the brightest souls can succumb to the allure of darkness.

"Your father, once a great warrior, made choices that led him astray. But we must not lose hope. We must cling to the love within us and fight for what is right. In time, the truth will be revealed, and you shall understand. But for now, we must focus on our mission to safely escape this treacherous place."

Mandodari's steps faltered, her eyes filled with determination and anguish, as she turned to face her beloved grandchildren. The weight of their journey pressed upon her heart, yet she stood tall, a beacon of strength in their darkest hour.

"My precious ones," she began, her voice quivering with a mother's love and unwavering resolve, "the path we walk is treacherous, filled with perils beyond our imagining. But now, I want you to know that you are not alone. We carry within us the indomitable spirit of our ancestors, the blessings bestowed upon us by the cosmos, and a legacy of love and resilience that will guide us through the darkest times. No matter what trials befall us, never doubt for a moment that I love you, and I will go to any length to protect you."

Tears welled in Alaya's eyes as she embraced her grandmother, her voice choked with emotion. "We love you, Grandma, and we believe in you. Your strength gives us the courage to face the unknown."

Aryan, his jaw set with determination, stood beside them, his voice filled with unwavering resolve. "We will fight alongside you, Grandma, shoulder to shoulder. We will not let darkness snuff out the light within us. Together, we will face whatever challenges lie ahead."

In that moment, their bond grew stronger, fortified by their shared love, determination, and the unshakeable belief that they were destined to overcome the shadows that threatened their realm.

Sensing the children and his mother Mandodari in danger, Kalkeyas vowed to distract his brother Malakar and Satan. He stood before Malakar, knowing that Malakar's ego would be badly impacted. He would never think his non-violent younger brother, Kalkeyas, who merely ever fought in one war, would dare to stand before the mighty Malakar.

Kalkeyas: "Malakar, please, listen to reason! This path you have chosen will only lead to destruction. There is still goodness within you. We can find a way to break free from this darkness."

Sensing Kalkeyas' interference, Satan intensified his efforts. Fearing that Malakar may again deviate from his path of darkness, Satan concentrated on influencing Malakar's mind through his malefic, eerie whispers.

Malakar: (laughs mockingly) "Oh, dear brother, how naive you are! You think you stand a chance against me? Look around you; see the chaos we have unleashed.

"Good or bad, who are you to decide? It's all a perception. From what you had been taught, you were compelled to believe that you stand for righteousness and the ways taught to you are only right. But wake up, dear little brother, Kalkeyas, it's all a sham to keep us checked and in control under the cosmic world.

"The greater beings are afraid that if we realize our true potential, we may easily dismiss them of their authority and that, they simply can't bear. But I, Malakar, have realized my true potential and have understood the vicious plan of light; I shall get my rightful place. I have embraced the power of darkness, while you cling to your futile hopes. With the blessings of the darkness, now even the light fears me. Join us and lead a powerful destiny as my right hand."

Kalkeyas's voice was desperate as he stood before his brother, Malakar. Their childhood memories echoed in his words. He pleaded with all his might, hoping to rekindle the bond they had once shared.

Kalkeyas: "Please, Malakar, don't let darkness devour you completely. Remember our childhood, the laughter, the love we shared as brothers. Our family needs you, Chhaya needs you. Don't let the allure of power blind you to the truth."

Malakar's voice, oozing with arrogance and disdain, scoffed at Kalkeyas' words and dismissed the importance of family.

Malakar: "Family? They are nothing but distractions, pawns in the grand game of power. The weak always depend on the strong. I have glimpsed the true potential within me, the promise of immortality, and power beyond your feeble comprehension. Why would I abandon such an enticing path for sentimental attachments?"

Kalkeyas, laced with compassion and sorrow, sought to break through Malakar's delusions.

Kalkeyas: "Power and immortality come at a great cost, Malakar. What good is a life devoid of love, family, and purpose? What satisfaction can you derive from a power that thrives on destruction and chaos? Open your eyes to the devastation you are causing, the lives you are tearing apart under the influence of Satan. This is not the path our family envisioned for you. Darkness is a deceitful mistress; she will ultimately betray you."

Malakar, consumed by his malevolent ambitions, lashed out with venomous words.

Malakar: "Betrayal? It is you who fails to see the truth. Darkness offers me everything I desire—dominance, control, and the ability to shape the world according to my whims. I have transcended the limitations of mortality, and I will ascend to unparalleled heights."

Undeterred, Kalkeyas stood firm, his unwavering belief in his brother's inner light shining through.

Kalkeyas: "You may have embraced darkness, brother, but I still see the flicker of goodness within you. I will fight for that spark of hope until my last breath. Remember, you were once a beacon of righteousness. We will not let darkness claim you completely. Together, we can vanquish this evil and restore the light within your heart."

Malakar's laughter dripping with icy disdain dismissed Kalkeyas' words with a heartless mockery.

Malakar: "Hope? Light? How feeble and pitiful. Prepare yourself, dear little brother, for I will unleash the full force of my power upon you. You shall witness the crushing might that awaits all those who dare to oppose me."

Amid this chilling exchange, Kalkeyas knew the urgency of the situation. Knowing that his primary goal was to buy time for his mother, Mandodari, and the safety of his innocent nephews and niece, with steely resolve, he continued to engage his brother and the Lord of Darkness, diverting their attention from the escape in progress.

As Kalkeyas skilfully danced through the shadows, his movements fluid and calculated, his mind raced with a concoction of strategies and sacrifices. Every taunt he uttered, every spell he cast, served a dual purpose: to keep his brother and the malevolent forces occupied and to ensure that Mandodari and the children could find solace in the embrace of safety.

Finally, after what felt like an eternity of navigating the perfidious tunnels, they arrived at the entrance of the secret chamber. Mandodari, her breath ragged but her resolve unyielding, stood before a massive stone door intricately carved with ancient symbols.

As Mandodari stood before the imposing stone doors, her hands gently cupped in front of her, she channelled her magical wisdom and energy into the ancient spells passed down through generations. Softly, she began to chant the incantations that would unravel the layers of security guarding the tunnel, each word infused with mystical power.

Guptamargaprakasya, reveal the hidden path,
Eldorian gates unlock and grant us passage through.
Let ancient magic guide our way,
Ward off darkness' wrath,
As I speak the words of power,
The doors shall yield anew.

The air crackled with energy as her spells intertwined with the very essence of the stone doors. Symbols etched upon their surface glowed with a vibrant luminescence, responding to the incantations and activating the enchantments that lay dormant within.

Adhyatmasaktayah Prakasayantu Margam, illuminate the way,
Banish shadows, grant us sight, with radiant display.
Let secrets of the hidden realm emerge into the light,
As we step through this portal,
Guided by the celestial might.

Mandodari's voice resonated with authority, commanding the doors to recognize her as their guardian and protector. With a resounding groan, the first layer of security relented, the stone doors slowly parting to reveal a glimpse of the passageway beyond. Undeterred, Mandodari continued her incantations, her voice carrying the weight of grit, while the children standing behind her stared in awe.

Purtana Bala Kavachah Raksantu Asman, shields of ancient strength,
Defend us from malevolence, its power's length.

Ward off minions of darkness, their wicked grasp,
As we tread this perilous path, protected in this clasp.

Her words echoed through the chamber, entwined with the magic that flowed through the tunnel. The second layer of security responded, shimmering waves of energy emanating from the doors as invisible barriers formed, shielding them from the lurking malevolent forces.

The ambience within the chamber was both awe-inspiring and foreboding. Soft, diaphanous light filtered through the cracks in the walls, casting a gentle glow that danced with the shadows. The air was heavy with ancient enchantments, and the faint scent of incense hung in the air, adding an otherworldly touch to the atmosphere.

The secret chamber itself was a marvel to behold. It was a vast space adorned with intricate murals depicting the history and legends of Eldoria. The walls shimmered with enchantments, their energy palpable, and alive. In the centre of the chamber stood a magnificent pedestal, atop which rested the ancient book of light—a book said to hold the preamble, the constitution, the secrets, and the wisdom of the ancient Eldorians.

***

Chitrangada suddenly interrupted Kalki with inquisitiveness and excitement, "Kalki, please tell me what I'm thinking is correct?"

Kalki, sensing Chitrangada's excitement, says, "Yes, Chitrangada, you're correct. It is the same chamber where you and I are standing now."

Chitrangada was stunned as she struggled to gather words.

"I do not know what it means."

Kalki: "Patience, Chitrangada, patience, everything will be clear to you shortly. You'll get the answers to all your queries. But you have to allow me to complete the story. Shall I?"

Chitrangada, her curiosity consuming her, nodded eagerly. The anticipation in her eyes pleaded with Kalki to continue, desperate to quench her thirst for knowledge. The weight of her curiosity hung in the air as she braced herself for the revellations that awaited her.

***

Advancing deeper into the chamber, Mandodari summoned her inner strength, her voice resonating with unhesitating resolve.

Atma-raksaya Svarga-margam Anugrhnatu, secrets of the ages unfold,

As I call upon ancestral wisdom,

Steadfast and bold.

Grant passage to this sanctuary, hidden from the world's gaze,

Through ancient knowledge's embrace,

Reveal the hidden ways.

As her words filled the air, the third layer of security responded. Symbols etched into the walls glowed radiantly, illuminating the passage, and dispelling the encroaching darkness. Invisible hands seemed to guide their steps, protecting them from the malevolent force that sought to impede their progress.

Finally, as they neared the heart of the chamber, Mandodari's voice rang out with unwavering conviction.

Antimavaranam Lanchayatu Margam, with the strength of love and the power of family,

I command the final barrier to yield.

Let the shadows scatter, the veil be lifted,

And the paths to freedom unfold.

Her words reverberated through the passage, mingling with the ancient echoes of those who had treaded this path before. The fourth and final layer of security yielded to her enchantments, dissolving into a cascade of shimmering energy. The tunnel ahead opened wide, revealing the path that would lead them to safety.

As they took their first steps towards the path shown by the chamber, their hearts heavy with the weight of their fractured family, they drew strength from their love for one another. Hand in hand, they entered the next phase of their destiny, prepared to face the trials that lay ahead, and hoping against hope that their love would be enough to withstand the darkness that threatened to consume them all.

At that moment, Mandodari, and the children stepped into the newfound passage, their hearts filled with pain, hope, and grit. They knew that their destiny demanded another war like never before, where the balance of the cosmos and the future of the universe lay.

The War Intensified

As Mandodari embarked into an unknown world, Satan's fury blazed like a raging inferno as he realized the children had eluded his grasp. He seethed with anger, his voice laced with venom as he turned to Malakar, his most trusted pawn.

"Malakar! You imbecile! You let them escape! Do you not understand the consequences of your incompetence?" Satan's eyes blazed with intensity, sending shivers down Malakar's spine.

Malakar, his head bowed, trembled before the wrath of his master. "Forgive me, my Lord. I never anticipated that they would find a way to escape. I swear, I will rectify my mistake and bring them back to you."

Satan's voice dripped with derision. "Oh, do you think it's that simple? The children are more than pawns in this game. The universe is protecting them, my daughter and your wife, Chhaya, is protecting them. I thought that you must be as good as my daughter Chhaya, and that's why she chose you, but I was wrong; you are a mere pawn in their hands. You can't be trusted with anything. Those children possess the power to end my reign of darkness, to destroy me, to destroy us, you fool! And I will not let that happen."

Malakar, sensing an opportunity to regain his master's favour, continued with hope in his eyes, "My Lord, while the children have slipped through our grasp for now, all is not lost. We have yet to find King Ravana's, my father's, blue sapphire ring. It contains unimaginable power and could tip the scales in our favour. If we possess such a powerful weapon, victory over the realms will be assured."

Satan's interest piqued, his eyes narrowing as he considered Malakar's words. "Oh yes, Malakar, I completely forgot about the blue sapphire ring. Its power is legendary, but its whereabouts remain a mystery. Countless have sought it, yet none have succeeded. For all we know, the cosmic world bestowed your father, the mighty King Ravana. Even you, being his son, are clueless about the ring's whereabouts."

Malakar's voice quivered with anticipation as he responded, "Indeed, my Lord, but we have the strength and resources to uncover its hidden location. With our forces unleashed upon Eldoria, we can search every corner, tear through every barrier until we find the ring and claim its power for ourselves."

Satan's lips curled into a wicked smile. "Very well, Malakar. This is your last chance. Bring me that ring, and perhaps you shall earn back my trust. Fail me again and your punishment will be unimaginable. Let the realms tremble before our might. Unleash war upon Eldoria with full throttle. Crush their feeble resistance and bring chaos and destruction to their lands. Let them witness the true extent of our power."

Malakar's heart swelled with newfound purpose. "As you command, my Lord. We shall unleash our forces, laying waste to Eldoria. The blue sapphire ring will be found, and once we have it in our possession, the children will have nowhere to hide. Their execution will be inevitable."

Their eyes locked in a malevolent pact, Satan and Malakar forged their sinister plan, vowing to bring the full might of darkness upon Eldoria. They relished the thought of victory in their hearts, fuelled by the anticipation of wielding the blue sapphire ring's formidable power.

As Malakar bowed deeply, his mind filled with apprehension and determination, he knew the quest for the blue sapphire ring would be perilous. Little did he realize that the ring held a power far greater than he could comprehend, and that destiny would ultimately decide its bearer.

The battlefield became a theatre of chaos and destruction as the forces of light clashed with the minions of darkness. The air was thick with the acrid scent of burning wood and the metallic tang of blood. Flames danced and devoured the once serene forests, while homes crumbled under the weight of powerful supernatural weapons.

Eldoria trembled under the weight of this epic confrontation, as the clash of forces unleashed a torrent of raw power. Lightning crackled across the sky, illuminating the harrowing scene below. Thunder roared, today louder than ever, in defiance, its echoes drowning out the cries of the battle.

Both sides unleashed their fury, casting spells that ripped the earth asunder and sent shockwaves rippling through the air. Elemental forces collided, causing whirlwinds and tsunamis to ravage the landscape. The clash of blades and the thunderous boom of mighty weapons reverberated through the war-torn land.

Amidst the chaos, warriors fought with villains, clashing in a whirlwind of speed and skill. Their bodies moved in fluid motions as they evaded deadly strikes and retaliated with lethal precision. The ground shook beneath their feet as they leapt, spun, and parried with supernatural agility.

The battlefield was a tapestry of contrasting colours and energies. Streams of light and darkness intertwined, creating dazzling displays of ethereal luminescence. Spells erupted in vibrant hues, painting the sky with red, blue, and purple explosions. The very fabric of reality seemed to warp and twist under the strain of these otherworldly forces.

Amidst the relentless onslaught, the determined band of warriors fought with unparalleled valour. Chhaya's illusions weaved through the chaos, bewildering their enemies and creating openings for her allies to strike. Ravana's mighty blows shattered defences, his tenacity unwavering in the face of overwhelming odds.

Vibhishana's strategic mind calculated every move, exploiting weaknesses and capitalizing on opportunities. Kumbhakaran's strength and resilience became unstoppable, toppling adversaries with each thunderous blow.

The battleground became a mosaic of shattered hopes and dreams, with the destiny of Eldoria hanging in the balance. Blood stained the land of the holy grounds of Eldoria, mingling with the tears of those who fought for their loved ones and the survival of their realm. Each clash of weapons echoed the resolve of the combatants, their spirits interlaced with the very essence of the land they fought to protect.

Chhaya, her eyes brimming with tears, caught a glimpse of Malakar, who was now unleashing every mode and form of darkness on Eldoria and his family as if he were on a mission to bring Armageddon on the land that he had once protected. Her heart ached at the sight of the man she had once loved, now lost to the clutches of evil.

She yearned for his redemption, for the reunion of their fractured family, for her father, Satan, the Lord of the Darkness, to return and leave her man and her beautiful world. But deep down, she knew that the darkness had consumed Malakar entirely.

While fighting alongside Chhaya, Ravana felt sorrow as he witnessed the turmoil within her. He saw the conflict in her eyes, torn between her love for Malakar and the duty to protect their children and Eldoria. With each swing of his sword, Ravana vowed to protect Chhaya, knowing that the battle against darkness demanded sacrifices beyond measure.

Ravana knew Chhaya needed to know that her entire family was standing with her. He understood that whatever happened, he must motivate Chhaya, and their allies, as sometimes it was the words of love, trust, and the mere fact that someone was there with you in your fight and struggle that could ignite unimaginable power and grit, which could be enough to win any battle, achieve any target. Sensing the morale of Chhaya and his fellow warriors sinking, the king of Eldoria, the mighty Ravana, spoke.

Standing tall amidst the chaos, Ravana raised his voice with commanding authority as he embedded his trident ferociously in the ground, his words echoing across the battlefield. "My fellow warriors hear me now," he declared, his voice carrying the weight of both a king and a father. "Today, we face a battle unlike any other. Our adversary is not just an enemy on the battlefield, but a shadow that has engulfed the heart of my flesh and blood."

He paused, his gaze sweeping across his loyal warriors' faces, filled with sorrow and unwavering resolve. "But let us not forget who we are," Ravana continued, his voice resonating with unyielding grit. "We are the defenders of Eldoria, the guardians of light in the face of overwhelming darkness. We are the manifestation of strength and resilience.

"With each swing of our swords and every spell cast, let us show the realms that the power of love, righteousness, and unity can conquer even the most insidious of evils," Ravana proclaimed, infused with an indomitable spirit. "We fight not just for victory, but for restoring faith and hope among those who have lost their way. Our duty as Eldorians is to bring Eldoria back from the abyss."

Ravana's voice quivered with emotion as he addressed Chhaya directly, his voice filled with a mixture of pain and determination.

"Chhaya, my child, the brave warrior of Eldoria, I understand the agony that tears your heart. But remember, a mother's love knows no boundaries, and a parent must protect their children, even from themselves. We will face Malakar with our mighty strength to keep our children and Eldoria safe from the clutches of Satan."

He looked deeply into Chhaya's eyes, his voice profoundly

sincere. "You, Chhaya, are the epitome of strength and resilience. Eldoria is blessed to have you as its protector, as the guiding light in this darkest hour," he continued, his words carrying the weight of admiration. Together, we will face the unimaginable pain that lies ahead. We will overcome the challenges, for the power of love and sacrifice knows no bounds."

Turning to his loyal comrades, Ravana's eyes blazed with a fire that could not be extinguished. "Today, we stand united against the forces threatening to tear Eldoria apart. Let our actions on this day be an anthem of defiance, a testament to the unyielding Spirit of Eldoria.

"As we charge into battle, let us remember that it is not just our physical strength that will pave the path to victory," Ravana exclaimed, with the command of a king, a leader. "Our unwavering belief in the power of love, sacrifice, and redemption will guide us through the darkest of hours. Let the legacy of Eldoria be one of triumph over adversity, of finding light in the depths of darkness. Today, we are fighting for the salvation of our trust that goodness wins over evil; we are fighting for the very soul of Eldoria. Let our courage be a beacon of inspiration for generations to come. For Eldoria!"

In the face of adversity, the warriors found solace in the inspiring words of their mighty king, Ravana. The war raged on, each side unleashing its supernatural weapons desperately bidding for victory. The clash of powers reverberated through the battlefield, setting the stage for a thrilling and intense confrontation.

Malakar, consumed by darkness, and with his newfound purpose of finding the blue sapphire ring, hurled his weapon of choice, the Jivaharastra, towards the forces of light. The Jivaharastra, a wicked scythe imbued with the essence of the eternal darkness, soared through the air with an eerie, almost sentient presence. It's very touch drained the life force from any mortal being struck, leaving behind a trail of desolation.

Chhaya, surrounded by the Rakshasas, and the valiant Eldorians, stood steadfast against this malevolent onslaught. Her illusions danced through the chaos, creating illusions of her weapons that struck with an otherworldly precision. Illusionary blades clashed with the destructive force of the Jivaharastra, each clash producing a shower of sparks illuminating the battlefield.

With his colossal strength and unmatched fury, Ravana wielded the Celestial Sunder with awe-inspiring power. With each swing, the radiant Trishul cleaved through the minions of darkness, severing their darkened souls from their twisted bodies. His presence alone inspired his allies, who fought alongside him with renewed vigour; their weapons alight with a burning determination.

Vibhishana, the strategic mastermind, orchestrated the battle with calculated precision. His Vidyutprerita Tatvastra crackled with elemental energy, summoning lightning bolts that struck down the minions of darkness with electrifying accuracy. Whirlwinds created by his staff swept through the enemy lines, disorienting, and scattering their forces, while his keen intellect guided his allies towards strategic advantages.

Kumbhakaran, the towering giant of immense strength, wielded the Mahabalastra with a devastating might. Each colossal punch sent shockwaves rippling through the ground, shattering the entities that dared to oppose him. The ground quaked beneath his footsteps as his sheer presence became a force to be reckoned with, inspiring fear and trepidation among his enemies.

The battlefield became a chaotic spectacle of light and darkness. Explosions erupted as spells collided, casting radiant bursts of energy and dark tendrils in every direction. The clash of weapons echoed like thunder, as swords, axes, and staffs clashed in a symphony of steel and magical forces.

Amidst the chaos, the warriors of light fought with unparalleled valour. Eldorian warriors, armed with their enchanted weapons and fuelled by the love for their land, engaged the minions of darkness in a fierce and unyielding battle. They stuck with precision and agility, their movements guided by the ancient teachings of their ancestors and blessed by the power of good and righteousness.

Chhaya, the epitome of resilience, weaved her illusions with skill and grace, confounding the minions of darkness at every turn. Illusory warriors fought alongside her allies, their attacks distracting, and disorienting the enemy. Shadows danced and twisted, creating a veil of confusion that gave her comrades an advantage in the relentless struggle.

The clash of weapons continued unabated, the battlefield soaked in blood and imbued with fallen warriors. Amidst the chaos and destruction, the forces of light fought on, vowed to defend Eldoria and its people from the encroaching darkness.

As the battle reached its crescendo, a surge of energy pulsed through the air. The combined might of Chhaya, Ravana, the Rakshasas, and their allies surged forth, pushing back the minions of darkness with a ferocity that seemed born of the very essence of light itself.

The thrilling battle scene unfolded with every swing, strike, and spell cast, as the clash of supernatural weapons and powers intensified.

The Ultimate Sacrifice of Love

The battle raged on for the final confrontation, with Malakar, Satan, and darkness on one side, determined to end the war with a final blow that would mean the end of Eldoria against the united Rakshasas and the Eldorians, who stood together, their hearts united in purpose, their souls aflame with determination to vanquish the darkness and let light reclaim its proper place.

Chhaya, her voice filled with an otherworldly calm, the type of calm that is felt before a storm hits, spoke softly yet resolutely, "I have witnessed the depth of darkness that has consumed Malakar, but I refuse to let it define our family. I've been running for too long now. I ran away from my malefic father instead of fighting him as I was scared, I ran away from my identity as I was scared of being judged, I ran away from accepting the fact that my love of life had a streak of darkness in him since the beginning, I refused to even think about the fact that I have to face my destiny ultimately.

"I kept longing for love, and I kept dodging my ultimate fate, but now no more, for I know now that this war is my destiny. It's time to confront my destiny, love, and sinister father for one last time. For the sake of our children and the future of Eldoria, let's end this darkness forever."

The atmosphere crackled with anticipation as the Rakshasas and their allies stood united, ready to unleash their final strike to protect their beloved land and to protect light over darkness. Chhaya, her voice filled with gratitude and calmness, turned to Kalkeyas, and uttered words that resonated with trust and urgency.

She held Kalkeyas' hands tightly; her eyes glistened with tears of contentment and a profound understanding.

"Brother, you have always been my confidante; you have always been there for us. I trust you and your selfless commitment towards us. As I speak about destiny, I always felt that when everything goes haywire, when everything is in utter chaos, it will be you, Kalkeyas, my dear brother-in-law, who is more like my real brother, who will be the one to end the war.

"I always felt that you are meant for a far greater purpose and will be the one Eldoria shall see as its guardian. I knew from the beginning that the real protector of Eldoria wasn't Malakar, but it is you, my brother. And now the time has come for you to live your destiny and end this war."

Kalkeyas stood there, perplexed. He struggled to comprehend the magnitude of the task entrusted to him. For him, it was a bizarre thing to hear that he was supposed to win the war for Eldoria, as he had never been considered a mighty warrior. While his commitment and love for Eldoria and his family were respected and known by everyone, his being the guardian of Eldoria and the one who was destined to end this war was beyond his comprehension.

Kalkeyas: "But how? How can I possibly end this war, dear sister?"

Chhaya: "Kalkeyas, listen to me now carefully. At this point, Malakar is entirely under the Lord of the Darkness's control. Whatever we say or whatever we do, Satan will manipulate, and use it to make Malakar go deeper into darkness and execute whatever comes their way. Malakar is Satan's vessel for darkness, and there's no returning for him. He either wins this war for Satan, or the Lord of the Darkness would ensure that Malakar's soul is trapped in hell forever.

"Even if we make our hearts strong and prepare ourselves mentally to deal with eliminating Malakar, killing him in his current state would trap his soul in the clutches of darkness. This would mean that my father would get the satisfaction of punishing me, as

I betrayed him and ran away from his clutches, either way. And I cannot let that happen.

"Today, my father, the evil Satan, will not win. Satan will not snatch away my family from me again, for this time, he shall see the wrath of my love, my sacrifice, and my pain. That evil Lord will lose to his daughter's light and grit this time.

"And to make this happen, I need you to promise me that whatever I ask of you, you'll do it without hesitation. Remember, this war is all about making difficult and painful choices, and I trust you, and only you who have the forbearance. Promise me, brother, you will not let my faith in you down."

Their eyes locked, and an unspoken understanding passed between them. What Kalkeyas didn't know was the magnitude of the work Chhaya was about to ask him.

Chhaya: "We must break the connection between Malakar and Satan. If we create that brief moment of vulnerability, there lies a chance, however small, to reach Malakar, to ignite a spark of his former self."

She took a deep breath, her voice laced with authority and hope as she looked deep into Kalkeyas' eyes without any doubt or hesitation. "In that fleeting instant, when doubt seeps into Malakar's heart, when the memories of our love and the warmth of our togetherness flicker in his mind, you must strike.

"I will embrace Malakar tightly, seeking to rekindle the flame of love within his heart, to rekindle the light that he once had within. As we embrace, our two souls entwined, you must plunge the trident into both of us, unifying our light and darkness in a final act of sacrifice."

Kalkeyas' eyes widened with a mix of disbelief and sorrow. He was shaken by what he had just heard. He struggled to comprehend the enormity of Chhaya's plan and the weight of the responsibility she placed on him.

"Chhaya, this is an immeasurable burden," he murmured, his voice quivering. "To pierce the trident into both of you, into the depths of your love and pain, it's a sacrifice that cuts to the core of my being. How could you even think that I would agree to do this? Do you think that little of me? Do you think my love for you is any less than the others? How can I do such a sinister act and kill my own family?"

Chhaya: "Brother Kalkeyas, you know that we know how much you love us. Your love and commitment to the family are unmatchable and run deep into your very fabric of existence. This sacrifice is only possible by someone as loyal and pure as you. This is my battle, the battle against the might and ego of my insidious father, Satan. My love for Malakar runs deep, and I vow not to let his soul face the wrath of hell. Please help me, help your brother."

Kalkeyas knelt down with folded hands as he cried inconsolably.

Kalkeyas: "Chhaya, please, I can't bear the burden of taking your lives. To protect Eldoria, I understand the necessity of defeating the darkness, but I cannot be the one to bring such tragedy upon our family."

His words trembled with a mix of sadness and love. "Think about your children, Chhaya. How can you ask me to make them orphans? How can you ask me to snatch the lives of their parents? How can I ever face them? The children need their mother. They are waiting for you, yearning for your warmth and guidance. How can we ask you to forsake them? They deserve to have their mother by their side, to witness their growth, and share in their joys.

"Please don't make me do this! I beg of you, Chhaya! Please free me from this burden. Please don't let my soul be impacted by such guilt. There's no turning back from such a grave sin. The guilt will haunt me till the end of my days. I cannot bear the weight of this sin, even if it means protecting Eldoria. Let me be the one to sacrifice. I shall confront Malakar, and you plunge the trident in us."

Chhaya: "As I said, brother, today, it's my battle; it's my destiny's call to sacrifice. My children are true warriors like you, and they will understand what you did and why you did it. I'm proud of my children and their survival and wisdom; I completely trust you and Mandodari. You two shall love them as your own. Under your love, care, and protection, they will remain the safest. I and Malakar complete each other, and only the light in me will help kill his darkness and make him attain salvation."

The pain etched upon Kalkeyas' face deepened, his eyes pleading with Chhaya to understand his agony.

Kalkeyas: "But Chhaya, Eldoria cannot bear to lose you. You are the anchor of our family, the source of strength and love. Without you, our lives would be shattered and directionless. Please, find another path that doesn't require such a sacrifice."

Chhaya's eyes glistened with tears, yet a sense of a higher purpose burned brightly within her.

Chhaya: "Brother Kalkeyas, I know this burden is heavy, and I never wanted to cause you pain, but you possess a strength that runs deeper than the pain. The path we tread is paved with pain and sacrifice, but it is through these sacrifices that true heroes are forged. I have seen your commitment and loyalty to our family and Eldoria.

"It is a burden that only you can bear, for you hold within you the love and loyalty that will guide you in the most critical moments of life's tests. But sometimes, the greatest acts of love require the greatest sacrifice. I trust in your strength and your ability to carry on and protect our family, for history shall be a testament that you, Kalkeyas, shall always protect Eldoria, and be its guardian till eternity. Please understand that this is a choice I make willingly, driven by love, and the hope of a brighter future for my children and Eldoria."

Kalkeyas cried dolorously. His heart ached as he looked into

Chhaya's eyes, seeing the depth of her sacrifice and the unwavering love she held for Malakar.

"Chhaya, I will do as you ask," he said, trembling. "But promise me, this sacrifice will not be in vain. Promise me that through our love and sacrifice, Malakar will find redemption, and Eldoria will be free from the clutches of darkness."

Chhaya's voice softened, filled with a mix of love and resolve. "I promise you, Kalkeyas," she whispered, her voice carrying the weight of her conviction. "In that fleeting moment, when our souls unite, the light that emanates from our sacrifice will engulf Malakar, overwhelming the darkness that holds him captive. Together, we shall offer him a chance at salvation, ending Satan's sinister plans, and Eldoria will stand victorious against the force of evil."

They stood there, united in purpose, their hearts intertwined in a bond that could withstand even the darkest trials. The path before them was treacherous and filled with unimaginable pain. Still, they drew strength from each other, knowing that their sacrifice was a testament to the power of love and the unwavering Spirit of Eldoria.

The battlefield trembled under the weight of the final confrontation. The clash between darkness and light intensified with each passing moment, mirroring the tumultuous skies above. Lightning crackled through the air, illuminating the ferocious faces of the warriors locked in combat. Thunder roared like the collective cry of both armies, a symphony of determination and defiance.

The Rakshasas and their allies fought with unparalleled valour, their weapons clashing against the force of darkness. Their eyes burned with inexorable resolve; their souls alight to protect Eldoria. Each strike, each spell cast, resonated with the weight of their love for their land and their absolute belief in the power of light.

The storm raged on, metaphorically representing the tempest that engulfed their hearts and souls. It seemed as if the very elements conspired to mirror the struggle between good and evil playing out on the battlefield. Rain poured in torrents, mingling with sweat and tears, drenching the warriors who fought with an unrelenting fury.

With each clash of their weapons, with each spell of incantation, the warriors of light sent forth a message to the forces of darkness. They proclaimed that even in the face of overwhelming odds, they would not falter. Their determination transcended the boundaries of fear and doubt, fuelling their every move and strike.

The deafening roars and growls pealed through the battlefield, as if the very realm of Eldoria groaned under the weight of the epic battle. The air crackled with an electric energy, charged with the clash between opposing forces. It was a moment where the destinies of warriors and land converged.

In the heart of the storm, Chhaya fought with an unremitting resolve, her eyes fixed on Malakar, now a vessel of darkness and a pawn of Satan. She held onto her love for him like an anchor, her perseverance to reach his fractured soul inexorable. Her every move was imbued with strength and tenderness, as if she fought with her physical prowess and the power of her unswerving love.

Vibhishana, Kumbhakaran, and Ravana skillfully distracted Satan, luring him with the illusion of the precious blue sapphire. Their plan unfolded flawlessly. Satan, consumed by his own greed, momentarily diverted his attention, breaking the connection between him and his vessel of darkness, Malakar.

Chhaya seized the opportunity in that crucial instant, her eyes filled with Dunkirk spirit and love. She gazed deeply into Malakar's eyes, desperately trying to reignite the spark of their shared memories. With every ounce of strength, she embraced him tightly, tears streaming down her face as she clung to the hope of rekindling the flame that had once burned so brightly.

In that profound moment of connection, Malakar, his soul

momentarily freed from the clutches of darkness, felt a surge of overwhelming emotions. He lifted Chhaya's head gently, his trembling hands cupping her tear-stained cheeks. The weight of his actions, the havoc he had wrought upon his family and their beloved land, weighed heavily upon him.

Tears cascaded down Malakar's face as he held Chhaya close, his voice choked with remorse. "I'm sorry," he whispered, his voice filled with anguish. "I know the depths of my sins, the irreparable damage I have caused. I'm unforgivable."

Their eyes locked, and in that unspoken moment, an understanding passed between them—a shared acceptance of the past and a glimmer of hope for the future. An unspoken contentment about Chhaya's plans made Malakar smile as he gripped her even more closely and whispered, "Thank you, my love, for choosing me, and fighting for my salvation till the end."

With their hearts intertwined, tears mingling, they turned their gaze towards Kalkeyas, their confidante in this pivotal moment. A bittersweet smile graced their lips as they spoke in unison, their voices a blend of tenacity and surrender. "Now, Kalkeyas," they urged, their words carrying the weight of destiny. "Plunge the trident. This fleeting second is our salvation, where our souls shall be forever entwined in an afterlife, in a realm where light prevails. Do not hesitate, for time is fleeting."

Kalkeyas' heart shattered as he witnessed the depth of their love and their willing sacrifice. Tears blurred his vision as he trembled with the weight of the trident in his hands. The magnitude of the task threatened to consume him, but he knew there was no turning back; he had to do it for the salvation of his beloved brother, who still had a ray of light in him.

Summoning every ounce of courage, Kalkeyas let out a guttural cry, a mixture of agony, hope and tenacity, and he plunged the trident into the hearts of Chhaya and Malakar, together. The blade pierced their bodies, a final act of selflessness and ultimate sacrifice.

A brilliant, blinding light erupted from the point of impact, enveloping the battlefield, and illuminating the darkened skies. The clash of weapons ceased, replaced by a hushed awe that settled over the warriors and onlookers alike.

In that transcendental moment, the souls of Chhaya and Malakar became one, their love and sacrifice forever etched in the tapestry of Eldoria's history. Their entwined spirits ascended, leaving a realm forever changed by their selfless act.

Kalkeyas collapsed to his knees, his body wracked with sobs and his soul impacted by the guilt of darkness forever, as he mourned the loss of his loved ones.

Overwhelmed by the weight of his actions, Kalkeyas cradled the lifeless bodies of his beloved brother and sister-in-law in his trembling arms. Inconsolable sobs racked his body as he whispered apologies through his tears, his guilt threatening to consume him. His anguish seemed insurmountable, as if he had committed an unforgivable sin.

A wave of sorrow and agony washed over the battlefield. The air resounded with the echoes of mournful cries, each voice a testament to the depth of their loss. Warriors and allies rushed towards Chhaya and Malakar, their hearts heavy with grief, their eyes blurred with tears.

In that moment of despair, Ravana, the wise, and venerable king of Eldoria, approached Kalkeyas, his hand resting gently on His quivering shoulder. With a voice filled with compassion, grief, and strength, he spoke words of solace amidst the sea of sorrow.

"Kalkeyas," he said, his voice steady and indurate, "Kalkeyas, my son, and the brave warrior of Eldoria, it takes the heart of a lion and the radiance of light to make the sacrifice you have made for your brother's salvation and the preservation of our land. Eldoria shall always remain indebted to the sacrifice of you three. You must not let the guilt of this sacrifice impact your soul. Chhaya entrusted you as she knew that only you have the light in you that can't be put off by darkness."

Ravana's words resonated deep within Kalkeyas' soul, offering a glimmer of solace amidst the darkness of his anguish. The weight of his guilt remained, but a flicker of hope ignited within him, fuelled by the recognition of the immense love and selflessness that had driven his actions.

As the news of Chhaya's sacrifice spread throughout Eldoria, a profound sense of loss engulfed the land. Every being, from the humblest creature to the mightiest deity, wept inconsolably, their tears mingling with the rain that poured from the heavens. It seemed as if the very realm itself mourned for Chhaya, recognizing her absolute devotion to her family and the sacred duty she had fulfilled.

The realization of his defeat consumed Satan; an infernal rage coursed through his veins. His bellowing voice echoed across the battlefield, filled with fury and contempt. In a fit of anger, he turned on his minions of shadows, lashing out, and obliterating them with a ferocity that sent shockwaves through the surrounding darkness.

Through clenched teeth, Satan unleashed his venomous words.

"Malakar, you pitiful fool!" Satan hissed, his eyes gleaming with malice. "Your feeble attempts to resist me have cost us everything. You proved to be nothing more than a disappointing traitor. And Chhaya, my deceitful daughter, you dared defy me, your love for this wretched land and your pathetic excuses for family and righteousness have blinded you to the true power of darkness. Don't think I've lost, you will pay for your betrayal, mark my words."

A grim smile crept across Satan's face as he revelled in his twisted triumph. His voice carried a chilling warning that sent shivers down the spines of those who heard it.

"Eldoria, take heed! Do not gloat on this meaningless victory, as I shall come back again. I shall return, more powerful than ever, and I will claim what is rightfully mine. The blue sapphire ring will be in my grasp, and those children destined to oppose me will know the true meaning of suffering. I shall return and unleash the gravest disaster this land has ever seen. Eldoria shall rot!"

Satan vanished into thin air as the echoes of his menacing threats hung. The people of Eldoria, still reeling from their profound loss, understood the gravity of the looming battle. The absence of Chhaya, their beloved protector, left an undeniable void, and the weight of Satan's imminent assault pressed upon their hearts.

Yet, amidst the darkness, and uncertainty, a flicker of defiance ignited within the hearts of Eldoria's warriors. They knew that the battle was far from over, that their land and very souls were still at stake. With each passing moment, their determination grew stronger, fuelled by the memory of Chhaya's sacrifice and the unbreakable bonds of love that had united them.

In the face of Satan's threats, the people of Eldoria embraced their grief and transformed it into a resolute spirit of resistance. They vowed to honour Chhaya's memory and protect the legacy she had left behind. Their hearts blazed with a newfound intensity, fortified by the knowledge that they carried the light of love within them, a light that could never be extinguished.

As they prepared for the imminent battle, Eldoria stood united, ready to face Satan's wrath head-on. They knew the road ahead would be perfidious, with unimaginable challenges and pain awaiting them. But their courage remained unshaken, for they carried within them the indomitable spirit of Chhaya, a spirit that would guide them through the darkest times.

And so, Eldoria braced itself for the battle ahead and the unshakeable pursuit of hope and the triumph of love over darkness.

The air around them grew still as a figure clothed in ethereal radiance descended from the light. It was Parvati, a divine being from the Astral Council, who had given refuge to their beloved Chhaya, known for her wisdom and benevolence. Her presence filled the hearts of all who beheld her, with a profound sense of peace and reverence.

Parvati approached Kalkeyas with gentle grace, her voice carrying a soothing melody, "Kalkeyas, son of Eldoria, Chhaya's spirit and love for this land have touched the very fabric of our realms. She has entrusted you with a great responsibility, one that shall shape the destiny of Eldoria."

Kalkeyas' eyes filled with sorrow and uncertainty, met Parvati's radiant gaze. He listened intently, hanging onto every word that passed her lips.

"Chhaya's final wish, a testament to her untiring devotion, is for you to become the guardian of Eldoria," Parvati continued, her voice imbued with a celestial warmth.

"She recognized your strength, loyalty, and unfaltering commitment to your family and land. You possess the courage to protect what is dear to you, just as she did. You shall wield the light of Chhaya's love, guiding and protecting Chhaya's children and this land until the end of time. Trust in the power that resides within you, for it is born with the love of those who sacrificed for this land and the strength of your lineage."

Kalkeyas's heart swelled with grit, and he nodded solemnly. He accepted the weight of his new role, understanding the magnitude of the task before him.

"I will honour Chhaya's wish," Kalkeyas vowed, his voice filled with newfound resolve. "I shall protect the children and Eldoria with all my being, for it is my duty and my eternal promise to Chhaya. No darkness shall prevail as long as I draw breath. But the weight of the guilt isn't easy to shed."

Parvati's smile was one of profound pride and assurance. "Go forth, Guardian of Eldoria. Embrace the path that lies ahead, for the love and courage of Chhaya shall guide you. The Astral Council and the divine realms shall watch over you, and the spirits of light shall rise to aid you in your noble quest."

Parvati gently smiled and motioned for Kalkeyas to look at his right palm. Curiosity and anticipation filled his eyes as he obeyed her instructions.

To his astonishment, engraved on his palm was a mark of the trident—the very weapon that played a crucial role in the destiny of the Rakshasas and Eldoria, ending the war, impacting Kalkeyas' soul, and giving salvation to his brother, Malakar. Kalkeyas' gaze shifted from his palm to Parvati, his voice filled with wonder.

"What does this symbol mean?"

Parvati's serene expression held a profound insight. She spoke with a voice that carried the weight of eternity. "This trident symbol shall be your guide, Kalkeyas," she explained. "It is a manifestation of your inner light and strength. Whenever your guilt and darkness threaten to consume you, this symbol will glow, guiding you towards redemption and inner peace."

Kalkeyas' eyes widened, his mind racing with the implications of Parvati's words. The trident symbol would serve as a beacon, a constant reminder of his duty to overcome the shadows within him and embrace the light that Chhaya had sacrificed her life to ignite.

With gratitude, Kalkeyas looked at the glowing symbol on his palm. It was a tangible connection to his past, a reminder of the sacrifices and battles yet to be fought. He understood that his journey would be filled with challenges, but with the trident symbol as his guide, he would find the strength to face his inner demons and emerge victorious.

With a final blessing, Parvati ascended back, leaving behind a sense of tranquillity and purpose in the hearts of all who witnessed the sacred moment.

Kalkeyas, infused with the responsibility of a guardian, stood tall amidst the battlefield's remnants and vowed to protect Eldoria until eternity.

The Legacy of the Rakshasas – Unveiling the Guardian

In the grand hall of the chamber, Chitrangada stood transfixed, her heart ablaze with a torrent of emotions. The tale she had just witnessed unfolded before her like a tapestry woven with strands of love, sacrifice, and an unwavering battle against the encroaching darkness. It resonated deep within her soul, stirring a fire that burned brighter with each passing moment.

The history of the Rakshasas, their valorous feats etched in the annals of time, danced vividly in Chitrangada's mind. She marvelled at their unyielding bravery and unbreakable spirit that defied the essence of darkness. And at the centre of it all stood Chhaya, a mythical, and real figure whose love knew no bounds. Her sacrifice, her unwavering devotion to her family and land, left Chitrangada spellbound, humbled by the weight of such selflessness.

Tears welled up in Chitrangada's eyes, cascading down her cheeks as a river of raw emotion. It was as if the floodgates of her heart had burst open, releasing a surge of admiration, pride, and a profound sense of connection. In that moment, the epic battle became her own, its echoes reverberating within her being.

Turning to Kalki, her eyes glistening with awe and gratitude, Chitrangada found solace in his presence. He had unveiled this extraordinary saga, weaving the threads of history into a tapestry of enlightenment. Their shared journey, now etched in their souls, bound them together in an unbreakable bond, forged by the power of the stories told and the legacy they inherited as descendants of the Rakshasas.

Overwhelmed by the intensity of Chitrangada's reaction,

Kalki felt his emotions surge like a tidal wave. Swallowing hard to contain the lump in his throat, he reached out, and gently clasped her trembling hand. With a silent gesture, he guided her towards a colossal portrait adorned in the grand hall – an embodiment of the Rakshasas' illustrious royal lineage, a testament to their glorious past.

As Chitrangada's eyes fell upon the mesmerizing details of the portrait, her breath hitched in her chest. Amongst the regal figures immortalized on the canvas, a face stood out, both familiar, and hauntingly profound. It was Kalkeyas, the legendary warrior, whose valour, and indomitable spirit had been etched into the very fabric of Eldoria's history. A surge of shock and exhilaration coursed through her veins, rendering her momentarily speechless.

Turning to Kalki, her voice quivering with disbelief and newfound understanding, Chitrangada uttered the words that reverberated through the chamber. Her eyes locked with his, searching for confirmation in the depths of his gaze.

"Kalki. Why do you and Kalkeyas bear such a striking resemblance? And that mark on your palm. You are not just a guardian, but a living embodiment of the Rakshasas' lineage. You are Kalkeyas himself, aren't you?" Her voice trembled with the weight of her revelation, a symphony of astonishment and realization echoing through the grand hall.

Chitrangada's eyes widened with astonishment as her gaze shifted from the portrait to Kalki. The puzzle pieces began to fall into place, revealing a revelation she could hardly comprehend. Her voice trembled with awe and disbelief as she uttered her realization.

"Oh, Holy God!" Chitrangada exclaimed, her voice filled with a combination of shock and wonder. "Rudrama, she is Mandodari, your mother, the esteemed Queen of Eldoria?"

The weight of this revellation bore down upon Chitrangada, her mind reeling with the implications of such a connection. The threads of fate seemed to weave an intricate tapestry, intertwining the destinies of Kalki, Rudrama, and the very fabric of Eldoria itself. It was a revellation that carried immense power and profound consequences, leaving Chitrangada grappling with the magnitude of her newfound knowledge.

Kalki's voice resonated with pain and determination as he revealed the depths of their intertwined destinies to Chitrangada. The weight of their shared history bore down on them, and the fate of Eldoria hung in the balance.

"Now, Chitrangada, you finally understand," Kalki's voice quivered with emotion. "You see why Rudrama and I share an unbreakable bond, why she is the only one who knows my true self, for she's my mother, the Queen of Eldoria – she's Mandodari, who Chhaya entrusted to keep the innocent children safe from Chhaya's father, Satan.

"Eldoria is not just a land to us; it is our home, and its people are our own. We owe them everything."

With every word, the gravity of their purpose grew, their intertwined destinies entangled in the legacy of Malakar's fall and Chhaya's selfless sacrifice. The weight of the past rested heavily upon their shoulders, a constant reminder of the debt they owed to Eldoria.

"Since that fateful day, Rudrama and I have dedicated our very existence to Eldoria," Kalki continued, his voice filled with a fierce determination. "We strive to protect our precious heirs, Alaya, Aryan, and Aks, for they hold the key to Satan's downfall. But Satan is relentless, ceaselessly searching for these innocent children. In his quest for invincibility, he seeks to extinguish their pure souls and devour their power."

As the truth unfolded, the air crackled with anticipation and the weight of their responsibility. Chitrangada promised to stand alongside Kalki and Rudrama, united by a shared purpose and an unwavering resolve to safeguard Eldoria. The battle against darkness had become their destiny, and the fate of their land and loved ones depended on their steadfast determination to prevail.

Chitrangada's voice quivered with awe and disbelief as she pieced together the intricate puzzle. The weight of revellation settled upon her, infusing her words with a newfound understanding.

"Now everything falls into place," Chitrangada uttered, her voice filled with wonder. "The unbreakable bond between you and Rudrama, the depths of her knowledge about you, and your unwavering devotion to Eldoria – it all becomes clear. The celestial deity Parvati chose and entrusted you with the sacred duty of safeguarding Eldoria. You are the guardian of this realm, its protector against the encroaching darkness."

Her words echoed through the chamber, carrying the resonance of ancient prophecies and celestial intervention. Chitrangada's eyes shone with realization as she continued, her voice trembling with reverence, "The Astral Council, the trident insignia etched upon your palm – a mark of your divine connection, a symbol of your profound purpose. And the glowing light it emanates when you grapple with the depths of guilt and darkness within you is the power displayed by Parvati herself. A beacon of hope and strength, guiding you back to reality when darkness threatens to ensnare your soul."

Chitrangada's revellation hung in the air, frozen in time, as the weight of their intertwined destinies settled upon them. In the clarity of understanding, the purpose of their meeting, their shared journey, became unmistakable.

But it was at this moment that a sudden guilt of doubting Kalki, doubting the entire cosmos, and almost succumbing to the illusions of darkness hit Chitrangada.

Kalki didn't need words to sense her guilt, and Kalki knew what guilt could do to a soul.

Kalki looked at her, his voice clear, and firm, like a truth that refused to be silenced.

"Don't do that to yourself, Chitrangada. Stop right away. Don't let the guilt of doubt make you feel sorry." His expression remained unchained – no comfort, no reaction.

"You faced the darkness – and that is nothing to apologize for. That is a gift.

"Yes, it hurt. Yes, it rattled something deep inside you. Still, isn't it wiser to recognize the face of what we stand against? You and I both know the history of Eldoria now. Isn't it better to feel the power of your enemy and live to speak of it?

"We train day and night, over and over, trying to mimic war. But practice… practice is predictable. Controlled. War never is. It strikes where we least expect it, with weapons we've never seen, through minds we never thought capable of cruelty."

He stepped forward, his words gaining weight.

"But now you carry something none of that training could've given you. You've felt the real thing. And that changes everything. Let it stay with you – not as fear or guilt, but as fire.

"Burn that moment into your memory. Let it live in your blood. Because when the time comes, when chaos reigns and the world turns on itself, that memory will guide you. It'll sharpen your instincts, steady your sword, and shield your spirit."

His tone dropped – calmer now, but heavier.

"You might not understand it today. But on the battlefield, you will. When you stand at the edge of everything, you'll see it clearly – this moment wasn't your defeat… It was the beginning of your strength."

Kalki smiled, "Welcome aboard, Chitrangada, to be a Yoddha who knows everything about Eldoria."

"Now it is clear," Chitrangada whispered, her voice filled with gratitude, "why I was guided to you, why our paths converged. United, we hold the strength to challenge the shadows and carry out what destiny demands. Let us embrace our destinies, united in purpose, and illuminate the path of Eldoria's future.

"But what I still don't understand," Chitrangada's voice trembled with confusion as she turned to Kalki, her eyes searching for answers, "is why Maya bears such an uncanny resemblance to Chhaya?"

Kalki's gaze met hers, his expression solemn yet resolute. "It's because Maya is Alaya," he revealed, his voice carrying the weight of a long-held secret. The revellation hung in the air, electrifying the chamber with its significance.

Chitrangada's eyes widened in shock, her breath catching in her throat. "You mean, you knew about Maya's origins all along?" Her voice caught between wonder and doubt. "And if Maya is Alaya, then does this mean Ayyappan is Aryan?"

Her voice quivered with sorrow and frustration as she continued, "Why would you keep such a momentous secret hidden? Why allow doubt to cloud their identities? Kalki, why?" Her words hung in the air, pregnant with the sting of broken trust and a silent plea to be understood.

Kalki's eyes bore the burden of regret, his voice laced with remorse. "I know the pain they have endured, the trials they have faced in the shadows of doubt. But there were reasons, Chitrangada, reasons I believed were necessary to protect them. The truth of their identities is key to extinguishing the darkness that seeks to consume Eldoria. My duty was to ensure their safety, even at the cost of their innocence."

A heavy silence settled between them, their minds grappling with the complexity of their intertwined fates. In that moment, the gravity of their choices and the consequences of their actions became all too apparent.

Chitrangada's eyes narrowed with determination as she pressed further, her voice resolute. "Then tell me, Kalki, where is Aks? The youngest prince of the Rakshasas' noble lineage. We cannot afford to hide anything if we are to stand united against the encroaching darkness."

Kalki's expression grew solemn, his voice taking on a weighty tone. "The whereabouts of Aks remain a closely guarded secret, one that will be revealed in due time," he replied, his words hanging in the air, pregnant with anticipation. "But for now, I have unveiled what you and Eldoria must know.

"It is now your responsibility to share this truth with the rest of our team, to dispel the clouds of doubt and uncertainty that threaten to weaken us. We must stand united, for darkness looms not only over Eldoria but also seeks to eliminate the heirs of Chhaya and Malakar, for they hold the key to maintaining the delicate balance of the realms."

Chitrangada's heart swelled with a newfound sense of purpose. She understood the gravity of the task and the weight of the responsibilities entrusted to them. It was now her duty to ensure that the Yodhas would no longer be plagued by doubts and uncertainties, for their unity was paramount in the face of impending darkness.

"We shall fight for Eldoria, the realms, and our Yodhas," she declared with unwavering resolve. Her voice reverberated with determination, carrying the echoes of ancient warriors who had stood against insurmountable odds. The path ahead may be fraught with challenges, but together, they would confront the darkness and safeguard their beloved realm.

As Chitrangada and Kalki locked eyes, a silent agreement passed between them. The fate of Eldoria and the destiny of its inhabitants rested in their hands. They would unveil the truth, rally their allies, and prepare for the ultimate battle that would determine their world's very existence.

A profound belief and understanding passed between Chitrangada and Kalki, a silent vow forged in their resolute gazes. In that moment, they knew that a shared purpose and an unyielding determination bound them together. With the knock of Kalyuga (Armageddon) echoing through Eldoria, they realized that the battle against darkness had already begun for the second time.

In the face of this impending catastrophe, Chitrangada and Kalki made a solemn pledge. They would prepare themselves, body, and soul, to confront the encroaching darkness that threatened to engulf their cherished realm. Their hearts burned with an unwavering resolve to save Eldoria, to protect it from the clutches of Kalyuga and the forces that sought to unleash chaos and destruction upon its lands.

In the haunting chambers of Eldoria's past, Maricha stood stunned as the veil of history unravelled before him. The secrets of yore lay bare, revealing the keys sought by his dark master, Satan, the Lord of Darkness – Maya and Ayyappan.

A sense of bitter regret gnawed at Maricha's conscience; he cursed himself for failing to eliminate Ayyappan when the opportunity had been so tantalisingly close.

Now, fuelled by fury and a resolve to rectify his lapse, Maricha spotted Ayyappan approaching, his quest leading him to the chamber Maricha occupied. Maricha, aware of Ayyappan's affection for Chitrangada, understood the catastrophic implications of their love. It was a vulnerability that could be exploited to shatter his master's grand design.

With a lethal determination, Maricha advanced towards Ayyappan, his movements echoing the impending destiny clash. The air crackled with tension as the two figures, draped in shadows, and touched by the essence of light, converged in a fateful dance.

Maricha's every step resonated with the urgency of his mission

– to thwart the blossoming love that could spell doom for the Lord of Darkness. In the dimly lit chamber, the stage was set for a collision of forces, a confrontation that transcended the physical realm. The fate of Eldoria hung in the balance as Maricha, driven by vengeful purpose, readied himself to extinguish the flickering spark of Ayyappan's existence.

Amidst the conversation, a foreboding gripped Chitrangada, an unsettling intuition that someone dear faced imminent peril.

Suddenly, the world outside began to mirror the chaos within, as if the very air could feel the tremble in her heart. The sky darkened, brooding and heavy, thick with an unseen weight.

The winds stilled. The silence screamed.

Anxiety crawled through like a living thing – sharp, suffocating. Each breath felt like inhaling smoke, like the oxygen had turned traitor.

The walls seemed to close in. The floor beneath her felt pulsing with a strange heat, waves rising and falling like a fevered tide.

It wasn't just tension – it was a warning. A pressure that pressed down on her skull, on her chest, like the realm itself was holding its breath.

Something has shifted, and whatever it was, it didn't feel right.

It echoed the strange sensation she experienced witnessing shadows torment Ayyappan. Trusting her instincts, she rushed out, discovering Maricha menacingly advancing towards Ayyappan.

In swift response, Chitrangada's urgent voice pierced the air, a warning that cut through the confusion. "Ayyappan, be cautious! Get away!" Before comprehension dawned on Kalki and Ayyappan, Chitrangada invoked the primordial forces. With unyielding command, she harnessed the wind, compelling it to intervene.

Maricha, mid-leap with lethal intent, found himself forcefully hurled away from Ayyappan.

Maricha was certain – this would be the end of all. He would crush the last flicker of resistance and offer the ruins as a tribute to his Lord—the greatest gift.

Maricha – the feared Chief of Darkness – stood tall in arrogance. But it seemed he had grown too confident…

He had underestimated the light.

He had dismissed the Astral Council.

He had forgotten the balance that governed the very fabric of the cosmos.

And in that fatal moment of pride, something shifted.

Chitrangada, the chosen warrior, felt it.

Whether it was the whispers of the cosmos guiding her, or the quiet, unspoken love of Ayyappan, stirring within her soul… she couldn't tell.

But something awakened.

And without thought, without hesitation, she moved.

Instinct became action. And the tide turned.

And then it happened.

With a scream that tore through realms, Chitrangada launched her final, blistering assault on Maricha – her body a world-wind of fury, her soul blazing with the fire of something deeper than rage. This was not just a warrior defending her comrade. This was a woman protecting the one soul who had unknowingly became her anchor in a crumbling world. Ayyappan. The one for whom she had begun to feel a love so profound that it transcended words, duty, and even destiny.

Stunned by the abrupt events, Kalki and Ayyappan beheld Chitrangada in awe.

In that searing moment, the universe seemed to shudder—almost as if it had always known, as if the stars themselves had written this tale long ago. Their fates were not just bound… but forged in the fire of time. Perhaps they were soulmates not of one lifetime but many.

And as her blade plunged deep into Maricha's chest, cleaving through centuries of darkness, blood exploded like a dying curse across the battlefield.

Maricha – the most feared of the dark commanders, the right hand of shadows, the monstrous sentinel of Satan – let out a howl that shook the realm. And then he fell. The land cracked. The skies wept embers. His ashes were scattered like a final omen.

Chitrangada had done more than end a warlord's life with that fatal blow – she had sealed a prophecy. Bound by blood and fate, her soul and Ayyappan's had been irrevocably entwined. The story – born in war, forged in fire – was about to echo through Eldoria like the immortal saga of Ayyappan's parents.

But this time, fate would not win.

Ayyappan would not fall like his father had. The abyss would not seduce him. His blood may carry the curse of the shadows, his lineage may lead back to the throne of evil itself – but his will and heart were unbreakable.

As Maricha's beastly form collapsed into ash, a deafening stillness swept over the battlefield.

And then, without a word, Chitrangada ran.

Maya and Kalki had already begun rushing toward Ayyappan but slowed, instinctively halting in their tracks. What they witnessed was no ordinary reunion. It was something sacred, raw, and honest. They exchanged a glance, hearts pounding—not from fear but from the weight of a moment that was never meant to be interrupted.

Chitrangada ran like her soul was on fire, like the world would collapse if she didn't reach him in time. Her armour clanked and scraped, blood and dust streaking her face – but her eyes were only on Ayyappan. Her emotions burst forth – not in words, but in the tears that streamed freely, unashamed.

She fell to her knees beside him, cradling his face in trembling hands.

"Are you alright?" Her voice slipped out, thin and uneven, trembling with the weight of unspoken pain and rising fury. "Did Maricha's attack harm you in any way?" Her fingertips hovered over the bruise, a quiet touch carrying more than words ever could. "I should have killed him in our first battle when I had the chance... I'm so sorry I didn't. I should've killed him the moment I had the chance... I'm so sorry I didn't. I should've ended it then – I should've protected you."

Ayyappan looked into her eyes – those fierce, tear-streaked eyes that had once stared down gods. And in that moment, the warrior in him gave way to the boy who had lived too long with pain and silence.

He pulled her into his arms without hesitation, holding her like the only truth in a world built on lies.

"Thank you," he whispered, his voice hoarse with emotion.

"Thank you for saving me. And I'm glad you didn't take his life earlier..."

He pulled back just enough to look at her again, eyes shimmering.

"If you had, I might've lost this soulful moment... to hold you... to have you in my arms. I'm so grateful that our paths crossed and brought you into my world."

Ayyappan, still cradling Chitrangada's trembling hand, locked eyes with her amidst the silence of the ravaged battlefield. His voice, deep and unwavering, broke the stillness: "Within your gaze, I see a fierce defiance – a promise of resurgence forged in our shared struggle. With you by my side, I rise not as a slave to a cursed lineage but as a warrior reborn to challenge the fate that dares condemn us."

Ayyappan continued, "Together, we shall lead Eldoria to triumph, banishing the ancient stain that once tainted the Rakshasas and restoring our clan's honour as it was always meant to be. We shall reclaim the trust and respect that belong to us by birthright, echoing the legacy of my great-grandfather Ravana, my revered grandmother Mandodari – now known as Rudrama – and my cherished uncle, the bravest of the brave and the wisest of the wise, Kalkeyas – now known as the great Kalki."

Chitrangada's eyes shimmered with untamed emotion as she stepped forward, her voice steady yet soft: "Every scar, every beat of our hearts, echoes the battle cry of destiny. I have waged wars against the dark and defied the gods' harsh decrees – but my strength finds its meaning for you. I vowed to shield you from the tempest and will continue to stand with you until the final breath."

In a silent corner of this charged moment, Maya observed with a storm of conflicting emotions stirring within her. Though her possessiveness as a sister and the deep wounds of the past ignited a fleeting moment of doubt, as she witnessed the fervour of their love intertwine so fiercely with their shared fate, she realized the truth.

Chitrangada wasn't just the chosen warrior; she was the destined soulmate of her dear brother. Ayyappan had now discovered love that could kindle hope on the darkest night.

For now, he had a purpose. A vengeance carved deep into his bones.

To destroy the architect of all.

His grandfather – Satan. The dark king. The origin of every nightmare.

For now, he had a mission—a resolute purpose to safeguard Eldoria and reclaim the Rakshasas' name as the 'Rakshaks' and not the 'Bhakshaks'.

But for now, as Chitrangada killed Maricha and won against the immediate threat that was looming over Eldoria, arm in arm, Chitrangada, and Kalki, alongside the Yodhas, and the Eldorians, embarked on their perilous quest to save Eldoria. With resolute determination burning in their hearts, they forged ahead into the unknown, their steps echoing with unwavering purpose.

Their determination blazed with renewed intensity as they armed themselves to defend Eldoria from the coming Armageddon. They had witnessed the sacrifices made by their ancestors, the unwavering love that fuelled their fight against darkness. Now, it was their turn to carry that torch, honour the legacy of those who came before them, and pave the way for a brighter future.

With their minds focused and their hearts aflame, Kalki, and the Yodhas vowed to save Eldoria, to defend it with every ounce of their being. Their journey had only begun, and the path ahead was uncertain. Still, they must face it with unfaltering courage and an unyielding determination to protect all they hold dear.

For Eldoria!

Acknowledgements

To my **Dadu** – my grandfather, my guiding star – this book is for you. I know you're up there, watching over me, smiling with pride, and wrapping me in your blessings. Your faith in me was exemplary, and your love eternal.

A heartfelt thanks to my **Dida**, the first storyteller I ever knew – the wellspring of creativity and the natural writer in our family.

Thank you, **Mom (Snigdha) and Dad** (**Barun**), for being the unshakeable pillars of my life. Your love, values, and strength shaped every word I wrote.

To **Naveen**, my husband, and confidant – thank you for your patience, your belief in my dreams, and for holding my hand through the chaos and the calm.

To **Abhilash**, my brother dear – you've always been my quiet strength, my buddy, and my secret keeper.

To **Mohona** (my sister-in-law) **and Raya** (my dearest niece), my bundles of joy – your laughter reminds me why imagination matters.

A heartfelt thank you to **Monima (Shraboni) and Shonama (Shanta)**, my dearest aunts, whose warmth and wisdom have been a compass in my life.
To my two lovely siblings, **Abhik** and **Arnavi** – thank you for being

there, always. You are a constant source of light and inspiration.

To my **in-laws** (papa, mommy, Nitin, Manni & didi), thank you for embracing me with love and being a part of this journey with your constant support.

A special thanks to my **Meshos** (Rajat and Sanjeev) – thank you for always being there, your quiet presence a constant source of warmth and comfort.

Thank you, **Rajani uncle, and Neerja aunty**, for being our constant guiding light.

To **Suhail**, my literary agent at **The Book Bakers** – thank you for being the first to truly see the potential in my story. Your belief in me, your honest guidance, and your steadfast support throughout this journey have meant more than words can express.

To the mentors, friends, and well-wishers who walked beside me during moments of doubt and discovery – your encouragement helped me keep going when the words felt heavy.

To **Arup** and the **Srishti Publishers** – thank you for believing in my voice and for giving this story a home. Your faith in this book helped bring it to life and into the hands of readers.

Each of you has played a role in this journey, and this book carries your presence in its very soul.

My gratitude is beyond words for the **Indian Armed forces**, whose honour, integrity, and selfless spirit breathe life into this story.

To every reader who holds this book in their hands: you are the reason I write. May these pages leave behind a whisper of truth, a flicker of thought, and a lingering sense of wonder.

And lastly, to the characters who spoke through me - thank you for choosing me as your vessel.